She landed on the floor w[...] a thud and a jarring of limbs. *Ouch.* She couldn't remember her carpeted floor being this hard and cold. What happened next convinced her that she must still be dreaming. Light suddenly filled the room and a man who looked a lot like Mark DeSanto stood looking down at her in concern.

Instead of screaming in terror, she began laughing hysterically. Couldn't she have just one hot sex dream? Maybe her riding Mark while he told her how perfect she was? Heck, she'd even be happy with a plain old missionary fantasy. But no, even in her dreams, she was awkward and always managed to embarrass herself. "Sorry about this," she mumbled to her dream Mark. "Just let me get back in bed and fall asleep. If I'm lucky, you'll be back and we'll try this again."

Also by Sydney Landon

The Danvers Series
Weekends Required
Not Planning on You
Fall for Me
Fighting for You
No Denying You
Always Loving You
Watch Over Me

THE ONE FOR ME

A DANVERS NOVEL

SYDNEY LANDON

A SIGNET ECLIPSE BOOK

SIGNET ECLIPSE
Published by New American Library,
an imprint of Penguin Random House LLC
375 Hudson Street, New York, New York 10014

This book is an original publication of New American Library.

First Printing, February 2016

For more information about Penguin Random House, visit penguin.com.

ISBN 978-0-451-47622-7

Printed in the United States of America
10 9 8 7 6 5 4 3 2 1

Penguin
Random
House

As always, for my husband, who will always be
The One for Me.

Chapter One

There are just days that suck, Crystal Webber thought as she used one hand to rub her aching head and the other to clutch her cramping stomach. Why in the world had she come to work this morning? True, she hadn't felt quite this sick when she'd left home, but she had been nauseous. She'd attributed it to skipping dinner the night before since she had fallen asleep on the sofa hours before her usual bedtime.

Now, though, she could no longer avoid the fact that she was ill. Her boss, Lydia, had gone to lunch, so Crystal sent her an e-mail explaining the situation before getting shakily to her feet. She quickly grabbed the edge of her desk and held on until the room stopped spinning. "You can do this," she mumbled under her breath as she put one foot in front of the other. She was grateful for her recent promotion to assistant to the director of marketing at Danvers International. Otherwise, she would be struggling to make it through the cube farm where her last desk had been located. There was little to no privacy there and someone would have certainly noticed that she was weaving as if she'd had one too many drinks. Thank God, things were quieter on the management side of the hallway.

She was relieved when the elevator doors opened as soon as she hit the DOWN button. The next few moments passed in something of a daze, and she had no idea that she'd actually made it to the sidewalk outside the building until the bright sunlight blinded her. As she blinked her eyes quickly to adjust, her stomach roiled alarmingly. The realization that she was going to be sick before she made it home had her so focused that she didn't notice anyone standing beside her until a hand touched her arm. "Are you okay?" Crystal jumped aside in shock at the sound of the voice, whirling around to see Mark DeSanto looking down at her with concern-filled eyes. *Please, no.* Fate couldn't be evil enough to throw the coworker she'd lusted after for months into her path at this moment. *Not today of all days.*

Using the last reserves of her strength, she pushed her shoulders back and attempted to give him a bright smile. "I'm fine," she replied in a voice that sounded scratchy, even to her own ears. He gave her a skeptical look and then, before she could do anything to stop it, the unthinkable happened. Her body went into a full revolt, and almost in slow motion, she threw up on a pair of shoes that likely cost more than her Volkswagen Beetle. Words of apology rose to her lips but before she could utter them, her world dimmed and then turned black.

As consciousness slipped away from her, all she could think was that she'd met the man of her dreams face-to-face and she wasn't going to live long enough to do a damn thing about it.

*   *   *

Mark DeSanto stood on the sidewalk in shock with the now-limp body of the woman who had just moments before ruined his favorite pair of Tom Ford shoes in his arms. He knew the effect that he had on most women. Hell, he'd had more than a few swoon at his feet, but the whole throwing-up thing was completely new. He had no idea what to do now with the unconscious woman whose weight he was supporting. It wasn't as if he could just lay her on one of the nearby benches for someone else to find—could he?

No, he discounted that option, despite how appealing it sounded.

When he'd seen her staggering out the door, he should have turned the other way and left her to be someone else's problem. He had walked out the doors of Danvers just steps behind her. Normally he preferred tall blondes with the occasional redhead thrown in for variety, so she wasn't his usual type. However, as if drawn by some unseen force, he had found himself reaching out and touching her arm, wanting a glimpse of the face that belonged to the enticing body.

But he'd caught glimpses of the woman he followed down the sidewalk in the hallways and lobby of the office many times in recent months. For some reason, she was always turning away by the time he became aware of her presence. He'd recognize her ass anywhere because that was the body part usually facing him as she walked in the opposite direction. She was petite but had curves in all of the right places. Her long brown hair hung in loose waves that stopped just inches from her delectable backside. Today, she was wearing a black skirt that reached her knees, but the slit in the middle had shown shapely thighs as she'd moved unsteadily. When she had lifted an arm, rubbing her neck, the top she wore had edged up, revealing a hint of skin. She seemed to be everywhere lately, and he was ready to meet his mystery woman so that he could move on.

Anything beyond that was doubtful. He didn't like to muddy the waters where he worked. That was not to say he'd never made an exception, but he tried not to. When she'd jerked around to face him a few moments ago, he'd felt a jolt of electricity shoot through his body. He wasn't a man prone to romantic foolishness, but there had been songs written to describe women like her. Wide eyes close to violet in color. Plump pink lips that made a man's cock sit up and take notice, and a flawless peaches-and-cream complexion that some paid millions for but never achieved.

He had still been gaping at her as she'd assured him that she was fine before she further shocked him by vomiting and promptly passing out. She had been seconds away from her beautiful face meeting the unforgiving concrete when he'd caught her. As he stood with her light weight in his arms, a black Bentley sedan pulled to the curb. His driver, Denny—who was also his cousin on his mother's side of the family—got out of the car gawking as if in disbelief of what he was seeing. As far as the employer/employee relationship, theirs was very informal. They'd grown up together, and although Mark's family had money from the DeSanto side, Denny's did not. So years ago Denny had proposed that he become Mark's driver and assistant when Mark had taken over the family business, and it had worked well for both of them. Mark compensated Denny more than probably anyone employed in a similar position, but he trusted him implicitly.

"I'm almost afraid to ask what you did to that girl, but if I'm going to become some kind of accessory, then I guess I need to know." Denny sighed in resignation.

Walking toward his driver in shoes that sloshed with every step, Mark shook his head helplessly. "I have no idea. She was weaving as she walked, and then she got sick and fainted."

Denny wrinkled up his nose as the smell finally reached him. "Shouldn't we do something with her? I mean, do you think she's drunk?"

"How in the hell am I supposed to know?" he snapped. "I didn't smell any alcohol, and it's barely midday. Also, she just left Danvers, so it seems unlikely."

"Then we need to get a doctor. She obviously has something wrong with her," Denny pointed out.

Rolling his eyes, Mark said, "You think? Open the car door so I can get her inside." Denny jogged ahead and had the door ajar when Mark reached him. "Here, you're going to have to hold her for a minute. Then you can give her back to me when I'm inside."

Denny held his hands up, trying to back away. "She's got puke on her. Can't you just get in with her? There's no need to ruin both of our clothes."

"Oh, for God's sake, Denny, I'll get you a new suit. Just take her for one second." Mark couldn't believe how hard it was for two men to juggle such a tiny woman. Finally, as Denny gently handed her off to him and shut the door, Mark slumped against the leather seat with her curled against him. Since he had no idea of her name, he rubbed his hand along her leg as he said, "Angel, open those eyes and look at me so I'll know you're okay."

He continued to say variations of the same thing as Denny started driving. He had almost given up when she finally shifted in his arms.

Suddenly, the violet eyes that had captivated him earlier were staring at him with an expression that was hard to decipher. He was too stunned to react when she lifted her hand and stroked it down the side of his face. "Oh, Mark, it's you—can we please have sex this time before I wake up?" No sooner had she finished the question than her head dropped back to his chest. If not for the soft snore that emitted from her mouth, he would have been checking her for a pulse.

He was chuckling at her words when it hit him. She'd called him by name. His angel wasn't deliriously asking for sex from a stranger. He had no idea who she was, but for the first time in so very long, he was interested in knowing more. This beauty seemed different from most of the women he'd met and with whom he had enjoyed a few hours of pleasure. As soon as she was conscious and coherent, he intended to find out who she was.

She'd already accomplished something that no one had in years.

Chapter Two

Crystal rolled over in bed, wincing at the wave of pain that one movement seemed to have caused. The glow of the clock on the bedside table showed that it was four in the morning, which would explain why the room was still pitch-black. Her limbs were heavy with fatigue as she curled around a pillow—and then she froze. She sniffed again just to make sure she hadn't imagined it—but no, her bedding smelled like a man. Considering she hadn't slept with anyone since her divorce, this was a very strange occurrence. Jerking upright, she fumbled on the bedside table for her lamp—but it wasn't within easy reach as it should be. She stretched farther until, with a shriek, she was falling out of the bed.

She landed on the floor with a thud and a jarring of limbs. *Ouch.* She couldn't remember her carpeted floor being this hard and cold. What happened next convinced her that she must still be dreaming. Light suddenly filled the room and a man who looked a lot like Mark DeSanto stood looking down at her in concern.

Instead of screaming in terror, she began laughing

hysterically. Couldn't she have just one hot sex dream? Maybe her riding Mark while he told her how perfect she was? Heck, she'd even be happy with a plain old missionary fantasy. But no, even in her dreams, she was awkward and always managed to embarrass herself. "Sorry about this," she mumbled to her dream Mark. "Just let me get back in bed and fall asleep. If I'm lucky, you'll be back and we'll try this again."

"Are you all right? Did you hit your head when you fell?" He sounded so real, his question caused her to frown. Her eyes widened as he squatted next to her.

Okay, this was officially freaky now. Dream Mark never talked this much. She quite liked this new development. He seemed so concerned for her. She decided to enjoy it while it lasted—or at least until she woke up. "I'm too weak to stand. Could you help me?" That wasn't a complete lie, as her limbs were heavy, and she was sore already from the fall. Her breath hitched when he slid one arm under her knees and the other around her back before straightening with her in his muscular arms. "Wow, you smell good," she moaned as she buried her face in the curve of his neck. When he didn't protest, she took it one step further—and licked at the throbbing pulse she felt there with the tip of her tongue. He shuddered, freezing with her in his arms.

Crystal felt like a kid in a candy store. Shouldn't she be awake by now? This felt so real. . . . And he smelled just like her pillow. She was pondering her next move when her stomach cramped. "What—?" she murmured in confusion. Then a wave of nausea rolled over her and she clamped a hand over her mouth.

"Oh no, not again," dream Mark said, sounding

panicked. He walked at a fast clip with her to the bathroom—only it definitely wasn't hers. This one was opulent, with gleaming marble double sinks, a huge shower, and a Jacuzzi bathtub big enough to swim in. Crystal was still gawking when he lowered her to her feet in front of the toilet. He made no move to leave, though; instead, he kept a supporting hand on her back. "How are you feeling, Angel? Are you going to be sick?"

"Um—I don't know," she answered absently. "I think I just need to sit here for a minute." He helped her down to the floor then seated himself just inches away. She could only stare at him since this whole dream was beginning to seem more like a walk into the twilight zone. Hesitantly, she reached out to touch his chest. She paused as she felt his heart beating against the palm of her hand. Jerking back as if burned, she began to notice little things like the fact that she was wearing what looked like a man's button-down shirt while Mark had on a pair of lounge pants and a T-shirt. When her eyes met his, she found him staring at her with equal parts concern and curiosity. It was then that his last words really registered. "'Angel'?"

The corners of his mouth turned up into a grin as he said, "Well, when you appeared to fall from the sky into my arms, I didn't know your name, so I just called you what seemed to suit you best. Of course, now that I know who you are, I find that I still prefer 'Angel.' There's something so innocent about you."

"Oh, my God," she wheezed. "This isn't a dream? I'm actually here with you. How—why?" Looking around frantically, Crystal desperately tried to remember what could have possibly brought her to Mark's apartment.

Shit, why couldn't she remember something as monumental as being with Mark DeSanto? Then a horrifying thought occurred to her. "If we had sex, I'm going to kill myself!"

A laugh erupted from his mouth, followed by a cough. "I must say, I've never had that reaction from a woman before."

She felt her face heating up as she imagined how he must have taken her comment. "No! Crap, that came out wrong. I just meant if we slept together and I didn't remember it, I'd be so pissed off." When he raised a brow in question, she quickly added, "You know, because I've been dreaming of doing that with you for so long—" Now he looked supremely amused as she continued to ramble, which only made the situation worse. Putting a hand over her face, she said from behind her palm, "Please forget I said any of that. I'd just like to know what I'm doing here."

Mark gave her an assessing look before saying, "I'd rather talk about that somewhere other than the bathroom. Are you going to be sick?"

Thankfully, her bout of nausea seemed to have passed during their conversation. "I—think I'm okay now."

Her growling stomach caused him to chuckle as he got to his feet and extended a hand to her. "Let's go find something to eat. You'll probably feel better after that."

Not only was her body letting her know it needed food, but her bladder was also making its presence known loud and clear. "I—er, could you wait outside for a minute?"

Looking adorably confused, he asked, "Why?"

Could the man not take a hint? "I need to use the bathroom," she mumbled, embarrassed to be having such a personal discussion with him.

Apparently, it wasn't something that bothered him, though, because instead of leaving, he leaned against the wall. "I don't think it's a good idea to leave you in here alone. These floors are stone. If you pass out again, they could do serious damage."

Her mouth dropped open, and she put her hands on her hips. "There is no way I'm peeing with you in here."

Giving her a chastising look, he said, "Angel, not only have you already done it in front of me, I kept you from falling off the toilet and onto the floor. Not to mention, I had to—"

"Oh, my God—please stop!" She moaned in horror, knowing exactly what he'd been about to say. How could that have happened? What was *wrong* with her?

Quirking an amused brow, he stepped back through the doorway. "I'll wait out here, but don't close the door all the way in case I need to rescue you—again."

Crystal pondered not only shutting the door but locking it as well. He'd probably just break the damn thing down, though. There was no way she could actually do her business with him so close. She was a timid tinkler at the best of times. Therefore, she turned the water on full blast in the sink and giggled as she imagined him wondering if she was flooding the bathroom.

After taking care of business, she washed her hands but left the water running. She needed a moment to process what had happened since she'd woken up here.

How in the world had she ended up with Mark DeSanto? In what world did someone like her find herself in this sort of situation? The last thing she remembered was leaving work early because she hadn't been feeling well and then throwing up on a pair of expensive shoes. *Shit!*

Please, no. Tell me I didn't toss my cookies all over my fantasy man. Fate could not be that cruel. Then there was the issue of her clothing—or lack thereof. She was wearing what she could only guess was one of Mark's shirts and her panties. She knew her bra was missing even before she confirmed that fact by pressing a hand against her chest. Had he—? No, surely she had been able to change her own clothing.

As her thoughts raced, she made the mistake of looking up and almost screamed at the sight of her reflection. Oh, sweet heaven, the image in the mirror staring back at her was beyond terrible. She looked like a rabid animal. Instead of nursing her to health, she was surprised he hadn't called animal control to have her put down. Her hair was sticking out in all directions, and her eyes were puffy, bloodshot, and rimmed in black like a koala bear's. Looking around frantically, she spotted a cabinet in the corner and said a silent prayer of thanks when she found a stack of washcloths as well as a comb inside it. She wet one and began washing her face.

Crystal was just attempting to tame her hair when Mark called out, "Are you all right in there?"

"I'm fine," she yelled back before turning the water off. Grimacing at her reflection, she put the comb down and decided there wasn't much more she could do at this point. She was in need of a shower, but that could wait until she got some answers from Mark. Schooling her features into an impassive line, she opened the door and tried not to drool in his direction. Did the man have to be so freaking hot? *You probably wouldn't have been stalking him for months at the office if he weren't quite so good-looking,* her inner voice chided.

She had been smitten with him practically from the first glimpse. Mia had caught her ogling him in the coffee shop of Danvers one morning. She'd unknowingly poured half a container of sugar in her coffee, while watching him add creamer to his. Then she'd done something completely juvenile and pulled her cell phone out to snap a picture of the unsuspecting hunk. She had thought him the most handsome man she'd ever seen. Tall, dark, and polished in his obviously expensive suit. He'd seemed so unaware of all of the female attention centered on him. One thing that had really drawn her attention was how he'd run a hand through his hair repeatedly as if stressed over something. Crystal had never been prone to developing crushes, but something had changed for her in that instant. There was no denying her attraction to him. She must have looked at the picture she had taken dozens of times, and her curiosity had been well and truly whetted.

Maybe it was the fact that she was more lonely than she would care to admit, but she found herself watching for him around the office from then on, even going so far as to go to his floor for no reason other than to catch a glimpse of him again. She'd also checked social media and been thrilled to find he had both Facebook and Twitter accounts. He wasn't a celebrity as such, but according to Google he was a wealthy business owner who attended high-profile charity events on a regular basis. He was photographed often at these gatherings, no doubt due to his drop-dead good looks. Possibly a big part of her attraction to him was the fact that he appeared so opposite from her ex-husband. Bill had never possessed the type of power and confidence that Mark seemed to emit so effortlessly.

She snapped from her daze as he looked her over as if checking for injuries before motioning for her to follow him. He flipped on the lights to dispel the darkness as they passed through a hallway that was made almost entirely of glass. She saw water in the distance and was just opening her mouth to ask about it when he glanced over his shoulder, saying, "The house is on the ocean. I live near Jason and Gray."

She'd been to both Jason Danvers's and Gray Merimon's homes since she was friends with their wives, Suzy and Claire. Well—technically, her sister, Ella, was friends with them. Crystal was more like an acquaintance through her family connection. She liked both women a lot, though, and sometimes had lunch with them along with Ella, Suzy's sister-in-law Beth, Mia, and more recently, Emma, Ava, and Gwen. Gwen Day and Mia Gentry were her best friends, and she was lucky enough to see them at work almost every day.

"I thought you lived in Charleston," Crystal blurted out before realizing that she wouldn't know that unless she'd been looking him up online.

He didn't seem to find anything strange about the question, though, saying simply, "I have homes in several places. Living in a hotel gets old after a while, and since I'm spending a great deal of time in Myrtle Beach now, it just made sense to have a more permanent place here."

Mark flipped on another light and she saw they were now in a gourmet kitchen straight from the pages of a magazine, with designer black granite countertops and a huge island. Next to it were a commercial-size stainless steel stove and refrigerator. The area was easily five times bigger than her galley kitchen in her own apartment. If she had this kind of space, she thought, then she might actually enjoy cooking, a pastime that had been spoiled for her during her marriage to her ex-husband. Bill had insisted on a full meat-and-potatoes type of meal each evening, which in itself might not have been bad if he hadn't felt the need to criticize her efforts the entire time he was cleaning his plate. No matter what she made, it was never good enough for him.

She perched on the edge of one of the barstools that he'd indicated before saying, "You have a really nice kitchen. Do you cook a lot?"

He smirked as if she'd said something amusing. "I'd like to say that I'm a whiz in the kitchen like the Merimon brothers, but my skills in that particular area are pretty basic. I can do enough to get by, but I'm on the go a lot, so I tend to eat before I come home."

Laughing, Crystal said, "I've heard Suzy and Beth talk about how Nick and Gray were raised to work out their problems in the kitchen. I guess they cooked with their mother while they talked. It sounds as if they could open their own bakery if they ever decided to change professions." Thinking of her own overbearing mother, she added, "I wish I had grown up with some-one that nurturing."

Mark paused for a moment in the act of adding bread to a toaster, then he said quietly, "Yeah, I wouldn't know a whole helluva lot about that either. Celine DeSanto's idea of parental bonding was to help my father remain upright until dinner was finished. Otherwise, he'd be passed out cold before the salad course was over."

Crystal didn't know what to say to the information that he'd just revealed. The stiff set of his shoulders said that he wouldn't welcome her sympathy, so instead, she changed the subject. "So, why am I here? I've put together enough to know that I must have gotten sick—possibly on your shoes," she added weakly. "But I don't recall anything other than that."

He worked silently for a moment before setting two pieces of dry toast in front of her along with a chilled bottle of water from the refrigerator. "I know it's not a great breakfast, but I think we should be cautious since you were still feeling nauseous just a short while ago." Pointing to the food, which she still hadn't touched, he added, "Now eat, while I talk." She began nibbling on the bread while he seated himself across from her. "I was walking a few steps behind you when you left Danvers two days ago."

"Two days?" she gasped out. "I've been here that long?"

"It was pretty late by the time we got here on Friday, so not quite two days. You were staggering, so I asked you if you were feeling okay. You said you were fine, but then you promptly puked on me before passing out. My driver and I managed to get you into my car with the intention of taking you to a hospital. In the end, my house was closer, and I decided to bring you here first. You seemed a bit better when we arrived, and I hated to move you again. Therefore, I paid an absurd amount of money for my personal physician to make a house call. He did some blood work and—"

"WHAT?" Crystal gasped. "You took my blood while I was out of it?"

He gave her a puzzled look before shaking his head in amusement. "Angel, I'm not a vampire, so I didn't personally take your blood. Dr. Francis handled that. I can assure you that he followed the same protocol here that he would have in the hospital. You'll be glad to know that you're not pregnant." Wiggling a brow, he added, "Good news for both of us, right?"

"You—I," she stuttered before managing to take a deep breath. "I could have saved you some money. I already knew that. You have to actually have sex to · get pregnant!" she snapped. "And I've only been here for two days. I don't think there was much risk of you being made a father this quickly. So I'm not sure why you're relieved at the news."

He began laughing, and dammit, she could only stare at him, admiring how sexy he looked when he smiled. It wasn't fair for one man to have so much going for him. His midnight-black hair was thick and just begged for a woman's hands to tug on the shiny strands. Even through the loose shirt he was wearing, she could see the defined muscles of his shoulders and chest. He would no doubt have a set of washboard abs that you'd yearn to lick, and his eyes were an intense shade of blue that glowed back at her like twin sapphires. Somehow, he managed to be pretty, sexy, and rugged all at the same time. Her clit throbbed with pent-up desire, and she had to fight the need to wrap herself around his waist and beg him to fuck her—hard. She'd never had a sexual experience like that before, but she'd read enough romance novels to know that was what she wanted in the worst way. And she knew instinctively that Mark was a man who could give it to her.

She was still lost in her fantasy when a hand on her bare leg jolted her back to the present. She was almost certain by the grin on Mark's face that he knew she was having dirty thoughts about him. "Well, it just clears the way, since you've expressed your desire to have sex with me several times in the last few days."

Mortified, she whispered, "Oh no," before dropping her head into her hands. It was fine to lust over him, stalk his Facebook and Twitter pages, and trail after him in the hallways of the Danvers building—as long as he didn't know about her interest. But now she'd made a complete fool out of herself. She'd seen enough pictures of him with women on Google to know that she wasn't even in the same league with them. He had been photographed at a lot of society charity events, but never with the same woman. "I was sick and didn't know what I was saying," she defended weakly.

"If you say so, Angel," he said with a straight face. "The doctor said you had a viral infection along with being anemic. That's probably what caused you to pass out. I had my driver pick you up a bottle of iron supplements. Dr. Francis suggested that you talk to your OB/GYN about birth control pills since some-times a heavy period can cause low iron levels."

Crystal could only gawk as he talked about some-thing completely personal as if they were discuss-ing the weather. Most men would be terrified even to mention a woman's menstrual cycle, but it didn't appear to bother Mark at all. She quickly raised her hands and clamped them over her ears while his mouth continued to move. "I'm not listening to any more from you," she said until he gave her an exasperated look. "Can we please not discuss my bodily functions? I don't even know you."

With a look that was hot enough to have her body tingling again, he said, "No, but you want to, don't you, Angel? I've seen you around the office—or at least glimpses of you. I have to say that seeing you up close was a surprise—a damn good one."

Dammit, he was charming and sexy. Crystal had no idea how to respond because she'd never really had a man compliment her before. Her ex's idea of saying something nice was *I guess you'll do*. Mark, though, looked at her as if he wanted to devour her. It was only fair since she'd wanted to eat him up from the first moment she saw him. Clearing her throat and break-ing eye contact, she asked huskily, "Can we get back to what's happened since I've been here? Did you stop to think that there are possibly people looking for me?"

"Being that it was Friday when you got sick, I didn't think anyone from work would notice. Plus, once Denny, my driver, found out who you were, I gave Brant a call and had him pass the information along to Declan."

"Ella and Declan are out of town," she murmured, remembering they were having a weekend away while Ava and Mac babysat for them.

"Yeah, I know. Ella called, though, and was rather freaked-out until I assured her that you were in good hands. She said to tell you that she'd cover with your mother."

"Oh crap—thank goodness." Crystal sighed.

"Do you still live at home or something?" Mark asked, looking confused.

Shaking her head, Crystal said, "No, but that doesn't stop my meddling parents and my husband from minding my business." When he appeared shocked, she quickly added, "I mean my ex-husband! We've been divorced for a while—but my mother chose him in the unofficial settlement and they gang up on me all the time."

"Hmm, I see," he murmured. "Well, back to what has transpired since you passed out at my feet. I brought you home, showered you off—clothes and all—then put you in one of my shirts. You don't seem to remember it, but you were awake for the most part. You were sick a lot, though. I was going to take you to the hospital after I cleaned us both up, but you begged me not to. Said you were afraid of staying there alone. So instead, I brought the doctor to you. He suspected you just had something viral but did blood work to verify it. That brings you up-to-date, as I've mentioned your mild anemia and negative pregnancy test."

Crystal's head was spinning as Mark finished running through the last two days at breakneck speed.

Puzzled, she asked, "Why would you do all of that? You don't even know me."

Giving her a roguish grin, he said, "I feel like we're pretty well acquainted now." When she narrowed her eyes at him, he added softly, "I couldn't take you to the hospital, Angel. You were so fucking scared for some reason when I mentioned it."

Looking beyond Mark's shoulder to where the sun was beginning to rise over the water, she rubbed her arm absently before saying, "I had my tonsils removed and had to stay in the hospital overnight when I was young. No one stayed with me, so I was alone, in pain, and scared out of my mind. My mom had told me before she left that I had better behave myself or the nurses would tell her in the morning and I would be in trouble. So every time they came to check on me and ask if I was in pain, I said no so that word wouldn't get back to my mother that I'd been bad." Trying to make light of what had been a terrifying experience, she forced out a laugh, adding, "It was a long night."

"Ah, I'm sorry, Angel. Your reaction makes a lot of sense to me now. That was a real shitty thing to do to a child. Is your mother still a heartless bitch?"

Crystal began choking on the sip of water she had just taken. He got up and walked over to pat her on the back until she managed to catch her breath. "Sorry about that," she said huskily. "It's just that no one is brave enough to call Dorothy Webber names. Most people are terrified of her."

"Trust me, Angel, I'm fully versed in bad parenting. Mine aren't exactly the type to give you the warm fuzzies either. Of course, I haven't seen either of them in a while, so maybe they've turned over a new leaf."

"How have you stayed away from them for that long?" Crystal asked incredulously. Considering her mother called her no fewer than ten times per week, it was hard to imagine going that long without her popping by for one of her awkward, unannounced visits.

Mark took her empty plate and put it in the sink before turning back to her. "It's not complicated. They only communicate with me when they want something. I only wish that weren't as often as it is."

"You're so lucky." She sighed before she could stop herself. Mark chuckled, nodding his head in agreement. Then she forced herself to say the last words that she wanted to utter. "I guess I should be getting home now. You must be so ready to see the last of me." *Please God, say no . . .*

He didn't speak for a moment. Instead, he studied her intently, as if looking for a sign of something from her. Just when she thought he wasn't going to say anything at all, he shrugged his broad shoulders and grinned. "What's one more night, Angel? I'd hate to take you home now and you have a relapse. Stay here and we'll leave early enough tomorrow morning to swing by your place before work. Today, we can take it easy and watch some movies."

Crystal could only gawk at his suggestion. She wanted to stay more than anything, and he was making it possible without her having to do something crazy like begging. So why was she hesitating? She'd never get the opportunity again to spend time with the man she had all but stalked for months now. She looked down at her hands, trying not to let her excitement show. "I guess that would be all right," she said, trying to sound flippant. She was on cloud nine until she remembered how she looked. "Um—do you think I could take a shower?"

He gave her a look that was pure wickedness. "Of course—but I should probably help you again. What if you get dizzy? I'll do your back—and front—if you like."

Down, girl—roll your tongue back into your mouth. "I—er, believe I'll be fine." She'd never wanted to scream *YES* before as she did now. She needed to remove herself immediately from the temptation he offered.

He rolled his eyes. "If you insist. After we've both showered, we'll go back to bed for a while. I don't know about you, but I'm exhausted."

Fighting back a yawn, Crystal nodded her head. "That sounds good."

Mark led her to the same bedroom and handed her more clothing from his closet—this time a soft T-shirt. He then pulled a pair of boxer briefs from a nearby drawer and passed them along to her as well. "Knowing you aren't wearing panties might be more than I can take. I'm only human, Angel. Hopefully, you can make those work."

Crystal knew her face was probably five shades of pink as she took the items and went into the bathroom, avoiding glancing at herself in the mirror. By the time she was finished with her shower and drying her hair, she was about ready to drop from exhaustion. When she opened the door and walked back into the bedroom, she was disappointed to find it empty. Mark had apparently decided to bathe elsewhere. Shrugging her shoulders, she crawled into the bed that she had so recently vacated and fell asleep almost immediately.

Mark stood staring down at the woman in his bed. It unnerved him that she looked so right lying there—as if she belonged. He rarely brought women to his home, and he certainly didn't do sleepovers. He'd broken all of the rules with her already. He'd nursed her back to health for the last two days and then asked her to stay with him for another night. Hell, he was pretty sure he'd have begged if she'd refused. He was drawn to her and he had no idea why. He fucked women—period. She was beautiful—but he could get that anywhere. She was sexy—again, that was a dime a dozen. She was also innocent—even though she'd apparently been married at some point.

She might not remember it now, but while she'd been sick, she had looked at him as if he was her hero. She had nestled into his arms between bouts of sickness, bringing out protective instincts that he didn't know he possessed. Dr. Francis had suggested Mark hire a nurse to care for Crystal until she had recovered, but Mark had brushed him off quickly. He didn't want anyone else taking care of her, which was fucking insane. Even having another man's hands on her creamy skin while the doctor examined her was torture. He'd excused himself from the room at that point to have a glass—or two—of bourbon.

Mark was an alpha male; he always had been. He was the one in control of sexual encounters. Being that way, he'd learned, kept emotional hassles to a minimum. He was a leader—never a follower. He was dominant in the bedroom and liked to push boundaries. He didn't cuddle, nor indulge in sweet talk. He'd never sent a woman flowers or anything even approaching a romantic gesture like that. So why was he so tempted to get in the bed and pull Crystal into his arms? He'd showered in one of the guest rooms with the intention of sleeping there as well, yet here he was. He couldn't stay away. He'd been with her almost constantly because she'd needed him since she'd been here. She seemed fine today, though.

He had turned, forcing himself to leave, when her voice brought him back around. "Mark?"

Going to the bed, he sat next to her. "It's me, Angel. I was just checking on you. Can I get you anything?" She didn't need to know that he'd been staring at her for the last ten minutes.

"No," she answered almost hesitantly. When he started to rise, her hand shot out and she grabbed his arm. "Do you—think you could stay with me for a while?" Before he could answer, she rushed on. "It's just that I get kind of nervous in new places sometimes."

He felt a wave of tenderness go through him as he remembered her telling him earlier about her ordeal in the hospital when she was younger. God knows he hadn't grown up with nurturing parents, but at least his nanny would have stayed with him had he been hospitalized. His poor Angel had been left alone to suffer. What a bunch of assholes. The decision made, he motioned her over, and settled in beside her under the comforter. Without a word, he lifted one arm and she was instantly under it and curled into his side. He dropped a kiss onto the top of her head as if it were the most natural thing in the world for him to be doing. He had no idea what was happening, but he had a bad feeling that he was in over his head with her.

The only thing he couldn't figure out was why he wasn't running the other way. He'd been so damn restless and edgy lately. Nothing seemed to excite or appeal to him anymore. He blamed it on stress, but his reaction to Crystal had him wondering if maybe it wasn't more. Spending time with someone who appeared so different from most of the women he met had been surprisingly appealing.

Always in the past if he was in bed with a woman, then there was sex involved. But now, he found himself content to hold the beauty who had literally fallen into his arms—just like an angel.

Chapter Three

The next morning, Crystal settled in the backseat of the car next to Mark. She vaguely remembered him getting in bed with her the night before, but he'd been gone when she woke at seven. She'd stumbled into the bathroom for a quick shower. When she'd walked back into the bedroom, she had been surprised to find a new dress with tags and matching shoes lying on the bed. A quick check showed both items were the correct size. The dress was a pale lilac color in a soft, whispery material. Crystal gasped in shock when she turned the tag over and saw that it was almost fifteen hundred dollars and the strappy sandals were well over a thousand. There was no way she could afford to pay Mark back all at once. She finally decided to leave the tags on the dress and tuck them out of sight. Hopefully, he'd be able to return it if she was careful with it today. The store would never take the shoes back, though, and God, she loved them. Surely, he'd be okay with her paying him in a couple of installments.

"You look beautiful." His words jarred her back to the present. His eyes were intense as he stared at her appreciatively.

"I—thank you," she stumbled over her words, sounding like an inexperienced teenager. "You didn't have to buy me clothes. You could have dropped me at home to change. I'll pay you back. I mean—not right away, but I left the tag on the dress so you can return it. And I'll reimburse you for the shoes as soon as I can."

"Angel, stop," Mark said quietly, placing a hand on her leg where the dress had ridden up. "Seeing you looking so exquisite this morning is more payback than I need. The outfit is yours. I don't want to be reimbursed."

"Bu-but Mark, do you know how much this whole thing cost you?" Crystal protested.

"Don't worry, honey. He can afford it," called a voice from the front of the car. "He wanted you in something that would bring out the color of your eyes and shoes that would accentuate your long legs. I think I followed directions pretty good, right, boss?"

Crystal gasped while Mark chuckled. "I couldn't have done better myself." The hand on her leg stroked her tender skin reassuringly as he added, "Angel, you probably don't remember him, but Denny is my assistant, my driver, and now your personal shopper. He's also my cousin."

"It's nice to meet you, Angel—er, I mean Crystal." The man in the front seat shot her a sideways grin before returning his full attention to the road. "Thanks to you, I got a new suit, so I'm grateful. It was definitely an upgrade."

"Oh no," she groaned. "I didn't throw up on you too, did I?"

"Nah." Denny waved one hand. "But I had to hold you while Mark got in the car—which was kinda messy, and then you puked all in the back floorboard. Don't feel too bad about that one, because I had someone else clean it. I have a weak stomach."

Crystal dropped her head forward in embarrassment. "I'm really sorry I put you both through so much. You should have ignored my protests and dropped me at the nearest hospital. Thank you so much for taking care of me."

Mark raised his hand from her leg and pulled her into his arms. Somehow, it felt as if he'd done that a hundred times before with her. He was still basically a stranger, but she'd never been so comfortable with anyone so fast, even her ex-husband. "You were no problem, Angel. Hell, you were pretty funny a few times—between the whole projectile-vomiting thing you had going on."

Crystal heard Denny snicker from the front, causing her to smile ruefully. She leaned her head against his chest and enjoyed the feeling of a man holding her. No one would ever believe that she was in Mark DeSanto's arms while being driven to work. Stuff like this just didn't happen to her. The embarrassing-herself part wasn't that big of a surprise—even though she'd never tossed her cookies on a man before. She was certainly socially awkward enough to make a fool of herself on a regular basis—and she did. "Well, you're both my heroes," she told them—and she meant every word of it. "I bet you do this sort of thing all the time."

Denny sounded like he was choking, causing her to eye the back of his head in concern until she figured out that he was actually laughing. "The women in and out of this car have problems, for sure—but in a whole different way."

"Denny—that's enough!" Mark snapped. Crystal could still hear Denny chuckling, but he didn't say anything else. She couldn't help but wonder what he had been talking about. She felt a crazy flicker of jealousy at the thought of how many women must have sat exactly where she was right now. It was quite possibly the reality check that she desperately needed before she cuddled further into his hard body and professed her undying love—and lust. When she started to move away, Mark's arms tightened around her. "Ignore him, Angel, and kiss me."

She turned her head to stare at him. "What?" Her shrill voice echoed around the car. She dropped it to a whisper as she said, "Are you crazy? We don't even know each other—plus we're not alone."

Looking amused, he asked, "So, exactly how well would I need to know you in order to taste that pouty mouth?" He tapped her lips, which, dammit, parted as if of their own volition.

Without thinking, Crystal pinched her arm. "Ouch!"

Mark grinned. "Are we going to have the dream-Mark chat again? That was one of the most entertaining moments of the weekend, Angel. Well, along with your confessions of stalking me."

"Oh, my God," she moaned. "This can't be happening."

"Ah, come on, baby, there's nothing to be ashamed of. I'm flattered as hell. Am I the only object of your obsession or are there others?" Giving her knee a quick squeeze, he added, "I'm not good at sharing, so you'll need to devote your complete attention to me from now on."

Keeping her head down, Crystal mumbled, "People say all kinds of things when they're sick, so you can't hold it against me." Before he could reply, the car slowed and they were pulling into the circular driveway in front of the Danvers headquarters. He didn't do anything to stop her this time as she scurried from his lap and onto the seat next to him. Denny put the car in park and got out to open the door. She took his proffered hand and stood uncertainly, waiting for Mark to join them.

To her surprise, Denny threw an arm over her shoulders. "Nice meeting you, Crystal. I feel like we're friends now, seeing as I've held your hair back while you were sick." When she gave him a confused look, he added, "Oh, not in the car. It was in Mark's flower bed while he unlocked the door at his house."

Crystal looked helplessly at Mark as he stepped closer. He rolled his eyes at his driver before saying, "Stop tormenting her and go park the car. I'll see you inside." Denny gave him a quick salute before getting back in the car and driving away.

Studying Mark's shiny shoes, she said, "So . . . um, thanks again for everything. Are you sure you don't want the clothes back? I can skip lunch to avoid staining the dress." Suddenly, a hand was under her chin, lifting her head until their eyes locked. Dear sweet Lord, she'd never thought of a man as lickable before, but oh, how she wanted to taste him. Then it happened . . . the ultimate mortification to put all other moments to shame.

His mouth dropped open in shock, and she realized suddenly that she had voiced her desire aloud. "No, no!" she hissed. "What are you doing to me? I can't stop making a fool out of myself where you're concerned."

Mark, seeming to notice that she was now close to tears, pulled her into his arms and rubbed a hand down her back. "Damn, Angel. The only thing you're doing is keeping me hard. I've never wanted to fuck anyone as badly as I want you. I've got a meeting with a roomful of men in about five minutes and my cock is hard enough to cut glass."

Crystal moved closer despite her embarrassment, wanting proof of his words. There it was . . . the unmistakable feel of him pressed against her stomach. He made a pained sound and it hit her that she was practically dry-humping him on the sidewalk. She reluctantly stepped back, breaking his hold on her. She needed to salvage what little pride she had left. She was acting like a teenager with her first crush, instead of a grown woman. Extending a hand to him, she strove for a strong tone as she said, "Thanks for everything. I—maybe we'll see each other around the office sometime."

She had gotten a few steps away when she heard him say, "No kiss good-bye, Angel, after all we've been through together?"

Before she could talk herself out of it, she whirled around and retraced her steps. Standing on her toes, she dropped a kiss onto his smooth-shaven cheek, causing him to inhale deeply. Then she scurried away like a frightened mouse.

When she reached the doorway of Danvers, she looked over her shoulder to see him still standing in the same place, looking confused. No doubt the poor man probably thought she was mental and was pondering relocation so he'd never have to see her again.

As soon as Mark opened the door to his office, he saw Denny sitting at his desk in the reception area with a big smirk on his face. "Don't even start," he growled as he walked past and shut his door. He'd given his assistant enough to keep him amused for the near future, and right now, he wasn't in the mood to be heckled. Hell, what could he say? Both he and Denny knew that he'd acted completely out of character for the last several days and even he didn't know why. It certainly wasn't like him to be content to play house, but strangely enough, he had been.

When she'd stood on the sidewalk and stared at him as if in some type of daze before saying how much she'd like to lick him, he'd almost lost it. As it was, he'd had the hard-on of a lifetime with her luscious body plastered against him. He should be grateful she'd had enough sense to pull away, because his hand had been about an inch from her ass and closing in fast. His cock still throbbed just thinking about it. He was adjusting his zipper, trying to ease his discomfort, when Denny buzzed to let him know that Brant Stone was there to see him. Grimacing, Mark stayed seated as his friend opened the door.

Brant crossed the room, extending a hand. If he thought it strange that Mark didn't get up to greet him, he didn't mention it. Dropping into one of the chairs in front of the desk, Brant asked, "So what's the deal with you and my sister-in-law?"

Mark was momentarily taken aback by the question. "Ella?"

With a snort of impatience, Brant said, "No—Crystal. I heard she was at your house all weekend. Something about her being sick." The narrowing of the other man's eyes told Mark that he didn't believe a damn word of it. That was the downside to being longtime friends with business associates. They tended to know far too much about your personal life. He and Brant had grown up in the same circles, so there weren't many secrets between them.

Trying not to look guilty that he was battling an erection at the sound of Crystal's name, Mark looked his friend in the eyes—and danced like a fucking ballerina. Speaking slowly and deliberately, he said, "Man, Ella is your sister-in-law. You are aware of that, right? I'm almost certain she's the only one you have."

Brant had always been a bit on the uptight side, and even though his fiancée, Emma, had loosened him up quite a bit, jokes still tended to fly over his head at times. Of course, he possibly didn't look amused because he knew Mark was bullshitting him. "You know what I mean," he said dryly. "I consider Crystal as much my family as Ella now. Declan was a little . . . . concerned about how she came to be at your house."

Mark couldn't help but be irritated over the fact that neither of his friends considered him trustworthy. Hadn't he always been there when they needed him, with no questions asked? Okay, maybe a few, but nothing like this inquisition. "For fuck's sake, Brant, I didn't chain her up in my basement. She threw up on me on her way out of the building, before passing out. What would you have had me do, leave her on the curb?"

Brant pursed his lips, before shaking his head. "I'm grateful you helped her. But I'm not clear on why you took care of her for so long. I know Declan and Ella were out of town, but you could have called her parents or me."

Mark gave a snort of disgust. "Her mother is one evil bitch. There's no way I would have put Angel at her mercy." Realizing his slip too late, he prayed that Brant hadn't noticed his nickname for Crystal.

Predictably, Brant parroted, "Angel?"

Shifting nervously, he muttered, "Um, sorry. Crystal, I mean." He could only hope that Brant thought he just couldn't keep up with all the women he interacted with. Before he could ask further questions, Mark launched into an explanation of his first statement. "I was going to take her to the hospital, but she got really upset. Said her mother had left her there overnight once when she was young. She'd been scared to death and in pain. Now she has some sort of phobia over it. So I took her to my house and called a doctor. It was a nasty viral bug, and she was really sick for almost forty-eight hours. Would you have wanted to move her in that condition if I had called?" Brant looked uneasy now. Since the other man was a bit of a neat freak, Mark couldn't imagine him dealing with what he had this weekend, and the look of horror on his face confirmed it.

"It sounds like we all owe you our gratitude," Brant admitted. "Plus, you may have a small point about Declan's mother-in-law. I haven't interacted much with her, but Dec says she's hell on wheels. I think Crystal's been in her line of fire since her divorce. I guess both her mother and ex-husband are trying to pressure her into reconciliation."

"Maybe they both need someone to spell it out for them. Ang—Crystal isn't interested," Mark retorted. What in the hell was he doing? He had no idea how she actually felt. For all he knew, she was dying to get back with her ex-husband. Even more worrisome was the fact that it pissed him off to even think about it. She wasn't Mark's, and he didn't want her to be. He was just feeling strangely territorial after taking care of her for a few days. He'd never done something like that before, so it was only natural that he would be concerned about her—right?

Brant studied him for what seemed like hours but was probably only seconds. "We're friends, Mark, and what you do in your personal life is your own business. Unless it involves someone that I care about." Indignant, Mark opened his mouth to protest, but Brant waved him off and continued. "Crystal is so far out of your league that you two might as well be from different worlds. She might have been married, but like Ella, she's led a very sheltered life. I know she's attractive and would appeal to most men—especially once someone spends some time alone with her. But she wouldn't know how to handle your world. You've got to know that, man."

Pinching the bridge of his nose, Mark attempted to regroup before he blasted his friend. He was sick and fucking tired of being judged. He'd always had a healthy sex drive, and yeah, he liked to be in control.

Was that a crime? He'd never had a woman complain. And he certainly didn't make promises, so he couldn't be accused of giving them false expectations. "Nothing happened between us," he said curtly. "Yes, she is beautiful, and of course, I'm attracted to her, but I didn't act on it. If I did decide to pursue something with her, though, that would be between us. But at this time, I have no intentions of doing so. Which makes this not-too-subtle warning unnecessary."

Brant didn't look like he believed a word that Mark was saying, but he simply responded, "Fair enough." Glancing down at his watch, he stood, saying, "We're running a few minutes late for our meeting. Are you ready to go?"

Mark gathered the papers that he needed and followed the other man out the door. His guilt lay like a heavy weight on his shoulders because he'd just done something that he hated. He'd lied to one of his best friends. He couldn't stay away from Angel. He missed her already and knew that it was just a matter of time before he sought her out.

Chapter Four

"Well, hello, Hollywood!" Mia wolf-whistled as Crystal made her way across the restaurant to where her friends were waiting. Mia Gentry handled the installations of new communications systems for Danvers and was dating Seth Jackson, who owned the luxurious Oceanix chain of hotels. She had actually met Seth while doing an installation at his hotel. Gwen Day also worked for Danvers in the accounting department and was engaged to Dominic Brady, one of the owners of East Coast Security. East Coast had offices in the building and also provided security for Danvers. Crystal had met both of them through work, and they'd become fast friends. Mia was outspoken and at times irreverent, while Gwen was sweet and funny. She was also noticeably pregnant, which Crystal could admit to herself that she envied. If only Bill hadn't been so . . . repressed in every way, maybe she would have had a family by now. Of course, he'd blamed their difficulties conceiving on her and had refused to even consider that he might have been the problem. Her doctor had mentioned when everything checked out fine with her that maybe Bill had a low sperm count. He'd completely shut down on her when she told him. As per usual, any problem in their marriage was always her fault. Heck, hadn't her own mother often agreed with him?

Gwen gave her an admiring look as she took her seat. "Wow, you look amazing. Is that a new dress?"

Shifting uneasily, she said, "Um—yes, it is."

Mia lifted the tablecloth to peek at her feet and let out a sigh of pleasure. "Damn, girl, those shoes are to die for. Actually, this whole look is sexy—but it's really different for you. You know I'm always up for a shopping trip, so why was I left out of this apparently epic one?" She stuck out her bottom lip in a pout.

Crystal had decided to keep her encounter with Mark to herself, but now she found that she desperately wanted to tell her friends what had happened. It wasn't every day that you spent the weekend with the man of your dreams. Why not enjoy it? "I didn't exactly do the shopping," she confessed. Both Mia and Gwen just looked confused now.

"Ohhh, you ordered it online," Gwen piped up. "It gives me a big thrill every time the UPS man shows up at our door with another package. Dominic says I'm way out of control, but God, I love Amazon."

Smiling in response, Crystal noticed that Mia looked disappointed. Well, that certainly wouldn't last for long. . . . "I didn't shop online," she added before taking a drink of the water their waiter had dropped off. "Someone bought this for me," she tossed out as she picked up her menu. "What's everyone having?"

The table was dead silent for a moment before Mia

pulled Crystal's menu from her hand and huffed out, "What we're having is an explanation. Who bought you that dress and those do-me shoes?"

Gwen choked out a laugh before looking around nervously to see if anyone was listening to them. "Don't make a pregnant woman beg. That's just cruel."

"I'll tell you," Crystal began, trying to control her own excitement, "but you're not going to believe me."

"Do you think we can get away with having a margarita with our lunch?" Mia asked, sounding half-serious. "It sounds like we need alcohol of some sort for this."

Rubbing her stomach ruefully, Gwen shook her head. "Oh no, I don't think so. If I have to go dry, then so do you. Now please put Mia out of her misery, Crystal, and tell us what's going on."

Unable to hold it in any longer, Crystal blurted out, "I spent the weekend with Mark DeSanto, and he bought me these clothes! Well, at least his assistant did, but I'm sure Mark paid for them."

"Holy shit sticks!" Gwen gasped out before turning red when all conversation nearby ceased. "Er . . . sorry," she murmured before dropping her voice.

"You slept with Mark?" Mia sounded as if she was being strangled as she choked out the words. "This is huge! You tramp, how in the world did that happen?"

Gwen snickered, wiggling her eyebrows. "I think we know how it happened. First, you both take off your clothes, then . . ."

Crystal looked down, knowing her cheeks had probably flamed bloodred, as Mia tossed a wadded-up napkin at Gwen. "Duh, I wasn't asking about that.

Believe me, Seth gave me a detailed demonstration of what goes where just hours ago. And I'm betting that Dominic did the same to you. So, since we've covered that, let's get back to Crystal—who has a lot of explaining to do."

Holding her hands up to quiet the questions her friends were tossing out, Crystal began to explain what had occurred. "It started off kind of badly—so don't get too excited." At their look of shock, she quickly added, "I mean, it wasn't like a normal date or anything."

"How in the world is that man so cocky if he's got a tiny dick?" Mia mused. "Sure, some might say it's not the size but how it's used—but damn. I would have guessed that Mark's was huge."

"Me too," Gwen whispered. "That just negates my belief in the 'swagger.'"

Feeling as if her eyes were going to cross as she tried to figure out what her friends were talking about, Crystal asked, "The what?"

Mia held her hands apart. "You know—men with big peckers have that certain kind of walk. At least we've all found that to be true." Gwen nodded her agreement as Mia continued. "So with you telling us that Mark has a petite package, it's blown all of our theories to hell. I will give the man full respect for owning his shortcomings, though. He walks around Danvers like he has a tree between his legs."

"But it's just like a limb instead," Gwen bemoaned solemnly as she patted Crystal's hand. "It's okay, sweetie. As long as he makes you happy—that's all that matters, right?"

Mia jumped in her seat, as if jolted. "Oh, of course.

Big ones are overrated. Sometimes a girl just wants to cuddle."

Crystal rubbed her forehead, wondering how the conversation got so far off track when it suddenly hit her. "Oh, my God." She started laughing. "Mark and I didn't have sex, so I never saw his—size. But I did feel it and I don't think there is any reason at all to call his manhood into question."

"I'm confused," Gwen said uncertainly. "I thought you spent the weekend with him?"

"I tossed my cookies all over him in front of the building on Friday and he took me home with him," Crystal revealed, trying to avoid any more crazy speculation.

In true Mia fashion, her friend skipped right over the truth and circled back to a certain body part. "Tell us more about your inspection of Mark's most valuable asset? How did that come about?"

Gwen, always being the more patient one, said, "Crys, just start from the beginning. I, for one, want to hear the entire story. You've been stalking the man for so long. This is like something from a romance novel."

"Thank you, Gwen," Crystal huffed out. "So, after our unfortunate meeting, Mark took me to his house and had a doctor come over to examine me. It was determined that it was just something viral, and sadly, I wasn't even aware of where I was until Sunday. Then Mark made me breakfast and asked me to stay until Monday. Just in case I had a relapse. He had his assistant, Denny, buy me this outfit to wear today—and that about sums it up." It was all she could do to keep a straight face as her friends looked at each other before turning pitiful eyes back to her.

"But what about getting close to Mark's love rod?" Mia asked beseechingly. Crystal wouldn't have been surprised to hear the woman's feet stomping on the floor. Mia had never been good at waiting. She would bet that poor Seth had his hands full with his girlfriend.

"Oh . . . did I forget to add the part about the ride to work this morning?" she asked innocently.

"I'm going to do something crazy if you don't tell us right now," Gwen threatened. When her chin wobbled, Crystal started to panic. She knew that her pregnant friend cried at the drop of a hat now. There was no way teasing them was worth that kind of risk.

"Hold your Kleenex waterworks," Mia said dryly. "Now, Crys, I don't know how long I can hold the floodgates closed, so you'd better spill—like now."

Giving Gwen a wary look, she said, "All right; I sat in his lap on the way to work this morning. Nothing happened, though, even though he asked me to kiss him."

"Why didn't you?" Mia asked incredulously. "Honey, I would have climbed that like a vine."

"Apparently, I said a few . . . embarrassing things while I was out of it. Like how he was my dream man. I think I even admitted to following him around Danvers. So I jumped out of the car as soon as we arrived and I was thinking to myself how I wanted to lick him—only I actually said it aloud! I, Crystal Webber, managed to shock superstud Mark DeSanto. When he recovered, he told me that he'd never wanted to fuck a woman as much as he did me—and then I humped his leg like a dog in heat, right in broad daylight for all to see."

"Holy . . ." Mia murmured.

"Shit," Gwen added absently.

Taking another gulp of her water, Crystal said, "Oh, and then I kissed him on the cheek and ran from him." The order of events might have happened a little differently, but that was the story in a nutshell.

"He wants you, Crys—bad," Mia squealed, finally breaking from her trance. "You're on his radar now, so you need to take advantage of it."

Crystal nodded before shrugging helplessly. "I don't know how. He was amazing to me and I loved the opportunity to spend time with him—even if I did embarrass myself a lot. But that's all I'm going to have, isn't it? Really, can either of you sit there and tell me that Mark and I will ride off into the sunset together in the very near future? Because as much as I'd like to believe that could happen, it's not very likely, is it?"

"Of course, it's possible," Gwen said immediately. "Trust me; I was the original unlucky in love before I met Dominic. My whole dating life was one failure after another. I always cared too much and got walked all over for my efforts. I would have never imagined finding a man who loved me through all of my insecurities. And look at Mia over there. She landed Seth Jackson. He's rich, hot, and puts up with her."

Mia stuck her tongue out at Gwen before nodding in agreement. "Just because Mark is wealthy doesn't make him any better than you, Crys, nor is he unattainable. Seth is the only one of the Jackson brothers and cousins in a relationship, and he swears they all envy him. Most men are like us. They want someone to connect with beyond the physical or financial aspect. Don't rule Mark out and believe that he's out of your league, because that's bullshit. You're a beautiful, intelligent woman, and he'd be lucky to have YOU."

Moved by the show of support, Crystal blinked back tears. "Is this where you tell me that he puts his pants on one leg at a time like the rest of the world?"

Nudging her in the side, Gwen winked. "Or we could say he takes them off that way. . . . Personally, I like that visual better."

"You would, horny pregnant woman," Mia teased. "I bet poor Dominic can barely keep up with you now."

Gwen's face flushed pink, but she gave a satisfied smile. "Trust me—he's not complaining. The man is like the Energizer Bunny. I was determined to see how many times he could do it in a row before begging for mercy, and let me say—I was the one who gave up first and he actually seemed disappointed."

"Seth's the same," Mia agreed. "The first few months we were together, I could barely walk straight. He goes at it hard." Looking proud, she added, "We've broken the bed—twice so far. God, I love that man."

"I have no idea why we're friends," Crystal pouted. "I pretty much hate you both most of the time. I've never been a part of anything being broken in the bedroom—well, unless you count speed records. Bill clocked in at less than five minutes on a regular basis."

Gwen shuddered, while Mia cringed. "Well . . ." Gwen finally said, "sometimes men get a little excited and the actual main event might not last long."

"I was talking about the whole thing—from start to finish. That includes any and all foreplay." Crystal sighed glumly.

"Please tell me you at least got off during that time," Mia pleaded.

"No," Crystal said. "I'm ashamed to admit that I didn't realize how it could feel until I—you know . . ."

"Took matters into your own hands," Mia guessed. "Crys, I would imagine that most women with a quick-draw man would feel that way. Heck, until Seth, my vibrator was the best I'd ever had. Some men just don't care if a woman gets hers or not."

"I was involved with a guy who was obsessed with making me orgasm," Gwen added. "The thing is, he wasn't really that . . . talented, and I felt like an old Buick that he was trying to fix up. I started faking it, just so he'd let it go. The point is, there are many things that can go wrong if you don't click with someone sexually. If you're attracted to Mark and he's said that he feels the same, then I say pull out all of the stops and go for it. You don't need to worry about what to do once you're with him again because a guy like that knows enough for both of you."

Crystal knew she probably sounded clueless, but she asked anyway. "So, how do I go after him?"

Mia put both elbows on the table and leaned forward to give her a confident smile. "You don't have to do anything. If I'm right about Mark, then he'll be coming after you shortly. Don't change anything. He's not going to be able to stay away now that he knows you exist. A man like that is going to be drawn to the innocent vibe you give off like a fly to honey. I give him a week, tops, before you hear from him. He'll spend a few days in denial, telling himself all the reasons why he shouldn't see you again. He may attempt to see other women to get you off his mind. When none of that works, he'll break."

"You really missed your calling," Gwen marveled. "If you put all of that into a book, I'd buy it. You have me dying to know what happens next."

"Me too," Crystal enthused. "It sounds so exciting that it couldn't possibly involve me."

"Oh, baby, you're the star of the show and only you will be able to script the ending," Mia predicted. "And when you do, there had better be full disclosure. After the scare earlier over Mark's package size, Gwen and I need to know that everything's okay in that area so we can sleep at night. The whole world-in-balance thing, if you know what I'm saying."

"You're nuts." Crystal laughed sheepishly. But she could only hope that Mia was right, although she couldn't see Mark ever pursuing her, regardless of what he'd said about wanting her. When she got home that evening, she was going to write down everything that had transpired between them while it was still fresh in her mind. At least then, she'd have something to look back on if Mark never spoke to her again.

"So no Snow White this evening?" Denny asked as Mark settled back for the drive home.

"Snow White?" Mark repeated, meanwhile knowing full well who he was referring to.

Denny grinned in the rearview mirror before saying, "Oh, I'm sorry; I believe you refer to her as your Angel."

Laying his head back against the seat and closing his eyes, Mark said, "I assume she's gone home by now."

Mark rolled his eyes as the other man said, "I'm not

one to stick my nose in your business, but you should keep that one around for a while."

"First of all," Mark began dryly, "when have you ever not had a comment on the women in my life? And second, nothing happened with Crystal. I helped her out and that's it. End of story."

Sounding far too serious, Denny said, "But you like her. I mean beyond the usual physical attraction. She spent more time with you this weekend than any female that I know of—other than your mother."

"And you see how enjoyable that long-term relationship has been," Mark pointed out.

Denny made a sound of disgust in his throat, being no fonder of Mark's mother than he was. "I'm just saying that you've been restless lately. Possibly, it's time for a change. There's this whole world of dating that you've yet to experience. There are things you can do with women outside of the bedroom, you know."

"How would you know?" Mark found himself asking, curious despite himself. He and Denny spent a great deal of time together and were close, but he didn't ask many questions about the other man's romantic life. His cousin mentioned having a date sometimes, but the concept of something that sounded so innocent had never appealed to Mark enough for him to express much interest.

"I've actually had several long-term relationships. You know, the whole going out to dinner, a movie, or some other form of entertainment. Anything that involves spending time with someone you care about. Heck, I don't even typically have sex on the first date, nor do I expect it. Believe it or not, the whole *let's get out of here* line doesn't work for most of us."

"I'm sorry to hear that," Mark smirked.

"If you'd like, I could help you with Crystal. A woman like that might not react as well to being invited over to fuck."

Mark thought back again to the way she had practically ridden his leg this morning, while rubbing against his cock. "You may be wrong, cousin. Angel may want many things that have never been asked of her. Often in order to think outside of the box, you just need a bit of instruction. Something I excel in offering to women."

"So you *are* interested in her?" Denny pounced on his statement like a dog with a bone. "I knew it. I could make a reservation for dinner tomorrow evening for you."

"I was speaking hypothetically." Mark denied any interest. He was content to let the rest of the ride pass in silence.

Later that night, though, he couldn't help but remember Angel mentioning the fact that she followed his Twitter feed. Picking up his phone, he typed out a tweet that said: *"Delay is the deadliest form of denial."* *C. Northcote Parkinson.* *#Angel.* Something about the quote seemed to hit the right note, and he wondered if she would see it. Then a wave of hesitation and indecision struck him. Shit, what was he even doing? He should delete the tweet and stay as far away from her as possible. In the big-picture view, she was all things virginal white, and in comparison, his soul was black and had been for years. Feeling unworthy was unfamiliar for him, and he had no idea how to handle these strange stirrings of inadequacy. He didn't do well with idle time, and it was obvious that he'd gone too long between women. He'd rectify that tomorrow and go back to what he knew best. For some reason, though, he couldn't make himself delete the tweet.

Crystal had barely closed the door of her apartment when she heard, "Where have you been, young lady?"

Spinning around, she saw her mother standing a few feet away with her hands on her hips. Crystal pressed a hand to her chest, trying to slow her heartbeat down. "Good Lord, Mom, you scared me to death!"

"Watch your attitude, young lady," her mother scolded.

It was on the tip of her tongue to tell her mother that if she didn't like it, then she should stop letting herself into her home uninvited. Frankly, though, the tirade that she would unleash would make Crystal sorry that she'd ever opened her mouth. With Dot Webber, it was best to pick your battles and hope to minimize the fallout. Making her voice as pleasant as possible, she asked, "What brings you by today?"

"I wanted to make sure you were still alive. Your sister said something about you staying the weekend with a friend. But you didn't answer any of my calls, so I thought for sure that something bad had happened to you."

Ella had told her today that she hadn't told their mother about her being sick at Mark's house. They both knew that would send her into DEFCON 5.

Instead, she'd tried to be vague and then avoided answering her phone. "As you can see, I'm fine, Mom. I know you're usually busy on the weekends, so I didn't think you'd miss me." Crystal knew she'd said the wrong thing as soon as the words left her mouth, but there was nothing to do but survive the coming explosion.

"Ohhh no, why would your mother be at all concerned about you? It's not as if I was in labor for eighteen hours with you or anything. Something that minor doesn't deserve common courtesy, does it?" Then, in a rapid-fire subject change, she tacked on, "Please tell me you weren't with that awful Gwen. She's living with some redneck and is pregnant yet again. All without being married. How many times do I have to tell you girls that if you roll with dogs, you get fleas? First Ella and now you. I have no idea where I went wrong."

Shit, the drama was in full swing tonight. It pissed her off that her mother continued to make nasty comments about Ella and Declan. Crystal was surprised that her sister still spoke to her. And Declan, he was bound to tell her off at some point soon. "You don't even know my friends, Mom, so you have no business passing judgment on them. Mia and Gwen are wonderfully supportive, and I am lucky to have them in my life. You should be happy that I have people who care for me."

Rolling her eyes, her mother snapped, "Mia, wow, there's another great example of what not to do. Living with some rich heathen who won't marry her. I bet they're part of that *Fifty Shades* lifestyle. The last thing an impressionable girl like you needs is to be friends with a swinger." Her mother grabbed her arm, and her voice rose when she shouted, "Heaven help us, were you doing that this weekend? You have a perfectly good husband waiting for you to come to your senses and you're off sleeping around? Crystal! I've never been so mortified in my whole life."

"What are you talking about?" Crystal gasped. "I'm not sleeping with anyone! Good grief, where do you get this stuff? And both Mia and Gwen are in committed relationships with men who love them. And Gwen is not pregnant again—this is her first child. How in the world can you manage to make that sound so ugly when it's not?"

Her mother jerked her purse from the nearby chair and tossed the strap over her shoulder. "I'm not standing here while you speak disrespectfully to me. When you've learned how to appreciate all that I do for you, then I expect an apology. Until then, you should stay home and reflect upon how you've screwed up your life."

With that parting shot, she hurried out the door, slamming it closed behind her. Crystal did something that was completely horrible. She flipped her middle finger up into the air and waved it around for good measure. There was no way she'd even tell Ella about this latest round of insults. She stayed upset enough over their mother's continued horrible behavior. Plus, Declan might actually make good on that bodily harm threat.

Since her appetite was completely gone now, she took her time undressing, taking care to gently place her new expensive outfit in the closet before making her way to the bathroom. She started the bathtub, throwing in some bath salts that promised instant relaxation. Except Crystal snorted at the description, thinking unless there was a fifth of whiskey and a couple of Xanax somewhere inside the salts, it probably wasn't happening. Instead, she grabbed her iPad from the bedroom and settled into the steaming water. She checked her e-mail first, finding nothing but the usual junk mail. She laughed when one of them offered her ten million dollars if only she sent them her banking information. Sadly, there were probably some people out there who actually fell for that.

Next, she looked through her Facebook feed and noted with a sigh of depression that another of her old friends had recently gotten married. They looked so ecstatic in the wedding pictures that the bride had posted. Crystal wondered if she'd even looked happy on her wedding day. In retrospect she figured "resigned" was a better word. After all, it had been as close to an arranged marriage as you could get in this day and age.

Closing Facebook, she turned next to Twitter. She wasn't really active on the platform but enjoyed seeing tweets from various celebrities. She'd had some serious lust over Taylor Kinney from *Chicago Fire*, but dammit, even he was getting married now. She couldn't imagine a life with Lady Gaga being boring—that was for sure.

She immediately looked up Mark's profile for her regular evening stalking session. For all she knew, Denny was doing all of Mark's posts, but it still made her feel closer to him to know what he was doing or thinking at a particular time. Tonight's post, though, had her fumbling with her iPad and grabbing it just seconds before it landed in the steaming water. *"Delay is the deadliest form of denial."* *C. Northcote Parkinson.* #Angel.

"Holy crap," she whispered to the empty room. Was this directed at her? God, it had to be. He'd never used that hashtag before. What did it mean? What was he delaying or denying himself? Her mind whirled as she tried to decipher the words. Her fingers flew furiously across the touch screen as she attempted to find a quote she could use in reply to his. In the back of her mind, the voice of reason said that she would be making a fool out of herself if his tweet wasn't directed at her, but it was a chance she was willing to take.

Finally, after ten minutes of searching on Google, she found the perfect one. Giggling to herself, she hit the REPLY button and then did a copy and paste. *"He who hesitates is a damned fool."* *Mae West.* #Angel.

Giddy at the interaction with Mark, she waited to see if he would respond—but after twenty minutes, she gave up and left the bath before she turned into a prune.

By bedtime, a few other people had added their own words or quotes about procrastination, but from Mark, there was nothing. Maybe she'd pissed him off. Men, she'd learned, were sensitive and often easily offended. At least Bill had been. She'd never have dared say anything like that to him. He would have struck out at her, and then afterward not spoken to her for days. Come to think of it, she should have said something daily to shock him. It would have forced some kind of reaction from him.

That ball was firmly in Mark's court now, and Mia

had seemed confident that he would make a move at some point soon. She'd shown him that she was interested; now she hoped that he would prove her friend right and approach her. If he didn't . . . then she was going after him.

Being a good girl had never gotten her anything that she wanted in life, so possibly it was time to try life on the other side of the fence for once. Wasn't the grass always greener there?

Chapter Five

Mark couldn't believe it. When was the last time he'd been asleep by nine in the evening? Apparently, he was more exhausted from his weekend of playing nurse than he had thought. It was almost six in the morning now, and he stretched in bed, feeling refreshed. Getting out of bed, he quickly tossed on a pair of running shorts, shoes, and a T-shirt. He usually ran about five miles in the morning before work. He had gym equipment at home but still chose mostly to use a health club near the office for his strength training. He found he enjoyed the bustle of the busy environment—plus he'd passed a few hours with more than one woman whom he'd met there. So far, they'd all been agreeable to the no-strings rule, and he hadn't been forced to change gyms as his friend Jacob had, more than once, after an encounter went sour.

There was still a chill in the air as he walked down to the beach and began loosening up. He'd been lucky to have lived on the water for most of his life, aside from when he was in college. First in Charleston and now Myrtle Beach. He even had a division in Hawaii and had thought at one time of relocating there. The

DeSanto Group designed and manufactured one of the best communication service routers in the world. When Jason Danvers had redesigned his top-of-the-line communications system, he had reached out to Mark and their partnership had been born. They had since upgraded most of the Danvers equipment to include the DeSanto routers and were looking at other ways in which their two companies could continue their collaboration together in the communication field.

His mind wandered to Angel again and he remembered the tweet he had posted the previous evening. Shit, he hadn't even thought to check it this morning. He hoped she'd made some sort of comment because he wanted to know her Twitter handle. Yeah, so maybe he was stalking her a bit in return. Nothing wrong with that if both parties were in agreement, right? With that in mind, he kicked up his speed and finished his run in record time.

Mark went straight for his iPad when he walked in the door and clicked to open the Twitter app. Looking through the replies, he did a double take when he reached a certain one. "Fuck," he groaned as he read a reply from @cryswebber. "'He who hesitates is a damned fool.' Mae West. #Angel."

The little minx was teasing him. Unbelievable. He hadn't been sure what, if anything, she'd do if she read his tweet. Now he had his answer. Crystal Webber, it appeared, had game. And dammit, he was even more intrigued than he had already been. His cock grew rock hard as he pondered her sexy response. He needed to get laid in the worse way if something like a freaking tweet had him on the verge of coming in his shorts like a schoolboy. If she'd attached a picture, then he wouldn't have been able to hold back. As it was, he knew damn well that he was going to jack off in the shower imagining himself buried balls deep in her hot little body.

Normally, he had sex frequently enough that he wasn't reduced to getting off by his own hand. He had a sinking feeling this wouldn't be the last time he would take matters into his own hands while thinking of Crystal Webber.

Feeling somewhat less tense, Mark walked down the hallway toward his kitchen, where he spotted Denny sitting on a barstool drinking a cup of coffee and holding his iPad. He shook his head as Mark approached, looking vastly amused. Maybe the little bastard got lucky this morning while he had had to jerk off alone.

"Dude, I can't believe you're flittering now."

Mark halted in the middle of pouring his own cup of coffee and raised a brow in question. Sometimes it seemed as if his cousin spoke a foreign language even though they were only a few years apart in age. "I'm sure I'll be sorry I asked, but what're you talking about?"

Denny turned his iPad around and pointed to Mark's tweet from the previous night. "Flirting on Twitter—flittering. You sent a quote loaded with double meaning out to Crystal, didn't you? I mean, come on—'hashtag Angel'? I felt sorry for you when I read it because I figured it would scare her off. Maybe make her think you're some kind of serial killer. But then a few replies down I see where she completely called you scared and a fool." By this point, Denny was almost falling on the floor, he was laughing so hard.

Mark barely resisted the urge to toss him out the door. The shit you had to put up with in the name of family was unreal. He'd fire anyone else for even a small piece of the daily insults that Denny heaped his way. Of course, he always gave as good as he got. That was what made their relationship work. Mark didn't have to put on airs with his cousin, and Denny damn sure didn't bother to adhere to the social codes of the employer–employee relationship.

"The only thing her reply proves is that she wants me to make a move on her. I sent the tweet to gauge her response, and it couldn't have worked better." Shooting Denny a pitying look, he added, "I'm sorry, my young friend, that you haven't learned the fine art of seduction. It doesn't all have to be dinner at McDonald's, a movie, and then home by nine. Verbal foreplay is highly underrated." He was actually pretty pleased with his slight until Denny began laughing even harder. The fucker was really starting to grate on his nerves this morning.

"Since when has the great Mark DeSanto bothered with seduction? They don't call you the one-night wonder for nothing. Don't get me wrong, I've always been rather envious of the ease with which you pick up women. I swear to God, they literally fall all over themselves to ride your sheets for a few hours. You'd clean up as a gigolo. And I also realize that since you've never had to put the slightest amount of effort into finding female company, the whole thought of anything outside of screwing might be overwhelming. But

I think if you decided to give it a try, then Crystal would be the perfect woman to help you remove your training wheels."

Mark had finished his coffee and set his cup in the sink before he turned back to see Denny. "Can we go now, Dear Abby? I've actually got some work to do today if this session of Dating Advice for Losers is over." The other man mumbled something under his breath as Mark tossed over his shoulder, "And I'm blocking you from my Twitter feed since you're using it for evil instead of good."

As they walked toward the car he figured he must be losing his mind because he couldn't wait to toss something else out into the Twitter-verse and see what his Angel had to say. *Hashtag pathetic*, he thought with a grimace.

It had been a quiet morning for Crystal since her boss, Lydia, was still out of town. She loved working with the other woman and missed their daily chats. Lydia Cross was single and had just turned thirty. Lydia didn't have anyone special in her life and wasn't in a hurry to change that. She had been engaged to her high school sweetheart when he was diagnosed with cancer, and he'd passed away a year later. That had been almost three years ago and Lydia said that she still couldn't imagine moving on with her life and dating someone else.

In that regard, Crystal had more in common with her than with Mia or Gwen, who were both in serious relationships. She hadn't worked with Lydia for very long, but they had bonded almost from the start.

Possibly, they each recognized that the other was lonely. They often went to a movie, dinner, or just to have a drink together in the evenings after work. Lydia was a beautiful woman with a fantastic personality. The only problem was that her heart seemed permanently broken. In her case, Crystal desperately hoped that time would heal her wounds or at least make them bearable.

She had opted to have a sandwich at her desk today instead of leaving the building for lunch. She took a bite of her ham and cheese while she pulled up her Twitter feed. When she looked through her feed, she almost choked on the suddenly much-too-dry bread. *"I generally avoid temptation unless I can't resist it."* Mae West. #Angel.

Oh, my God, he'd actually responded to her tweet, and with a quote from Mae West, no less. Crystal's body felt warm all over as she pondered the meaning behind the passage he'd picked. Was he saying that he could or couldn't resist her? Surely, he was leaning toward the latter if he was continuing to play this Twitter game with her. Heck, he'd started the whole thing. Should she answer right away? Or would it be better if she waited until tonight? How sad was it that this was the most excitement she'd had in her life in . . . maybe ever? She so desperately wanted to see him again, but she hadn't caught even a glimpse of him around the hallways of Danvers. Shit, she couldn't wait. Typing "Mae West quotes" into Google, she started looking for one to get his attention.

After several minutes, she had the perfect one. *"An ounce of performance is worth pounds of promises."* Mae

West. #Angel. Giggling under her breath, she closed out Twitter and forcibly turned her attention back to her work.

She was putting together a marketing packet for Lydia when there was a tap on her door. Looking up, she smiled as her sister glided into her office. That was actually how the other woman appeared to walk now. Ella was so happy with her husband and new baby that her feet didn't seem to touch the floor anymore. If she didn't love her sister so much, then she would be jealous that she seemed to have it all now. A hot-as-hell husband who doted on her, an adorable baby, and a beautiful home near the beach. Yet Crystal couldn't think of anyone who deserved it more.

Ella had been the preferred target of their meddling mother for years, while Crystal had been the favorite when she was married to Bill. She was embarrassed to admit that she'd actually felt special to her mother during that time. It was the only time in her life that she'd ever felt as if she wasn't a complete disappointment. Sadly, she'd let herself be pushed into marrying Bill, and she'd stayed with him, even though she was miserable during the marriage. It had seemed easier than dealing with her mother's disapproval. And even worse, she wasn't sure if she would have ever had the courage to leave Bill if not for seeing Ella break away from her mother's control and live her life the way she wanted to. Crystal would never be able to repay her sister for showing her that there could be more to life than what she'd had.

Ella dropped into a chair, giving her a wary look. "Did Mom track you down yesterday?"

Crystal held up an imaginary gun to her head. "Oh yeah, and in person no less. She let herself into my apartment and was waiting for me when I got home."

"Crap." Ella winced. "I hate those surprise visits. She did that to me a lot before Declan and I got married. Now he's told me that I had better never give her a key to our home. He says he'll be pleasant as long as she acts that way to him, but there is no way she's walking in unannounced again."

Crystal started snickering. "Remember when Mom walked in on you and Declan in bed together while you were dating?"

Ella shuddered. "How could I ever forget that? She almost caught us a few other times as well. She e-mailed me quotes on the evils of fornication for months after that. Declan was afraid he'd never be able to perform again, just remembering her staring at him." Giving an impish wink, Ella added, "Trust me, his fears were completely unfounded."

Crystal laughed, still amazed that her shy sister could talk about sex now with only a slight blush. "Thanks for sharing that. Maybe if you'd said something along those lines to our mother, she would have been too distracted with you to ambush me."

"Was it bad?" Ella asked, even though she already knew the answer. Parental time was never pleasant for them.

"Just the usual." Crystal shrugged. "I'm a disappointment, more than likely a slut, and I have horrible friends. I've ruined my life by not begging Bill to forgive me. Oh, and she's not speaking to me again until I ask her forgiveness for being a disrespectful smart-ass."

Wincing, Ella said, "Boy, she gave you the works. How long do you think the whole not-speaking-to-you thing will last before she shows up again?"

Clicking her tongue as if deep in thought, she finally said, "I give her a week—max. She's too curious about where I was over the weekend. There's no way she'll drop that this soon."

Ella's eyes appeared to cross for a moment before she breathed out. "You sure don't believe in taking baby steps, do you? I mean, I know you told me what happened with Mark, but I still can't believe he took care of you like that. I've spent a little time around him at various business functions, and he's always charming. But he's so—gorgeous. He looks like Matthew Bomer. All dark, sexy, and mysterious. I've heard he never sees the same woman twice either. Crys, you're like a long-term relationship to him!"

Lifting a brow, Crystal asked, "Why are you over there lusting after Mark when you're married to Declan Stone? Your hubby is a serious stud muffin. You know I stare at his ass at all our family functions, right?"

Ella grabbed a paper clip from her desk and tossed it at Crystal. "I'd have to be blind to miss that. The only person's butt he stares at, though, is mine, so that's all that matters."

"You've got that right," Crystal conceded. "He's totally whipped, Ells, so good for you."

Suddenly, her sister snapped her fingers together and literally jumped up and down in her seat. "I'm going to have a barbecue this weekend, and we'll invite everyone—including Mark. That way, you'll be able to see him again without looking like you're stalking him. Are you still doing that, by the way?"

Trying hard to look offended, but failing, Crystal nodded. "Just a tad, and only on his Twitter account. I haven't resorted to walking up and down the hallway outside his office yet. It was easier before when he didn't know me. Now it would look too obvious."

"No, really?" Ella said dryly. "Anyway, I'll get with the others and make this happen. Don't make any plans for Saturday evening."

Crystal didn't bother to point out that she rarely had anything to do on the weekend. After Ella had left, she wondered why she hadn't told her about the tweets that she'd been exchanging with Mark. Something about it just seemed too personal to share. For now, she wanted to keep it between them. It was almost too good to be true, and she didn't want to tempt fate by over-analyzing it.

At least now she had a reason to see him again, and she had to hope that the week would pass by quickly before she resorted to driving by his house.

Chapter Six

Mark had gone straight home after work and given Denny the night off. He generally used the drive to and from the office to return calls and e-mails, but still preferred to drive himself when the workday was over. After changing into something more casual, he'd grabbed the keys to his Porsche and driven across town to his favorite bar, Rivers. It was a popular meeting place for college students and professionals. He'd been chatting with the bartender, Jason, while enjoying a scotch and water, when a blond-haired beauty settled on the stool beside him. A quick glance told him that she was around twenty-five and had a spectacular set of fake tits. She had the perpetual tan common to so many living in a beach town. He had the sudden urge to lecture her about the dangers of sun exposure. What the *hell* was wrong with him? The only stern warnings he was usually interested in giving were in the bedroom. He had certainly never cared enough to go beyond that.

She was now turning sideways to face him, flashing her best flirty grin, and he felt . . . absolutely nothing. Nada. She was the exact replica of most of the women he picked to fuck for a few hours, and he wasn't interested. Maybe it was the whole skin thing. Yeah, that had to be it. She'd turned him off by being too . . . tan. He angled his seat away from hers, and she stalked off.

"Man, I can't believe you just blew Ashley off." Jason laughed. "I've heard that she goes above and beyond. I'd kill for a shot at that."

Mark shrugged, not in the least sorry. He was looking for something different tonight. After another thirty minutes, a brunette took the place of Ashley. This one looked to be a few years older, and she was a knockout. He was considering speaking to her, when she reached out and touched his arm, stroking up and down. He was immediately turned off. She was too forward. He didn't like aggressive women. At least not tonight.

Things continued along the same lines for the next couple of hours. Jason was openly staring at him in confusion, probably questioning his sexual orientation by this point. He didn't want to examine why, but no one appealed to him tonight. This was surprising because he'd been hard more often than not since Crystal crashed into his life. Why wasn't he doing something about it? Just thinking of her again had him pulling his phone out and checking his Twitter account. *"An ounce of performance is worth pounds of promises."* Mae West. #Angel.

"Damn," he hissed as his cock strained against his zipper. She was killing him. He hadn't lied to her when he'd admitted to wanting to fuck her more than he ever had another woman. It was fast becoming an obsession. Just picturing those plump lips of hers sucking his cock was enough to make him blow his load in this very public bar. Before he could embarrass himself, he dropped some money next to his drink and made a hasty retreat.

As soon as he walked in the door at home, he picked up his iPad and Googled quotes. There was no way he could sleep until he replied to her little tease. A grin spread across his face as he found the perfect one. *"When I'm good, I'm very good. But when I'm bad, I'm better." Mae West. #Angel.*

It was already close to midnight, but he stayed up another few hours in hopes that she'd respond. When she didn't, he thought it was probably for the best. He'd have begged for her address, and then gone there and fucked her until she couldn't walk for a week. Unless he was very wrong, sex with Angel wouldn't be a one-time thing. That was reason alone enough to stay away from the woman who was rapidly turning his life upside down.

Mark was edgy and wired the next morning after tossing and turning most of the night. Denny dropped him at the gym with threats to leave his grouchy ass stranded if he didn't exit in a better mood. He stopped at the juice bar to buy a bottle of water. He was paying when someone clapped him on the back. He jerked around, still in a foul mood, to see Seth Jackson giving him a questioning look. Mark felt some of his tension drain as he greeted his friend. Seth ran the Oceanix Resort in Myrtle Beach and had been a friend for years.

They had been talking for a few minutes, when his

friend and coworker Jacob Hay strolled up to join them. Jacob was vice-president of operations for the DeSanto Group, as well as Mark's right hand. He divided his time between their headquarters in Charleston and Myrtle Beach, with a liberal amount of travel in between.

Mark broke into a grin, as Asher Jackson was next through the door and immediately walked over to punch him in the shoulder. "I didn't know you were in town again," he said after they shook hands. At one time, he and Ash had hung out a good bit. They ran in the same circles and had similar . . . interests. Hell, they'd even shared those interests a few times in the past. If Mark was considered a hit-it-and-quit-it, as Denny often called him, then he wasn't sure what that made Ash. The other man had some strange hang-ups, and if women wanted to spend time with him, then they had to accept those aspects.

"For a few weeks." Ash nodded. "I try to get down and see Mia as often as possible," he added slyly, while watching his brother Seth for his reaction. Mia was Seth's girlfriend, and the guy was crazy about her. Mark saw her occasionally at Danvers, and she was a beauty.

Instead of looking jealous, Seth just laughed. "My woman is perfectly happy and satisfied. She thinks of you as the brother she never had, Ash."

Giving a wolfish grin, Ash said, "I'm trying to encourage that. She gives her hugs more freely to family members."

Jacob grabbed a towel off a nearby table and wiped his face before asking, "So what's up with all this

Angel stuff on Twitter? My assistant seems to think you're doing some kind of Internet dating now. Who's cryswebber?"

Dead silence settled between them as Seth and Ash joined Jacob in staring at him. *Well, hell. Social death by hashtag—how original.* "Er—it's nothing. Just joking around with a friend." Mark began edging away, trying to break the focus of the group. Who knew that so many people followed his fucking Twitter feed?

"Crys Webber," Seth repeated slowly before snapping his finger. "That's not Crystal Webber from Danvers, is it? Declan Stone's sister-in-law?"

"Not sure," Mark said vaguely. "Are we going to work out today or stand around chatting?"

Both Ash and Jacob were looking at him in surprise, while Seth looked uneasy. "Crystal's a good friend of Mia's. From what I gather, she's rather—innocent, for lack of a better word."

Exasperated, Mark said, "She's been married before, Seth. It's not like she's never been around a man."

"Doesn't sound like your usual kind of woman," Ash added.

"Listen, there's nothing going on," Mark snapped, tired of defending himself. For God's sake, did his friends think that he was Jack the Ripper or something? Every one of the men surrounding him worked hard and played harder. A common interest had made them friends. He wasn't sure where all of the judgment was coming from, but he was tired of it. He stalked away but had only gone a few steps when Jacob tossed an arm over his shoulders.

"PMS today or something? Sorry about tossing you

under the bus. I didn't think it was a secret or any-thing."

"It's not," Mark replied, still annoyed. "As I've said, she's just a friend."

"All right, brother, whatever you say. But if you end up marrying her, I'm going to lose money." At his ques-tioning look, Jack added, "All of the women in the office are betting that you've met 'the one.' We may have placed a few friendly wagers. So whatever you do—keep it casual."

Elbowing his friend in the side, he shook his head. "You've got problems. And don't bother losing any sleep over your money—we both know I'll never settle down."

Seth and Ash joined them, and they worked out steadily for an hour before hitting the showers. After his recent round of teasing from the guys about his Twitter activity, he shouldn't be dying to see if Crystal had replied yet. He knew that if she had, he wouldn't be able to resist continuing the verbal foreplay, no mat-ter how much his friends were enjoying his social media embarrassment.

Her palms were sweaty and her heart was racing—again. Enclosed in the restroom at Danvers with her cell phone, Crystal stared at Mark's latest tweet. She'd overslept that morning and had no time to look before rushing to work. She normally didn't check her social media while at work, but she felt like it was acceptable since she was taking a restroom break.

Once again, she was looking through Mae West quotes on Google and trying to find a reply for Mark.

She was on the verge of giving up and doing it later when she spotted the perfect one. Giving a fist pump to the empty room, she quickly composed a new tweet. *"I'll try anything once, twice if I like it, three times to make sure."* Mae West. #Angel.

Someone was frantically trying the door handle, so she washed her hands and hoped that she'd transferred the quote correctly. There was no time to check now. The person waiting was a blur of action as she hurried into the room behind her and slammed the door. *Geez.* It made her want to knock on the door and remind them that there were in fact several more restrooms on this floor. When she returned to her office, she had an e-mail from Ella, inviting her to lunch at noon.

Crystal spent the next few hours handling tasks for Lydia before collecting her purse for lunch with her sister. She'd invited Mia along as well. Gwen was having an ultrasound today and wouldn't be in until later. They were all excited to hear if she and Dominic would be having a girl or boy. The couple had pondered letting it be a surprise, but in the end, they were just too excited to find out.

When she reached the lobby, not only were Ella and Mia waiting, but also Suzy, Claire, Beth, Emma, and Ava were gathered there. Suzy's husband, Gray, was a vice-president at Danvers along with his brother, Nick. To make matters more interesting, Suzy's sister, Beth, was married to Nick. Emma Davis was engaged to Brant Stone, who also worked for Danvers along with his sister, Ava Powers. Ava was married to Mac, who ran a security company based out of the Danvers building. To add even more confusion to the mix, Gwen had dated Mac briefly before falling in love with Mac's business partner, Dominic Brady. Crystal could barely keep up with all of it in her head. When the women had lunch together, Crystal found herself overwhelmed at times by the details of who was with whom. If love was in the air at Danvers International, then Crystal had to wonder why it seemed to be overlooking her when so many others had found "the one" at the office.

Since there were so many of them, they decided to walk to the sandwich shop next door instead of splitting up into different cars to drive. Crystal walked beside her sister, getting an update on her niece, Sofia, on the way.

When they were finally settled into a large table, Crystal had Ella on one side and Mia on the other. It seemed as if every time they had a group lunch, she ended up directly across from Suzy—which made her more than a little nervous. The woman was gorgeous and sophisticated, but that wasn't the unsettling part. She was also a bit of a loose cannon. Mia had a similar personality, but Crystal had been around her friend enough to be comfortable discussing most anything. She didn't know Suzy as well and was usually caught off guard by some of her questions or comments.

Ella had obviously invited everyone to her barbecue on Saturday, and they were discussing the details. Crystal almost swallowed her tongue when her traitor of a sister blurted out, "And we need to make sure that Mark attends. I've had Declan invite him, but, Emma, if you could have Brant follow up that would be great."

Licking her lips, Suzy asked, "So, beyond the obvious reasons, why do we want him to attend so badly?"

Crystal kicked Ella under the table—which was a huge mistake. Instead of shutting up, Ella just started sputtering as if she'd lost her mind. She might as well be holding up a guilty sign. "I—er—um . . . trying to be nice?"

Dammit. Crystal winced. This was what happened when you had someone like Ella try to play matchmaker. All eyes were on her stuttering sister as if trying to figure out what she was hiding. Then, just as she'd feared, Suzy's gaze settled on her. "You're the only unattached one at this table. So unless someone has a confession to make about the state of their relationship, I'd say your sister is recruiting Mark for you."

"God, yes!" Mia exclaimed. "My girl here is completely gone on 'DeStudo.'"

Ava made a sound that was a cross between laughter and choking. "DeStudo?"

With a dreamy expression, Emma nodded. "That's actually pretty accurate. I was in line behind him at the coffee shop last week, and man, is he sexy. He smelled so good that I found myself inhaling too fast and I was getting dizzy. And that voice. All manly and rough . . . I love Brant, but I secretly wouldn't mind Mark for my work husband. I wouldn't even need to touch him. Maybe an hour a day of sniffing and staring at him would do for me."

"He is something," Claire admitted shyly. "Jason has had him over for dinner a few times, and he's so charming. He's even good with our daughter, which I wouldn't have expected since he doesn't have children. I guess I wasn't too good at hiding my admiration on his last visit because after he left, Jason waved a hand in front of my face and told me that I could go ahead and blink."

Suzy chuckled at Claire's story before saying, "Gray knows that I can't help but appreciate a hot guy. Luckily, he's secure enough to where he laughs it off. I also know he's a man and will admire a beautiful woman—but that's all it is. Now, if I were in the market for a threesome, Mark would be right up there at the top of the list. I mean, it's not as if I could pick Nick, since he's my brother-in-law. And Jason signs my paychecks, so that could get complicated. Declan looks like he knows his way around the bedroom, but I wouldn't be able to choose between him and Brant, so they're out. That leaves me with Mac, Dominic, and Gage—who wear those cargo pants well. But they are all in new relationships—which could be messy. That brings me to Mark. So yeah, if I were in the market, that bad boy would be my pick. I've heard some interesting rumors about him being a bit of a freak in the bedroom as well." Staring at Crystal, Suzy asked, "Honey, are you sure you're ready to make the leap from a Honda to a Lamborghini? Maybe you should start with . . . say, a Cadillac or even a Mercedes? While I admire you for going straight to a sports car, I have to wonder if you know how much horsepower that baby has."

Beth's eyes widened as she looked at her sister. "Just to be clear, we're still talking about Mark, right?"

"Crap, I don't know," Mia murmured. "I'm still processing the whole threesome thing." Then, raising her hand like a schoolgirl, Mia giggled. "I think I've mentioned that Suzy and Gray were at the top of my list of threesome dream teams."

"Please don't encourage her," Beth moaned.

"Hey, I'd do you, Suzy," Emma piped in. "You even used to have my favorite ass before Gwen came along."

"Everyone wants Gwen's ass," Claire inserted before covering her face. "I think that came out wrong."

Suzy bumped shoulders with Claire. "Hey, no judgment here. It's a safe zone. And thank you, Emma, for your kind words. I'd be looking more for a man-man-woman kind of thing, but you never know."

Ava cleared her throat as the laughter died down at the table. "Crystal, you do know that Mark doesn't really do relationships, right? I'm not trying to dissuade you, but to my knowledge, Mark has never been involved with a woman beyond an evening." Giving Crystal a look of concern, she added, "If you're looking for something like that, you know, to experiment, then that's great."

"Oh, I'm not looking to marry him," Crystal said breezily. She only hoped that the other women wouldn't notice how forced her smile was. Of course she tried not to harbor any romantic delusions where Mark was concerned—but didn't every woman have the Cinderella fantasy from time to time? Possibly, that was her whole problem. She grew up feeling subservient to first her mother and then to her husband. She'd barely been capable of making a decision on her own, and even when she did decide something for herself, she had to wonder if someone in her life hadn't influenced it. "So . . . a question for all of you," she began before she could chicken out. "If my being so . . . different from Mark's usual kind of woman is a problem, should I show him that I can . . . change?" she stuttered out, no doubt sounding like an idiot. That hadn't come out right at all.

Before anyone could answer, Ava spoke up again. "When I decided to go after Mac, I had to reinvent myself. It's not that he didn't love me as I was, because he did—for years. But I'd lost him because I wasn't ready to be in a relationship with him. So in order to get his attention, I went a complete one eighty from who I'd always been. Instead of repressed and cautious, I became more of a daredevil. I did stuff that I knew would push every button that he had. I figured negative attention was good so long as he was thinking about me. Even if he only wanted to wring my neck. So I know what you're trying to say."

"Just to be clear here," Suzy asked, sounding fascinated, "are you advising her to go buy some handcuffs and beat Mark at his own game?"

"There's nothing wrong with that." Beth grinned, wiggling her eyebrows.

"Oh, dear God"—Suzy groaned—"must everything lead back to images of you and my brother-in-law? Please don't traumatize my nephew by doing kinky sex stuff."

"Duh, that's why there's a lock on the bedroom door," Claire added. "Just because you have children doesn't mean you don't still . . . do things. Right, Ella?"

Ella's face went up in flames, but the twinkle in her eyes said that she knew exactly what the other women were talking about. "Um—sure."

"I don't know Mark," Mia began, "but don't you think he'd be a little surprised if Crystal suddenly showed up at his house wearing leather and carrying a whip?" Winking, she added, "Even Seth would do a double take if I did that, and trust me, the man likes his kink."

Emma reached over and put her hands over Ava's

ears. "Brant is on the dominant side and likes to be in control of the bedroom action."

"I know you're talking about sex with my brother," Ava snapped but didn't try to remove Emma's hands.

"Anyway, as I was saying, Brant has those tendencies, but he also likes to be surprised. I don't think you need to go as far as going all *Fifty Shades* on his ass, but a few assertive things to throw him off his game would probably be good. If he considers you a good girl, then he won't be expecting you to make any moves on him. So I would do that. Even something small would get his attention."

"I agree." Suzy nodded. "Girl, grab that ass if he gets within arm's reach. I mean really get in there and get yourself a handful of that fine piece."

Emma, who had been in the middle of taking a drink of water, sprayed Ava as she began choking. Ava wore a disgusted expression as she took a napkin and began mopping herself up before doing the same to her future sister-in-law. When Emma had recovered, she blotted her lips and said, "Well, that would be one way to get his attention, for sure. I was thinking something a bit more subtle to begin with, like being all touchy-feely when he's around."

"But I rarely ever see him, unless I'm trying to. . . ."

"You mean stalking." Mia giggled. "Now that you've spent a weekend with him, you're a step ahead. You can actually speak when you see him."

"Whoa! Hold the phone," Suzy interrupted. "You've slept with DeStudo and you're trying to get advice from us? Honey, it seems like you've left some key parts out here, and I, for one, need an explanation."

Mia whispered a quick "I'm sorry" for spilling the beans.

Crystal figured at this point that she didn't have anything to lose by telling everyone about her time with Mark. If she wanted their help, then she owed them the full story. So she quickly filled them in on what had transpired after she'd gotten sick and how Mark had taken care of her. She left out their Twitter flirtation, still wanting to keep that to herself.

When she was finished, Ava murmured, "Wow, that's unbelievable. While I would haven't called him an uncaring bastard, I'm shocked he didn't hand you off at the first opportunity."

"Sometimes a man can surprise you," Emma pointed out. "Brant and I are still complete opposites, but it works. Oh, baby, does it ever. . . ."

Ava made a gagging sound, causing Emma to laugh.

"Well, you have an opportunity coming up with the barbecue," Ella said. "And trust me: even if I have to go drag the man myself, he's going to be there."

The rest of the lunch was filled with funny dating or sex stories, making Crystal that much more aware of what was missing from her life. Even if she'd stayed married to her ex, she'd have nothing to share now—which she found completely depressing and unacceptable.

Chapter Seven

Crystal checked Mark's Twitter page yet again. He'd gone silent after her last tweet, and it was driving her crazy. She'd broken down on Friday and taken the elevator to his floor, hoping to run into him, but no such luck. Ella's barbecue was only hours away, and she had no idea if he'd be there. Ella promised that she'd done everything short of threatening Declan to make sure that his friend showed up.

Updating the page one last time, she almost dropped her iPad when she saw a tweet from only seconds earlier on his page. *"Too much of a good thing can be taxing."* Mae West. #Angel.

"What the hell?" she whispered as she reread the quote. Was he telling her that he didn't have any interest in her? He'd never even given her a chance, so why would he assume that she was too good? She tossed her iPad down on her sofa in disgust. Screw the bastard. She didn't have to prove anything to him.

Then she stalked around her apartment, raging over what assholes men were. Suddenly, she grabbed her tablet, and began frantically searching quotes, hoping to find one that would make him eat his words. She'd almost given up when she found it. The perfect way to let him know how wrong he was about her. She typed out, *"I used to be Snow White, but I drifted."* Mae West. #Angel. She thought it sounded so much better than #kissmyassMark!

Crystal ran to her closet, more determined than ever to look her best for the barbecue. She wanted Mark to swallow his damn tongue when he saw her today. She needed to strike the right balance between casual and sexy without appearing to have dressed up for the occasion.

After ten minutes of frantic digging through her closet, she found something that she'd bought on clearance last year but never had anywhere to wear it. It was a white strapless sundress. She paired it with a jean jacket and a brown leather belt. She was reaching for sandals when a pair of cowboy boots that she'd worn only a few times caught her eye. She'd seen similar outfits in magazines and always thought they looked fun and flirty.

When she was finished dressing, she stared at herself in the mirror. She had to admit that she looked hot. Just the right blend of sweet and sexy. Before she could talk herself into changing, she quickly added a touch of pink lip gloss and ran a brush through her loose waves.

The dress was much shorter than she normally wore, and she could only hope there wasn't a big gust of wind tonight. Just in case, though, she'd worn her sexiest underwear. A girl had to be prepared for anything when going to war, right?

Before the voice of reason could send her into the

closet to change outfits, she ran out to her car and was on her way to Ella's. She spent the entire twenty minutes of the ride trying to bolster her courage to knock Mark for a flip—and then leave him hanging, since that was essentially what he'd done to her with his Twitter flirting.

"Brace yourself, because you're mine tonight, DeStudo."

This is a mistake, Mark thought yet again, as he pulled into Declan and Ella's already crowded driveway. He'd tried to decline the invitation with some half-hearted business excuse, but Declan had been unusually insistent that he attend. Mark socialized often, as was expected of someone in his position, but he wasn't much for the smaller, intimate gatherings such as this. These people not only worked together, but they were also either related by blood or extended family by choice. Something that was almost a foreign concept to him. Denny was the only one who could even remotely fall into that category in his life.

He also hadn't been too eager to face Crystal after his brush-off Twitter post—because that's exactly what it had been. She'd been occupying far too many of his thoughts during the past week, and he'd needed to break her hold on him. At first, he'd decided not to reply to her last tweet. Then when it had become apparent that he'd have to attend the barbecue this evening or piss off his friend, he'd felt it might be better to let Crystal know where things stood before seeing her again. He had little doubt that she would be here, even though he hadn't come right out and asked Declan.

Now, though, he felt a little guilty and wondered if he hadn't perhaps been hasty in his dumping via Twitter. *For fuck's sake, I've reverted into a teenager.* It struck him suddenly that he hadn't looked to see if she'd made any reply to his tweet, so he hastily pulled his phone from the front pocket of his jeans and opened the application. What he read there made his cock jump and his hand cramp as his grip tightened. *Holy fucking shit.* Denny having nicknamed her "Snow White" was ironic, considering her post. But the part about her drifting was enough to have him crawling out of his skin. He'd essentially called her a good girl, and she'd come right back letting him know she no longer was.

Mark paced for another few minutes, trying to get himself under control. He wanted to stomp through the door, get his hands on Crystal, and take her somewhere until he could breathe again. The rational part of his brain said that she was just teasing him. He'd probably hurt her feelings, and she had lashed out. Likely he'd go in and she'd spend the whole evening avoiding him. Which was about the only way he'd survive, so he hoped like hell that happened.

He was pondering getting back in his car and leaving, when an SUV pulled in behind him, effectively cutting off his exit. He saw Mac get out of his Tahoe and cross to the other side to help his wife, Ava.

Mark was unable to hide his smile when the stunning blonde walked toward him. "What are you doing out here by yourself?" she teased as he leaned down to drop a kiss on her cheek.

"Hiding like a coward," he answered honestly. She gave him a funny look, which made him wonder if he was more transparent than he'd thought. She couldn't possibly know about his attraction to Crystal unless she'd been stalking his Twitter profile as well.

Turning to Mac, he extended his hand, saying, "It's good to see you again."

"You too, Mark," Mac replied as he pulled Ava back against him in a possessive gesture. Mark knew Ava's family well and considered them friends—a fact that Mac could clearly live without even though he had chosen the nonverbal approach to get his message across. "Are you going inside?" Mac asked, pointing to the front door.

Before he could answer, Ava stepped forward and curled her arm around his, while keeping her other hand on her husband. "Of course he is. Who could resist an evening with such stimulating company?"

Mac looked confused as he stared at his wife, while Mark again had to wonder if she didn't know more than she should. Was she friends with Angel? "That's right," he agreed, letting her pull him along. He'd make the rounds and then slip out early. No big deal at all.

His pep talk lasted him all of five minutes—until the moment he saw her. She was Snow White tonight. A sexy cowgirl version, at least, and he was screwed. His good intentions were already shot. Those plump lips would wrap around his cock and then she'd dig those cowboy boots into his back as he fucked her out of his system. He could assign some of the blame to her—she should have been smart enough to realize that you can't tease a tiger as if he's a house cat without getting mauled.

Chapter Eight

Crystal was on her second glass of wine when she saw Mark walk in with Ava and Mac. The other women in attendance had already been teasing her for bringing out the big guns tonight. Suzy had even given her a big seal of approval by asking to borrow her outfit at a later date. "The sexual tension between you two is making me horny," Mia remarked as she looked at Crystal and Mark. "DeStudo hasn't taken his eyes off you, girl. He's yours for the taking tonight."

"Huh—what?" Crystal asked distractedly.

"Yeah—exactly." Mia snickered. "Just walk around and let him follow. He's definitely going to."

Crystal started down a nearby hallway, intending to wipe her sweaty palms and take a breath before approaching Mark. She barely had time to register the sound of footsteps, before her arm was in his grasp and she was swung around and pushed into an empty room. She started to struggle until she heard a masculine voice say, "Angel, it's me."

That was it for her. Those words were the equivalent of gas on a flame. She used her hands to locate him in the darkness. "Mark . . ." He made what sounded like a grunt of surprise as she blindly pressed her lips against what she hoped was his mouth. Actually, it turned out to be his cheek, but she moved to the right until she found what she was looking for and her lips met his.

"What do you need, Angel?" he asked huskily as he rocked against her.

"Touch me," she begged. He took a couple of steps forward until he'd braced her back against a wall. He pulled her strapless dress down and her bra along with it. Her breasts sprang free into his waiting hands.

"Fuck, I want to see you, baby. But right now, I'll settle for tasting." With that, he sucked a bud into his mouth while flicking the tip of the other one. When she moaned, he whispered, "You have to be quiet, Angel, or someone will hear us."

Moments passed in sheer bliss, as Mark pinched and teased her nipples, while his tongue was back in her mouth. She was hanging on the edge, when suddenly a sliver of light lit up the small space. Before either of them could pull apart, the door flung open and she was gaping at her brother-in-law in horror.

Crystal had to give Declan credit for not being easily shocked, because he simply blinked a couple of times before shutting the door without saying a word. She heard him yell down the hallway, "The broom's not in the closet. I'll get the one from the garage." Apparently, Ella was determined to check for herself because a second later, because Declan, in a voice heavy with amusement, said, "Trust me, Ellie—there's nothing in that closet that you need to see right now."

As their voices faded away, Crystal slumped against

Mark. "Oh, my God," she moaned in horror. "My brother-in-law just saw my boobs. Maybe even worse."

"He left pretty quickly, so I doubt he saw much," Mark murmured reassuringly.

Maybe she should be utterly embarrassed by what had just happened, but Crystal was surprised to feel a giggle escape, followed quickly by another. Before she knew it, she was slumped back against Mark's broad chest, shaking with laughter. "This is totally my luck," she managed to wheeze out. "I mean, I finally throw caution to the wind and decide to go for it, and I bare my tits to Declan!" She heard Mark chuckle in her ear before he nipped it with his teeth. "Ouch!" she yelped, sticking her elbow in his stomach to defend against his love bites.

"Careful, Angel," he warned. "I have something wedged up against my ass that I suspect is the broom Declan was hunting. If you force me back another step, I'm probably going to become intimately acquainted with it."

"Oops, sorry," she replied, trying to stifle a snicker.

"We'd better get presentable and out of here before someone else comes along," Mark said as he began pulling first her bra and then her dress back up. "I have no idea where the light switch is in here, so we'll have to check to make sure everything's as it should be when we step out."

"Mark . . . I want to go home with you tonight," Crystal found herself saying as she stared at his outline in the dark. Wait—had she really just asked to have sex with him? Well, yes, she had. Heck, who was she kidding, she'd do it right now, even knowing that Declan was probably watching the door by this point.

"Angel," Mark said, sounding both surprised and uncertain. "When and if you're ever in my home again, it won't be for another sleepover and it won't be to make love. We'll fuck—because that's what I do. And you don't strike me as a woman who goes for that type of entertainment."

"That's exactly what I want," Crystal found herself replying. "I've never had that before. Actually, I've never made love either, if I'm being honest."

"Wait—what? You've been married, Angel. How could you possibly be a virgin?"

"Um, what are you talking about?" she asked. "I didn't say I was a virgin."

She heard him sigh in the darkness before he said, "Honey, if you haven't made love and you haven't fucked—then what have you done? That about covers it, I believe. Shit, surely you didn't just do oral while you were married, did you?"

Crystal's mouth fell open at his statement. "No!" she sputtered. "Bill didn't do stuff . . . you know . . . down there. What I meant was that my ex-husband wasn't very good at sex. At least, I don't think he was. He was my first and only, so I have nothing to compare him to. But I don't think what we did could be classified as either lovemaking or the other thing. From the things that my friends say, though, there's a lot more than I've experienced, and I want it—with you." *Oh crap, I didn't mean for that to come out sounding so desperate.*

His voice sounded strained when he finally said, "Angel, I can't be your white knight, and, baby, you deserve to have one. I'm not capable of giving you what you're looking for."

Crystal felt his arm move around her, and she knew he was looking for the door handle. She had just seconds to get his attention before the moment was lost, so she gave it her best shot. "Mark, I want to know what it feels like to be fucked—just the way you'd do it. I don't want rose petals and champagne. I want dirty, sweat-soaked sheets. I want aches in places I've never imagined, and I want to take a man in my mouth for the first time ever." Stiffening her spine, she added, "If you aren't interested, then I'll find someone who is."

The last word had barely left her mouth when the door was wrenched open once again. She blinked against the light to find Mark's driver, Denny, standing there grinning. "Let me be the first to toss my name in the mix. Because if my cousin is crazy enough to turn you down, then I'm happy to be your backup plan."

She could only gape at the other man, mortified. Mark stepped up behind her, putting a hand on her waist. "What in the hell are you doing here?" he gritted out.

Looking completely unaffected by his boss's biting tone, Denny held up his phone. "Well, actually, you invited me, if you recall, and also ordered me to bring a case of your favorite wine. So I made my delivery but couldn't seem to locate you anywhere." Putting a hand on his heart, he continued. "I was so worried that I tracked your phone. Imagine my surprise when your little red dot led me right to the broom closet."

Having gotten over the initial embarrassment, Crystal was enjoying the sparring going on between the two men. She had liked Denny right away. And the way he teased Mark was nothing short of hilarious. "Thanks for saving us." She grinned at the other man. "Mark was under attack by an overeager broom."

"Oh, my pleasure, beautiful." Denny grinned before extending his elbow to her. "Shall we join the others while my cousin sulks?"

She looked over her shoulder at Mark to find him glaring at them. When he met her eyes, his expression softened slightly before becoming perplexed. He didn't know what to do with her. It was written all over his face. She had a feeling that he didn't often suffer from any kind of indecision. Well, while she had him off balance, she'd do everything in her power to keep him that way. He'd wanted her in that closet, and tonight, she would use all of her limited knowledge to entice him further.

When she walked out onto the back deck with Denny, Ella came over at a fast clip. "Where have you been?" she whisper-shouted before pulling her away from Denny with a smile of apology.

"Making out in your closet," she replied to a stunned Ella. "Oh, and Declan totally busted us, as I'm sure you'll be hearing about later."

"Did you have someone in there with you?" Ella asked, looking hopeful.

"Els, of course. Even I'm not desperate enough to masturbate at your barbecue."

Ella started choking, while Crystal reached over to thump her on the back. A few feet away, Declan caught her eye and lifted a beer as if saluting her. Ella, noticing the interaction, looked back and forth between them before exclaiming, "How in the world does my husband know something like that before me?"

"Er—he might have walked in on us," Crystal admitted sheepishly.

Before Ella could respond, most of their female friends had surrounded them. Mia smirked then elbowed Suzy. "You got lucky, didn't you, Crys?"

Suzy gave her an appraising look before saying, "She certainly did something. She has the rosy, sexy glow going on."

"What'd I miss?" Gwen waddled up to the group, holding her back.

Crystal saw an opportunity for a distraction, and she jumped on it. "Gwen! You've been avoiding us since your ultrasound appointment. I'm dying to know whether I'm having a niece or nephew, so spill."

Gwen shook her head before dropping it. "We chickened out."

"Pardon?" Claire asked, looking confused.

Emma pointed to Gwen's stomach. "You do realize that you've got a little person in there and it's too late for backing out, right?"

Beth gave a rueful smile. "I had some of those moments of panic myself. But Nick kept telling me that returns were illegal."

"Oh no, that's not what I meant," Gwen sputtered out with laughter. "We've decided to wait until the baby is born to find out the sex. We'll probably be moving to a bigger place shortly afterward anyway, so it doesn't make a lot of sense to go all out on a baby room. Our families are disappointed, but it's something we both wanted."

"Well, if you ask me, there's not enough mystery left in the world," Suzy agreed. Pointing to Ella, she added, "Just please don't go all Linda Blair when you're in labor like that one did."

"She scared the holy hell out of me!" Ava giggled. "I've told Mac not to even think about having children until I get that memory out of my head."

"At least you were the skinny skank," Suzy said dryly. "Although I'm pretty happy being the queen of the whores." Everyone laughed, having heard the story of Ella going into labor while she was with Suzy and Ava and calling them all kinds of horrible things from the pain she was in.

Then Mia pushed her under the bus. "Crys, your lipstick is smudged all around your mouth and the seam of your dress is askew."

Crystal looked down to find that yes, indeed, when Mark had helped her with her dress, he hadn't exactly done a great job in the dark. The side seam now ran down the middle of her chest. Why hadn't she gone to the bathroom after leaving the closet? She might as well be holding up a sign that said I JUST GOT GROPED IN THE CLOSET.

"And Declan busted them," Ella blurted out.

"Way to have my back there, sis," Crystal deadpanned. "All right," she said in resignation, "Mark pushed me into Ella's broom closet, and we kind of made out."

"Shut the fluck up!" Beth squealed excitedly.

Suzy rolled her eyes. "I swear, with all of these kids around now, we can't even curse anymore. I've been reduced to 'mothertrucker' and 'duckhead.' It just doesn't give me the same feeling of satisfaction."

"No kidding," Claire agreed. "Jason rolled out the *F* word in front of Chrissy a while back and she was like a parrot. She must have said it in front of my mom and Louise a dozen times. It got to the point that they were giving me dirty looks and suggesting I go to church more often."

"So, we already know that Mark had his hands either down or up your dress, since it's all turned around." Mia laughed. "Dare I hope that he had them both places?"

Crystal knew that her blush was giving her away when Mia's eyes widened. Throwing up her hand in a high five, she said, "You go, girl!"

"It was amazing," Crystal confessed before adding the part that worried her. "But he said that he couldn't be what I was looking for. I tried to assure him that I only wanted hot sex, but he seems to believe I'm looking for a wedding ring. A relationship down the road would be good, of course, but I'd be happy with a man who actually puts me first—even if it's only for a night."

"Honey, every woman deserves to have her toes curled." Suzy nodded. "You just need to take the reins here and make it happen. If he shoved you in a closet, then his composure is hanging on by a thread. All you have to do is reel him in. Take this time to torture his ass."

"Suzy's right," Mia agreed. "He's sitting over there talking to Seth. So you're going to follow me, and when I sit on Seth's lap, you sit on Mark's."

"Okay—Wh-what?" Crystal's eyes widened. "I can't do that. He'll think I've lost my mind."

"Trust me." Claire smiled. "That's not going to be what's on his mind."

Gwen clapped her hands and bounced up and down in excitement, causing the other women to look at her in alarm. "Cool your jets there, baby mama, or something's gonna fall out," Emma advised, looking wary.

Before Crystal could run in the other direction, Mia grabbed her arm and pulled her toward where her boyfriend sat. Seth started to get to his feet, but Mia pressed him back down then settled across his lap. *I can't believe I'm doing this*, Crystal thought before she followed suit and perched gently on Mark's lap. She heard his quick intake of breath before his arms encircled her, almost as if by reflex.

Then her traitor of a friend smoothly got to her feet and tugged her boyfriend up with her. "Come on, babe. I need a drink." In the blink of an eye, they were gone and she was left alone in the corner with Mark.

"You have no idea who you're dealing with, baby." Mark sighed as he tightened his grip on her.

Stroking her fingers through his thick dark hair, she said earnestly, "I know you think I'm some sort of goody two-shoes, but I can be bad—I want to be. I've never been given the opportunity before—but I know I can do it."

Looking pained, Mark laughed—although it came out sounding more like a wheeze. "Baby, this isn't some kind of baking contest. There is nothing wrong with being a good girl. Hell, that's one of the reasons

I can't keep my hands off you. Your innocence must be like some sort of crazy bat signal to me. I've never spent time with a woman like you, and frankly, it's messing with my head," he admitted wryly.

She had no idea how to respond to his confession. He'd both pushed her away and pulled her closer with just a few words. Other than his good looks, she was attracted to him because instinctively she knew he would take her places in the bedroom that she'd only imagined in her dreams. If he asked her to leave right now and go have sex with him, she would do it without question. After all, she'd spent her adult years making first her mother and then Bill happy. She'd paid her dues, and she was damn well tired of waiting around for what she wanted. Instead of her life finally starting, it felt some days as if everything was passing her by instead. "Then stop fighting it," she advised. "I want you, and you seem to feel the same. We're both adults and free from any other obligations. Er—you don't have a girlfriend or a wife, right?"

Mark tapped her chin, shaking his head. "Angel, of course not. I thought I'd covered the fact that I didn't do the relationship thing."

Smiling brightly, she said, "So we're good, then. Do you have like a toy drawer with all of the supplies we'll need or should I buy them? Do you think they sell that kind of thing at Walmart? I usually buy my KY Jelly there, but it's in the pharmacy section." Snapping her fingers, she added, "Amazon! That's where I purchased my—thing, so I can just order what we need. I have a Prime account, so I get free shipping."

His head slumped against her neck as his body shook. "Are you all right?" she asked as she looked at him in concern.

"Baby, what 'thing' did you order from Amazon, and why do you need KY Jelly?" he asked in a tight voice. "Shit, if you're talking about a vibrator, then don't tell me. I can't handle knowing." Crystal looked away, not saying anything. He'd said he didn't want to know, after all. "Fuck, that's what you bought, wasn't it? Do you ever use it and imagine it's me inside of you, Angel?"

She shifted uneasily on his lap, knowing her face had to be bright red once again. She didn't dare admit that she'd even named her battery-operated boyfriend Mark. He'd think she was some kind of weirdo for sure.

They were locked in their own little world until a loud voice jerked them apart. "Mark, can I talk to you for a minute?" She looked up to see Declan scowling down at them. Actually, a quick glance around showed most everyone shooting them curious looks. She could only hope that no one else had been close enough to hear their conversation. This day had probably taught him more about his sister-in-law than he'd ever wanted to know. Ella was going to kill her.

"Um—sure," Mark agreed as Crystal scrambled from his lap. He got up slowly, putting his hands in his pockets. He gave her a wink before following Declan into the house. She didn't want to answer all of the questions that she knew the other women would have, so she stayed where she was, waiting to see if he'd come back.

She'd barely had time to start worrying when she

felt a hand on her shoulder. "Sorry, Angel, but I've got to run. I received a call while I was talking to Declan. It's nothing major, but I need to take care of something." Crystal noticed Denny standing a few feet away, obviously waiting for his boss.

"Oh—okay," she murmured, trying to hide her disappointment. For some reason, she'd had it in her head that tonight would be a turning point for them. Now it looked as if she'd be a party of one—as usual. "Drive safely," she added, knowing it sounded lame. What she actually wanted to do was stick out her lower lip and sulk like a teenage girl with her first crush.

As she was turning away, Mark touched her shoulder before clearing his throat. "Would you—I mean, do you want to do something tomorrow night?" She could only gape at him in shock as his words hung heavily between them. Had he just asked her out? Or did he mean sex?

"Like a date?" she asked uncertainly. "If it's the other thing that we discussed, we'll have to make do with what you have because Amazon doesn't deliver on Sunday. I have my Rabbit, though—so I could bring that. If you don't have handcuffs, we could use one of your ties. I like that teal blue one that you wear sometimes." When he continued to stare at her with his mouth now hanging open, she rushed to reassure him. "You don't have to make a decision now. You can text me—or call me later. Or even send me a private message on Twitter." *Oh God, I'm rambling and making a fool out of myself. Shut up, Crystal—don't say another word!*

He rubbed his temple, saying, "Angel, I'm talking about dinner. Isn't that what normal people do when they go out together? Possibly a movie as well." Behind them, Denny coughed loudly, although Crystal suspected it was actually to keep from laughing. She and Mark probably sounded pathetic. Both of them uncertain and fumbling around with something so simple. "Although I'd be lying if I said I wasn't intrigued by the other stuff you mentioned." His eyes widened for a moment before he took a deep breath. "I'm trying to do this right, Angel, so stop distracting me. May I pick you up at seven tomorrow night?"

Unable to contain her grin, she said primly, "Yes, please." At the same time, she fought the urge to run around and do some cartwheels. She had a freaking date with Mark DeSanto. Stuff like this didn't happen to girls like her. But it was happening—ahhh!

He leaned down to brush a kiss onto her cheek before moving his lips to her ear. "No need for the tie, Angel—I have handcuffs." With that statement, he gave her a quick salute and followed Denny out.

Since every head at the barbecue was still turned to her, she playfully held up her fingers in a V for "victory." "That's right, I've got a date tomorrow night!" After a few seconds of silence that felt more like minutes, the applause started and she took a bow.

Who knew that all it took was the promise of dinner with a sexy man and two glasses of wine for Crystal Webber to turn into a wild woman? Dear Lord, had the answer to her happiness been that simple all along?

Denny smirked as they walked into Mark's house an hour later with Chinese takeout. "'At last, your love has come along. Your tying-up days are overrr . . .'"

"Shut up, asshole," Mark snapped as he listened to his assistant butcher a classic love song.

"Oh, come on, man, I was just getting to the part about not turning any more asses red. That was my best verse. I worked on this for the entire trip." He pouted.

"I knew I should have gone through the fucking McDonald's drive-thru," Mark grumbled.

"Well, if you hadn't lied and made us leave before the actual food was served at Declan's, we wouldn't be in need of food. Why'd you bother to tuck tail and run after making out in the closet, talking dirty, and then asking her out? Heck, it was all smooth sailing and you panicked." Looking suddenly serious, Denny asked, "What made you do that, by the way? The date, that is. . . ."

Mark dropped on a barstool and lowered his head onto his folded arms. "I don't know. I caved to pressure. Declan was warning me off, like I was going to defile her or something."

Denny raised his brows and Mark flipped him off. "Yeah, so maybe he had a small point. But for once, I was trying to be a good guy—and she wouldn't let me. If I didn't know better, I'd swear she was taking a BDSM training class."

"Maybe she bought some self-help books," Denny interjected. "You know, *Spankings for Dummies* or *Bondage 101 for Beginners*."

Mark rubbed his eyes before chuckling. "I wouldn't doubt it at all," he admitted. "There's something about her, though. She makes me want shit I've never desired before, and it's scary as hell."

"That doesn't mean it's wrong," Denny said. "You've been different with her from the beginning. If she were one of your usual women, then we wouldn't even be having this discussion because you'd have already slept with her and she'd be long gone. The fact that you haven't, even though you obviously want her, should tell you something."

"That I'm losing it?" Mark asked ruefully. "Or maybe I'm just getting too old for the crap I've always favored."

"Yeah, a bad case of arthritis and you're out of business," Denny snickered. "Imagine having to rub on the joint cream before you crack the whip. Talk about ruining the moment. And don't even get me started on the smell. You remember how the grandparents' house smelled like a mixture of mothballs and mint toothpaste?"

"This is beyond depressing." Mark groaned. "It's Saturday night and I'm sitting here discussing old age with my cousin. Let's hurry up and eat so I can be asleep by nine. That's what old bastards do, right?"

"You're really pathetic," Denny said sarcastically. "Might I point out that your dry spell can be measured in weeks? Plus, you have a date with a beautiful woman tomorrow night. All men should have your kind of problems."

Mark nodded, grabbing a container of shrimp lo mein. "I am pretty amazing, aren't I?"

Denny snorted. "Thank God. The conversation was beginning to sound like a category on *Jeopardy!* called 'Things That Losers Say.' I'm glad you're back to your humble self again."

They polished off their meal along with a couple of beers each while joking around. He'd never admit it to the other man, but it was one of his better Saturday nights on record. He'd been restless for a while, and when having sex with a variety of women came in second to a night with your cousin, it was definitely time for a change. He was in no way talking about settling down and buying a fucking minivan, but the possibility of trying a relationship with one woman was almost intriguing. He'd never known that before, so how could he judge whether or not it was right for him? And he couldn't think of anyone better to fill that position than Crystal Webber. He'd already established that he wanted her around—hell, he was making an ass out of himself for her and the world at large to witness.

Tomorrow night, he would show her he could do sweet. He'd be a gentleman and attempt not to sleep with her on the first date. She would have to stop saying shit about being tied up for him to succeed, though. He'd been so hard when Declan had the come-to-Jesus talk with him, he'd been forced to keep his hands jammed in his pockets to hide the evidence. The random kinky stuff that tumbled from those plump lips drove him nuts. And the Rabbit she mentioned? He was almost certain that she wasn't referring to a pet bunny.

His Angel was going to test all of his newfound resolve, and no amount of jerking off before the date was going to help if she didn't lay off the sex-toy talk.

Chapter Nine

Crystal had checked her watch again before she returned to pacing the floor of her living room. Mia was late—which wasn't unusual. Normally, it wouldn't be a big deal, but her friend was lending her a dress for her date with Mark, and she didn't want to find out at the last moment that it didn't fit.

She almost jumped out of her skin when a knock sounded at the door. In the middle of her mad dash, she stubbed her toe on the carpet and ended up hopping the rest of the way. *Damn, what else today?*

Mia stood there, holding up a gorgeous black dress—that looked a little on the short side. "Sorry I'm late," the other woman tossed out as she walked in. "I couldn't find my keys. I finally checked the car and I'd left them in the ignition." Wrinkling her nose, she added, "I'd never hear the end of that if Seth found out." Looking Crystal up and down, she grimaced. "Um—yeah, you look . . . low-maintenance."

Crystal started laughing at her friend's subtle put-down. "I was waiting for you to get here with the dress. I didn't want to mess my hair up while I was dressing."

"Oh, thank goodness." Mia sighed. "This isn't your

finished look. I was a bit worried there for a moment. Have you showered and shaved—everything?"

Turning away before Mia could see her blush, she mumbled, "Yes, I'm all groomed." She didn't want to admit it, but she'd done something that she'd never dared before. She'd gone completely bare—downstairs. In the midst of her usual trim session, she'd had the crazy urge for something different. She'd mentioned trying it to her ex-husband one time, and he'd almost passed out. Then he'd gone into great detail on why it was wrong that she'd even considered it. That was Bill, though. Anytime she'd ever wanted to try anything new in the bedroom, he'd made her feel like some kind of cheap slut. Eventually, she'd just stopped trying or caring. That had been the beginning of the end of their marriage. She couldn't imagine Mark ever belittling her for something like that. He made her want to be adventurous and step outside of her comfort zone. And unbelievably, tonight she had a chance to do just that with him. An official date—just the two of them. A shot for her at fulfilling one of her many fantasies involving him.

Mia handed her the dress then pulled some type of brochure from her purse. Giving Crystal a wicked grin, she waved it in the air. "Guess what I wanted to tell you? My friend Becca is now a representative for Naughty Nights, and I'm hosting a party for her!"

"Naughty Nights?" Crystal asked, wondering if this was some kind of sex club. Was it wrong that the idea wasn't as scary as it should be?

"You've never heard of it?" Mia asked, while she thumbed through what Crystal could now see was a booklet. "It's the newest thing. You get a bunch of your girlfriends together, have a few glasses of wine, and buy sex toys. I've been to one of the parties before. It's actually a lot of fun. And I brought you one of the catalogs. You can do a little window-shopping before the party next week."

"Bu-but everyone would know that I bought a vibrator," Crystal whispered. Sure, she'd mentioned her Rabbit to Mark, but that was different. She planned to have sex with him. But to pick out stuff like that in front of a bunch of strangers—or even worse, friends— was something she couldn't imagine.

"Who the hell cares?" Mia waved her worries away. "Honey, everyone there will be doing the same thing. Becca will even bring some with her so that you can test the look, feel, and most important—the size. I mean, nothing's more disappointing than thinking you're buying a big hot one online only to find out that it looks like some pecker reject when it arrives. Yeah, realistic, my ass. If you can't get your fantasy cock in rubber, then where can you?"

Crystal sagged back onto her sofa, dropping her head in her hands. "You're nuts," she managed to choke out between embarrassed laughter. "What does Seth think about you trying to buy your dream penis online?"

Mia licked her lips. "We like our toys, but trust me, none of them measure up to what he's got going on. My man is hung, and I've got the bowed legs to prove it."

"Oh, my God!" Crystal collapsed into a fit of giggles. "He'd die if he knew the things you said about him."

"Why?" Mia smirked. "Do you think any man would actually care if his woman told her friends that he had a big one? Hell, he'd probably be thrilled. Oh—and I can tell that Mark does as well. Have you noticed that outline going down his leg? He's packing—seriously."

"You looked at his crotch?" Crystal gaped at her in disbelief.

"Well, duh. You had him so worked up last night that it practically had its own zip code when he left. I wasn't staring the whole time, but Suzy and I were near the doorway as he was walking out and it was kind of hard to miss."

"It did . . . feel that way," Crystal admitted. "Not that I've had much experience in gauging a man's size."

"Well, you're going to tell me all about it tomorrow." Mia grinned before taking Crystal's hand and pulling her to her feet. "Now let's go pull you together for DeStudo. When I get finished with you, he'll be bringing that monster out of his pants to play."

Mark stood uncertainly on Crystal's doorstep, feeling like he was on the verge of a panic attack, which was completely unlike him. What was wrong with him? He was never nervous where women were concerned. He'd been standing here damn near five minutes and had straightened his clothing a dozen times. Why was meaningless sex easier than a simple date? Sure, there wasn't a lot of conversation when you were fucking—so actually talking to his date would be different. Plus, there was the whole goal of not sleeping with her tonight. He wasn't sure what he'd been thinking when he made that resolution. It just sounded stupid now. He wanted her and she felt the same. Why deprive either of them?

He was in the middle of talking to himself like an

idiot when the door suddenly swung open and there she was. His Angel in a short black dress that made her look sinfully good. Rather like a fallen Angel.

"I—um, thought I heard something out here, and since you were a few minutes late, I decided to check." Shit, he'd stood out here so long stressing like a pussy that he'd lost track of time.

Shaking off his insecurities, he took a step forward and dropped a kiss on her cheek. "You look amazing, Angel." *Heaven help me, she smells good enough to eat.*

"Thank you," she replied softly. "You look really good."

Did she just look at my cock when she said that? Clearing his throat, he asked, "Are you ready to go?"

"All set." She smiled shyly, stepping out and locking her apartment door. He reached down to thread his fingers through hers as if it were the most natural thing in the world. Weird, something else he didn't normally do. He'd put a hand in the small of a woman's back, but holding hands felt too intimate. It was something you'd do on a vanilla kind of date, though, wasn't it?

Denny had offered—begged—to drive them tonight, but Mark had politely refused. On their first date, he didn't need the other man laughing at him as he tried to do the whole normal thing with Angel. "So, how was your day today?" he asked as he opened the passenger door of the Porsche for her.

"It was good." She laughed softly. "I was really nervous, though."

Surprised, he kept hold of her hand as he asked, "Was it because of me?"

Instead of shying away, she looked him in the eye

and simply said, "Yes." He found that he liked that answer a lot since he'd been feeling the same way. Heck, he'd changed his clothes three times, which was beyond absurd. He wasn't sure regular dating was something that he needed to pursue if it was going to turn him into some kind of bumbling fool. Somehow smacking a woman's ass was simple and straightforward, but calling it a date made it complex and complicated.

Unable to resist, he pulled her close, lowering his mouth to hers. A low moan sounded from her throat as he licked into her mouth. The sound was enough to have him instantly hard. When her tongue darted out to touch his, he was on the verge of pulling her back to her apartment and ordering a damn pizza for dinner after he'd sated his hunger that burned for her. The scary part was that he knew deep down that once would be only the beginning. His Angel was fast becoming an addiction that had thrown his life in disarray.

They were pulled from the moment when a car passed by, honking the horn repeatedly. "Well, crap," she snapped crossly as she glared at the retreating vehicle. Apparently, she didn't like the interruption any more than he did.

He tapped her chin, smiling at her disgruntled expression. "Don't worry, baby. We'll pick that up again later if you're a good girl."

She blushed, which he found adorable. Most of the women who came to his bed weren't capable of that kind of innocent embarrassment anymore. Innocence was a heady thing, and hers captivated him. "I thought you liked your women bad."

Shit, had she really just said that? *Lighten up, she's just joking around. Everything isn't a sexual innuendo.* He directed most of his pep talk toward his wayward cock as he crossed the front of the car and settled into the seat beside Crystal. Her sweet scent filled the small space around him, and he had his next epiphany. He should have let Denny drive. She was so close now, and there was no way to put distance between them. *Don't stare at her tits and don't put your hand between her legs. Dear God, just look away from her. Pretend she's Denny.* His good intentions lasted until he pulled out of her parking lot. Then somehow, his hand ended up on her bare knee. It was all her fault. Her damn dress was way too short. How was he supposed to resist touching so much exposed skin?

When she started laughing, he realized that he'd voiced his question aloud. *Real smooth, man.* "Sorry," he mumbled, feeling like some kind of socially awkward reject. When she put her hand on his, moving it up higher, his heart rate accelerated into the danger zone. *Great, I'm going to have a stroke from a little contact with her bare leg.*

"I wanted to wear a dress that would make you want me," she confessed shyly.

Inhaling a jerky breath, he said hoarsely, "Angel, I couldn't give a fuck what you wear. I'd want you if you were wearing granny panties and a burlap sack. Trust me: it's the woman, not the clothes, that attracts me." Her grip tightened on his hand as she asked a question that had him weaving all over the road. "Can we . . . just skip dinner and go to your place?"

"Angel," he groaned as he righted the car. At this

rate, he'd be pulled over for DUI without ever touching a drop of alcohol. "Let me just go ahead and tell you that we're not having sex tonight. Now that it's out there, we don't have to stress about it all evening." *What in the hell did I just say? It's as if Angel and I have switched bodies. I'm the virginal girl and she's the horny guy.*

She crossed her arms and gave what sounded like a huff of irritation. "But why not? I mean, you know I'm receptive, right?"

Mark wanted to beat his head against the steering wheel. This wasn't going at all as he'd planned. She was testing his resolve, and he wasn't even sure why he wanted to resist in the first place. Now it was almost like some sort of contest that he was determined to win—or at least survive. "Baby, can you just please let me be the better man for once? I'm trying so hard not to treat you like I have other women, and you're making it hard—like really hard." When she opened her mouth to say what was probably something else that would blow his mind, he quickly added, "Let's wait until we're at the restaurant to finish this conversation, okay? I'd like to avoid wrapping the car around a pole tonight if that's okay with you."

He switched on the stereo to a soft-rock station and tried to relax as the music filled the car. Maybe this was the grown-up version of a time-out, because that was exactly what he needed right now. A moment to regroup and start thinking about stuff like his parents, grandparents, and anyone else who would be a complete turnoff. Because focusing on Angel was out of the question right now or he'd do something crazy like park behind a deserted building and take her on the hood of his car. His mind raced with the least sexy images he could come up with: *Denny, the little old lady at Starbucks, bad sushi, Angel throwing up on his shoes . . .*

I must have said something wrong, Crystal thought glumly as Mark sprinted from the driver's seat as soon as they reached the restaurant. Mia had advised that she should simply be honest with him about what she wanted, and she figured asking to go to his house made her feelings pretty clear. Only something about it had freaked him out. He'd almost run off the road, but even more alarming was the fact that he was chanting something under his breath repeatedly. She thought she caught Denny's name and something about his mother. Was he on some type of medication? If not, maybe he needed to look into that, because he was acting kind of crazy.

She saw a valet approaching her door, before Mark waved him away. She reached for the handle just as he flung it open. The result was her almost tumbling from the low-slung seat and onto the pavement. Luckily, he managed to catch her before that happened. Dear God, so far, they were almost a disaster together. She was awkward enough on her own; she certainly didn't need any help in that area from a man who normally seemed so smooth and polished. He mumbled an apology before helping her to stand.

"Oh wow, I've always wanted to come here." She beamed at him once she noticed they'd arrived at a seafood restaurant located on one of the quieter piers in Myrtle Beach. He smiled in reply before putting a hand on the small of her back and leading her toward the door.

"Mr. DeSanto," the hostess gushed. "How wonderful to see you again, and you've brought company this evening. I have a quiet table in the corner that would be perfect."

Both the hostess and Crystal gawked at Mark when he said loudly, "No! Er—I mean, how about that one right there?" he asked, pointing toward a small table in the middle of the room with absolutely no privacy.

Nonplussed, the hostess stammered for a few moments before finally saying, "Of course, Mr. DeSanto, if that's your preference. Right this way, please."

Mark could barely pull her seat away from the table thanks to a rather large man behind them, but he somehow managed. Why in the world would he have wanted to sit here? Maybe he was one of those people who liked to herd with others. She'd never pictured Mark as a pack animal, but then again she wouldn't have imagined him panicking over having sex either.

"This is great, don't you think?" he enthused, as he appeared not to notice that she was wedged up in her corner with barely an inch to spare.

"Sure," she agreed, determined to make the best of it. So Mark had some strange quirks. That was to be expected, right? Lord knows Bill had issues. Maybe she attracted that type of man. Looking at how handsome he was across the table, she decided that even if she had a permanent indentation in her side after their cramped meal, it was a small price to pay for a night out with the man of her dreams. After all, he looked delectable in the suit he wore so well. Needing a diversion to keep from drooling, she craned her head to see the view from the wall of windows. "Wow, what a beautiful place. Do you come here often?" Probably a stupid question since the hostess knew him by name.

Mark took a sip from his water glass. "I have dinner meetings here occasionally. I'm glad you like it." They continued to do well with their polite conversation after ordering their entrees when her first embarrassing moment of the evening occurred. The waiter was adding fresh ground pepper to her Caesar salad when she made the mistake of taking a deep breath and inadvertently inhaling what seemed like half of the shaker. Instantly, her eyes watered and her nose burned. Then the sneezing started. Considering where they sat in the restaurant, it was impossible for those nearby to miss her attack. Sadly, she'd never been a dainty sneezer and tonight was no exception. She grabbed her napkin, trying to cover her face while fumbling in her purse for a tissue. The waiter was apologizing profusely even though it hadn't been his fault, while Mark jumped to his feet to offer his assistance.

"Kleenex," she managed to choke out between rounds of both coughing and sneezing. He took her purse and upended it on the table until he found what he was looking for. Considering how close they sat to the other diners, she had little choice but to blow her nose right there for all to see and hear. Mark handed her a glass of water, and she managed to take a couple of small sips without spraying the table. Finally, she was able to regain control and wanted nothing more than to climb under their table and hide.

Mark was rubbing her shoulder, looking down at her in concern. "Are you all right now?"

She nodded, giving him a rueful smile. "Other than

being mortified, I'm fine," she added. "I can't believe that happened."

Mark returned to his side of the table and took his seat. "You certainly keep life interesting," he acknowledged. Crystal was surprised to see that he still looked concerned, but there was also a flash of amusement in his eyes as he looked at her. Bill would have spent the rest of the meal berating her for causing a scene, but it appeared that Mark couldn't care less what others thought. She'd yet to catch him looking at anyone other than her.

Within moments, he'd had her salad and water replaced with fresh ones and she'd put the items that had been thrown from her purse back inside. He was sweet, considerate, and thoughtful—in other words, the perfect guy. She was relaxed and enjoying her meal when their waiter—possibly trying to atone for the pepper incident—bent to pick up something from the floor. He had glanced at it, his eyes widening as he hastily handed it to Mark, and then left without a word. Mark looked at the paper curiously before dropping his fork. The sound of it hitting the glass plate echoed loudly, causing Crystal to jump in her seat. "Are you—is everything okay?" she asked in concern. He shifted in his seat, before swallowing a few times.

He tucked the paper into his jacket pocket and asked, "Are you almost finished, Angel?"

She looked down at her half-eaten meal before shrugging. "Sure, if you are."

He paid the bill quickly, and they were outside once again. He put a hand on her back, helping her down the steps. Not a word was spoken between them until they were in his Porsche. Instead of leaving though, he pulled the paper from his pocket and carefully unfolded it. "Angel . . . is this yours?" he asked, sounding stressed.

She noticed that it was actually some kind of booklet instead of a single sheet of paper. She took it from his hands, and then gasped in horror. "Oh crap! I—Mia—I mean . . . you weren't supposed to—God!"

Dropping his head onto the steering wheel, he said softly, "I was afraid of that."

"Mark—I can explain. Mia brought it by earlier. One of her friends sells this stuff, and Mia is hosting a party for her. It was lying on the table when you got to my apartment earlier, and I stuck it inside my purse so you wouldn't see it." Putting her hand over her eyes, she whispered, "But now both you and the waiter think I'm some kind of pervert."

Without looking at her, Mark asked thickly, "Did you make those notes?"

Crystal looked down at the page that the booklet was open to and cringed. She'd been thumbing through it while waiting for Mark and had listed a question down beside one particular product. It was intended as a joke for Mia—not for Mark's eyes. "Yes," she finally squeaked out. "I was going to tease Mia about it."

"Did you get wet when you were looking at this book, Angel?" Mark asked as he turned to look at her intently.

Her mouth dropped open as she stared at him. "Wh-what?"

He put a hand on her exposed knee, slowly trailing his fingers up her thigh. "You heard me. Were you turned on when you imagined using one of these on yourself? Did you imagine me using them on you?"

Crystal was in serious danger of swallowing her tongue as his words ignited a fire of desire within her. She straightened her spine and forced herself to maintain eye contact with him as she admitted, "Yes—to both questions."

He took the booklet back from her nerveless fingers and pointed to the item that she'd written beside. "To answer your question, baby, that toy is for double penetration."

Gawking at him, she asked, "How can you put them both in at the same time?"

He squirmed in his seat before turning the key in the ignition. "Baby, one of them is for your ass."

When his meaning hit her, she breathed, "Ohhh."

"Exactly." He grinned as he pulled out into traffic. "Angel, I want you to know that I really tried to behave tonight. I had every intention of taking you to dinner and then delivering you back to your door. But you've made that impossible."

Uncertain what he was getting at, she timidly asked, "What do you mean?" Without answering, he took her hand and pulled it across the console, putting it against his crotch.

She hissed as her fingers wandered over the steely length.

He did a combination of a laugh and a groan as he gently pushed her hand away. "Do you want to come home with me and help me take care of that?"

Sitting up straight, she tried to hide her sudden giddiness as she asked, "Tonight?"

"Yes, Angel, you broke my resolve. I couldn't even make it through the first date with you. If this isn't what you want, then tell me now and I'll take you home. Otherwise, I'm going to lick and suck every inch of your body before I fuck you—all night."

Eyes going large, she mouthed, *Oh wow.* "That's the best thing that anyone's ever said to me, and I'd like to accept your offer of everything you just mentioned. Plus anything else you might want to throw in." Then remembering his earlier explanation of the sex toy in the catalog, she hastily added, "But not the rear thing, if you don't mind. I mean, I'm not saying it's an absolute no, but that's something I'd need to think about—a lot. And maybe do some research. Do they have books with detailed descriptions of how that would happen and what it would feel like? And with a pain level listing?" When she realized that she was rambling, she abruptly stopped and saw that Mark was shaking with laughter in his seat as he drove.

"Angel," he managed to get out. "Baby, I don't know if they have books like that or not, but you don't have to worry about it. There is no way I'd expect that our first time together. If everything we do in bed isn't a ten, then I'm not doing something right. I'm not a selfish lover, so you can be assured that you'll get yours—several times—before I do."

Rubbing her thighs together in an attempt to relieve some of the pressure building within her, she admitted, "That sounds amazing. I—please don't be disappointed if that doesn't happen. I can't have one of those during sex. It's a more common problem than you know," she added, not wanting to sound like there was something wrong with her. She had read that many women couldn't come through intercourse.

"That's a fucking cop-out." Mark shook his head. "A man needs to make sure a woman is satisfied. I promise you that you'll come on my tongue, my fingers, and my cock. I'll never leave you hanging unless it's just to delay your pleasure."

Dazzled by his promises, she asked unsteadily, "Are we almost at your house?"

Mark laughed softly as they turned into his driveway. Before he turned off the car, he asked softly, "Last chance, Angel. Do you really want this?"

Instead of answering verbally, she opened her car door and stepped out. Sometimes actions spoke louder than words, and Mark seemed to have no trouble interrupting hers.

Chapter Ten

He'd never been this hard in his life. He needed to dominate and devour her, but a part of him wanted to make love to her in a way that neither of them had ever experienced before. They were standing in his foyer and he was back to that odd, awkward feeling. She was different from any woman he'd ever known. He didn't know why she had come to matter to him, but she had. He'd known deep down in his gut from the moment she passed out in his arms that she was special and would be a game changer for him. He'd proven his own point that day by taking her home and watching over her. It was inevitable that they would end up at this point. The fact that he'd waited as long as he had was a testament to his confusion and denial over what she made him feel—and the things he longed for when he was with her.

She was looking at him now in a kind of nervous anticipation. Funny—that was exactly how he would describe his present state of mind as well. His body was raring to go, but the rest of him was jittery, as if afraid of screwing up something vitally important.

Clearing his throat, he asked, "Would you like something to drink?"

She looked surprised by the question. Shaking her head, she murmured, "No, I'm fine." Then she blurted out something that had his jaw dropping open. "Did you know that your nickname at the office is DeStudo?" As if thinking better of her revelation after the fact, she slapped her hand over her mouth. "Oh, my God, I shouldn't have said that. It's just when I get nervous, I lose the filter between my mouth and my brain and things pop out without me thinking them through. Please ignore that."

After his initial surprise, Mark couldn't control the grin that spread across his face. "'DeStudo'? Did you come up with that name, Angel?" he asked, prowling closer to her.

"What? No! I don't know who did," she stammered.

"So you don't think I'm attractive?" he asked, watching her gulp at his question. Teasing her was fast becoming one of his favorite pastimes.

A few seconds later, the joke was on him, though, as she admitted in a rush, "I think you're the sexiest man I've ever seen. I've never lusted after anyone before, but I can't stop thinking about trying out all of my secret fantasies with you."

"Ah hell," he groaned as he stopped just inches away from her. He raised a hand, stroking a finger down her soft cheek before cupping her face. "I'll tell you again, baby, that you had your chance to let me run the other way. But since you didn't, you're mine."

"Yes, please," she replied sweetly as she stood up on

her toes to press her mouth against his. That was it; he was gone. There was no Declan to discover them together and interfere this time.

Mark forced himself to remain still as she licked at his lips until he parted them and let her inside. When her questing tongue met his, he lost it. Without breaking contact, he leaned down and picked her up in his arms before striding down the hallway.

When they reached his room, he walked forward to the end of his bed before easing her gently down onto the soft surface. He positioned himself on top of her, carefully bracing his weight on his forearms. For now, he simply wanted to devour her mouth. With Angel, he felt like he could happily kiss her for hours. When she wrapped a leg around his and ground her hips against him, the kiss became pure carnal activity.

"I want our clothes off," she moaned in his ear.

Ah fuck! Me too, baby. He reluctantly pulled back, getting to his feet and tugging her up with him. He walked quickly to one of the bedside lamps and clicked it on before returning to her. He lowered the zipper on her dress and he pulled it from her shoulders. The material slid past her hips and into a pool at her feet. "Sweet Christ," he said feeling dizzy. "You're beautiful, Angel—simply stunning." And she was. Standing before him in a lacy black bra and tiny matching panties, she would fuel any man's fantasies. Flawless skin, legs that seemed to go on for miles, a flat stomach, and breasts that were more than a handful.

"Can I?" she asked, pointing to his shirt. He'd imagined her being shy in the bedroom, so he was blown away that she was asking to undress him.

"Hell yes, baby; I'm all yours." He'd worn a suit tonight but skipped the tie and left a couple of buttons undone on his dress shirt. Her fingers went straight to the next ones in line and began slipping them through the holes until she reached his slacks. He remained quiet, wanting to see what she'd do next—and she didn't disappoint. With barely a pause, she unbuckled his belt and released the hook closure on his pants. He fought to keep a straight face as she chewed her lower lip while she concentrated on her task. *Too fucking adorable.* He had to give her credit because within moments—with no help from him— she had his dress shirt on the floor and was tugging his undershirt over his head.

Then her hands went to his zipper, and his legs went weak. His cock was already peeping from the top of his boxers. Her fingertips were all over it, and he had a horrifying moment of fear that he would blow his load before he was fully undressed. That was only acceptable if your pants were around your ankles while you were buried deep inside a woman. Having it happen from some very light contact was strictly a high school mistake. One he'd never made, even back then. So—he grabbed her hands and held them in one of his while he finished the job for her. His cock sprang free. "Oh, my goodness," she said, looking astonished, before licking her lips. And there it went—the last of his self-control. He had to have her—now. There'd be time to take it slow later.

Dropping her wrists, he walked to the bedside table, pulled out a strip of condoms, and tossed them on the bed. He returned to her and settled his hands on her hips.

"I can't hold off long, Angel. I'll make sure you're there with me first, though, even if it kills me, baby. Okay?" She nodded her agreement and used one hand to open the front clasp of her bra. Her breasts tumbled free as she stepped back from his hold and positioned herself half-sitting, half-lying on his bed. *How could anyone have ever let this woman go?* he wondered as he climbed into bed beside her. He made quick work of removing her panties before sliding his hands up her inner thighs until he reached her core. His fingers found her slick folds, and he whispered in wonder, "You're ready for me, aren't you, baby? You're so hot and wet." His thumb slid easily around her clit while he eased his index finger inside of her.

"Hurry, Mark—hurry," she cried out as her body quivered with need. He could tell she was already close to coming, just from the small amount of stimulation that he'd given her. He wanted to taste her—to see her come apart again and again—but right now, they both needed a release. Instead, he pulled back, rolled on a condom, and positioned his hands under her knees. Pulling her closer to him, he lined up his cock and thrust inside. When she screamed loud enough to wake his neighbors, he immediately stilled, gritting his teeth. "Why are you stopping?" she snapped. Her hips pushed back impatiently, taking him deeper. "Go—please," she pleaded.

With no handcuffs or sex toys in sight, Mark had the wildest sexual experience of his life. He couldn't even fathom the fact that she claimed to have never orgasmed during sex because she'd come within seconds of his plunging into her wet heat.

Her nails had scored his arms as she'd attempted to top from the bottom. He'd had a lot of vocal women, but most sounded as if they exaggerated it just for entertainment value. His Angel, though, seemed to genuinely love his cock, and she let her appreciation be known. It reminded him of the saying *a lady in the living room and a whore in the bedroom*. He didn't want to offend her by commenting on it, because he freaking loved it. He'd given it to her hard, and she'd begged for more. She was a greedy little thing in bed, as the fact that he was now lying next to her panting would attest to.

He leaned down to kiss her mouth, and then the tip of her nose. Her eyes, which had been closed, fluttered open. He saw surprise, along with satisfaction there. "That was amazeballs," she murmured, before kicking her arms and legs in a way that made Mark think she was having some kind of attack. As he gawked down at her, she suddenly grabbed her breasts and squeezed them. "Oh, my God, I want to do that again and again!" Then it was as if she deflated in front of him. Her lower lip quivered as she said, "But we won't, will we? I mean everyone says that you don't repeat—things. So now that we've . . . done it, we're finished."

Mark felt his chest clench at her words. He had no idea how everyone at Danvers knew his sexual tendencies since he'd always tried to keep that rather private, but she wasn't wrong, and that stung. This should be it for them. This was the point where he'd take home the woman he'd slept with and say a few meaningless words. However, he would never promise to call again, because he wouldn't. The thought of Crystal leaving now sent something close to panic racing through him.

Hell, he wanted her to stay the night with him. He didn't want to analyze why he was feeling what he was, because then he'd do something stupid like distancing himself and hurting her. And that he couldn't live with. Not with her.

"Baby, the only thing I'm going to do is go toss this condom and grab us something to drink. After that, I'm going to taste that beautiful body of yours, and then you're going to ride me. Sound like a plan?"

Her eyes searched his before she gave him a huge grin. "Yeah, I can go along with that." Mark left the bed and disposed of the condom before grabbing two bottles of water from the kitchen. His voice of reason was screaming that he was in over his head, but for once, something beyond physical desire was ruling his decisions.

Crystal tried to keep a straight face as Mark walked back in the room and handed her a bottle of water. *This is really happening! I had sex with Mark DeSanto, and we're going to do it again!* While he was gone, she'd slid under the comforter and propped her back on a few of his pillows. She was so sated and boneless that she'd barely been able to make herself move, but it had seemed kind of . . . slutty to remain sprawled across his bed naked. When you weren't having sex, you were supposed to cover your lady bits up. At least that was the way Bill saw it. The first time they'd had sex and she'd thought she was supposed to sleep in the nude afterward, he'd quickly let her know differently. He'd made her feel as if it was a dirty deed that should never be spoken of.

So, she was dumbfounded when Mark walked into the bathroom and came back with a washcloth. He pulled the comforter away from her and nudged her legs apart. He was so gentle that it brought tears to her eyes. She would have never imagined a man doing something so intimate, and while a part of her was embarrassed, another part was entranced. Maybe she was being silly and he did this for all of his women—but she didn't think so. Somehow, she felt she was unique to him. Possibly, it was the novelty of being with a woman who he considered innocent. Whatever it was, she found that she liked being taken care of.

And heaven help her . . . the sex. She hadn't been able to get enough of him. He'd ignited nerve endings that she hadn't known existed. Heck, even his touching her belly button sent spasms of pleasure through her sex. He had been everywhere. When she'd been close to going over the edge, he'd switch directions and come at her in another way. His cock was so big that she ached—but in a good way. He'd licked her nipples, and then bit down on them while he pounded away. Dear God, she'd even found herself rubbing her clit while he went deep. She'd never touched her body in front of a man before, but Mark made her lose all of her inhibitions. She was a total sexual being with him, and she'd held nothing back.

When he collapsed next to her and pulled her to his chest, she put one arm around his waist and snuggled closer. The room was quiet as he ran his fingers through her hair, massaging her scalp. Mark, it appeared, was very comfortable in his skin. He was still nude, and a quick glance down showed that he was hard. Unable to resist, she dropped a hand to fist around his cock, marveling at how smooth and satiny the skin there felt.

Her thumb moved across the lush head, rubbing the moisture that had gathered there. He drew in a ragged breath before growling, "That's it, Angel. Tighten your grip and pump me harder."

She clasped him as firmly as she could since her fingers wouldn't meet and jacked his length. He groaned, making her feel as if she was doing something right. She wanted nothing more than to taste him, so with that in mind, she pulled away from his arms until she was kneeling over his dick. His essence exploded against her tongue as she twirled it around his head. She pumped the base with her hand while taking as much of his length as she could into her mouth. He raised his hips, sliding his cock between her lips and hitting the back of her throat. She choked momentarily as her gag reflex was triggered, causing him to moan as he felt the vibration. "Mmm," she whimpered, so turned on by the pleasure she was giving him. She really had no idea what she was doing, but he guided her by placing a hand on her head. When he abruptly pulled out, she looked at him in confusion. "What?"

"My turn, Angel," he rasped as with a few movements of his hands, she was flat on her back and her legs were over his shoulders. She was sputtering out a protest when he licked her slit and sucked her clit into his mouth. After that, she was unable to form any more coherent thoughts as he devoured her through another couple of orgasms before rolling on a condom and pulling her on top of him, impaling her down onto his hard cock. Once again, she screamed and moved against him in ways that would do a porn star proud. If Mark

DeSanto was a bad boy, then she'd never want a good guy again. He'd ruined her for all other men.

Now that she knew what was possible between a man and woman, she never wanted it to end. The problem was that everyone knew Mark didn't do serious relationships. She surprised herself with what she was capable of in his bed. Was she strong enough to smile and wish him well when he walked away? Because he would, right? He always did.

Chapter Eleven

Monday morning seemed to arrive in the blink of an eye. Both she and Mark had fallen asleep after their last round of acrobatic sex, and she'd been surprised to open her eyes and see the morning light streaming through his bedroom windows. He'd insisted they save time and water by bathing together, where she'd experienced another first—against-the-wall shower sex.

When she walked into the kitchen in search of Mark after getting dressed, she found him there, sipping a cup of coffee with Denny. She'd wanted to back down the hallway and hide from the knowing smile on the other man's face, but Mark had spotted her. "Coffee, Angel?" he asked, already pouring her a cup.

"Thanks," she replied softly as she used the cream and sugar sitting nearby. In the light of day, she felt awkward and unsure of how to act around Mark after the previous night. When he pulled her against his chest and dropped a kiss on her temple, it shocked her. From the look on Denny's face, he felt the same way. It was obvious he wasn't used to seeing this side of his boss. As she was enjoying the closeness between them, a phone chimed. Both Denny and Mark checked theirs before looking at her. She shrugged and pulled her iPhone from her purse to find a text from her mother.

Mandatory family dinner. Seven tonight, don't be late.

"Well, shit," she grumbled.

Mark raised a brow in amusement, asking, "What's wrong, baby?" She turned her phone to let him read the message and saw his expression darken.

"Tell her where she can put that order," he advised.

Sighing, she shook her head. "It's easier to just go and get it over with. Otherwise, I'd have to hear about what a lousy daughter I am for weeks."

Mark put his hand under her chin, lifting it to study her. "Don't let her do that to you. You're playing right into her hands."

Forgetting all about Denny, she snuggled closer, saying glumly, "I know, but it's a hard habit to break. She's my mother, after all. I'll just head straight there from work and get it over with. Then I'll go home and stare at the walls for eight hours or so until I've recovered."

"Come here afterward," Mark said against her ear. "I'll give you something to take your mind off things for the night."

She grinned against his chest, feeling suddenly giddy, while Denny made a gagging sound. "I hate to break up this lovefest that you two have going on, but if we don't hit the road, we'll be late for your first meeting, cousin."

Mark glanced down at his watch and grimaced. "You ready, Angel?" he asked as he gently released her from his hold.

Trying to sound far more enthusiastic than she felt,

she said a bright "Yep, let's get this Monday started." She refrained from adding that her mother had ruined any chance of this being a good day. Mark, sensing her somber mood, simply tucked her into his side on the ride across town—letting her know that he was there, but also giving her time with her thoughts before he dropped her at home.

He stepped out with her when they reached her apartment and insisted on walking her to the door. "I've got several meetings today, so I'll probably be tied up until this evening. Call me when you're leaving your parents' house and we'll go from there."

Despite being depressed over her evening plans, she felt the urge to do some kind of crazy victory dance at his casual mention of an evening together. She was going to see Mark again, and it wasn't even a weekend night. God, she felt like such a rebel. A new and improved model of herself, thanks to DeStudo. A giggle escaped her throat before she could hold it back. He gave her an inquiring look, to which she just shrugged her shoulders. "Trust me, it's a woman thing. You don't want to know."

Pulling her into his arms, he kissed the side of her neck and purred, "Oh, but I do, since I know it involves me. We're both going to be late though, so I'll let it go—for now." Dropping a kiss on her lips, he added, "Have a good day, Angel. Drive safely." As he was turning away, he suddenly swung back around. "Why don't I have Denny circle back after he drops me at the office? He can pick you up so that you can relax on the drive this morning."

Going to him, she curled her arms around his

stomach and gave him a squeeze. "I'm leaving from work for my parents'. I'll be fine. It's sweet that you care, though."

"Sweet?" he repeated as if the word felt foreign on his tongue. Considering his reputation with women, it probably wasn't one used to describe him often. He kissed the top of her head and pulled away. "Talk to you tonight," he murmured before walking toward his car. Maybe she should have left that last part off. It might not have been smart to bring that to his attention. She didn't want to scare him off, but she loved that he was concerned enough about her well-being to want to send Denny for her. Whether he wanted to acknowledge it or not, Mark DeSanto was a good guy. She only hoped he could accept that before he pushed her away.

Mark had spent the ride to work from Crystal's apartment dealing with issues at the Boston branch of his company. As with any type of business, the most challenging problem was finding strong people that you didn't have to constantly micromanage. Normally, he'd get on his private plane and be there in a few hours to deal with the issue in person. But the thought of traveling right now didn't appeal to him. That was strange considering he'd lived out of a suitcase for years. He'd always kept a base in Charleston, but hell, everyone needed an official place that they called home—even if they were rarely there.

Switching home base from Charleston to Myrtle Beach had seemed logical considering his continued partnership with Jason Danvers. He'd been quietly putting down roots here, which was a testament to how weary he had become of the nonstop business travel. He'd never liked staying in one place for long, thus the reason he'd finally purchased his own plane. Flying commercial sucked when you were doing it so often.

Now here he was with a house and an actual office where he spent weeks at a stretch. Jacob had been encouraging him for ages to turn over more of the travel to him, but Mark had been resistant. He liked maintaining control in all areas of his life, and to him, if you wanted something done right, then you did it yourself. Seemed easier than taking the time to train someone else. He'd been reconsidering his stance though in the last year. He was burned-out—so fucking tired of it all. Usually, when that kind of feeling threatened to engulf him, he'd find a woman and channel his frustrations into a more pleasurable outlet.

He hadn't been lying when he'd told Angel that he had handcuffs. Hell, he had a drawer full of the sorts of toys that had been in that surprising little booklet of hers. He liked to use props during sex. To him, it depersonalized the act and made it into something less intimate. It was physical release in the basest of terms.

Mark hadn't wanted any of that last night with his Angel. He was a man; of course, he'd get off on tying her down and having her at his mercy, but for once, that hadn't been his first thought. No, instead he'd wanted to hold her and see the expression in her eyes as they came together for the first time. His touch had set her aflame, and she'd made no attempt to hide it from him. There was no artifice in her. She gave her body to him as if she trusted implicitly that he would take care of her.

Even as anxiety and uncertainty had clawed at him while she'd lain sleeping in his arms, he'd only pulled her closer and fought off his misgivings. His self-preservation instincts had been screaming to push her away. To send her home and put some distance between them. But for once, the part of him that was tired of being alone was stronger. So he'd allowed himself to curl his body around hers and let the rest of the world fall away.

He'd woken to her sleeping soundly against his chest, and it had felt good. It had felt right in a way he hadn't experienced before. He'd had her in the shower, again pushing away the voice in his head that was bellowing in alarm. Then he'd invited—no, demanded—that she come to him after she'd had dinner with her bitch of a mother so that he could soothe the hurt that she would no doubt be feeling.

What was he doing? Where was this going with her? In the end, she'd be hurt and he'd be the bastard who did it. Fuck, he should walk away now before either of them got in over their head any further. *Too late—you're barely treading water now.*

Even as those thoughts swirled in his head, he picked up his phone again and called Jacob. "I need you to fly to Boston today and take care of some problems there. Denny will make arrangements to have the jet fueled and the pilot waiting for you by noon."

"No problem, boss," Jacob said easily. Mark detected the note of satisfaction in the other man's voice and knew that he was pleased that Mark was finally utilizing him in the full capacity in which he was hired. "I'll be in touch when I land." The call ended as abruptly as it began. Like him, Jacob was a man of few words. He didn't need hand-holding, and for the first time, Mark was grateful for someone to share the load of responsibilities.

What disturbed him most about delegating was that he wasn't sure who he was if not a workaholic. Women worked around his schedule—always had, and they never complained. His life revolved around two things—working and fucking. One had never interfered with the other, so why was he trying to fix what wasn't broken? Why was he in the midst of making more time for a life he didn't even have? *Because you're going to end up either alone or like your parents.*

"Is she messing with your head?" Mark jumped at the sound of Denny's voice, having been completely lost in thought.

"What're you talking about?" he asked, looking at the other man in the rearview mirror.

"Crystal has you wound pretty tight. Don't get me wrong—I think she's good for you. I'm just wondering how you're handling it."

Mark rolled his eyes sarcastically. "I'm not a virgin with his first girlfriend here. I have no idea why you would think I'm having some nervous breakdown over Angel."

Denny looked around, and then chuckled. "Um—maybe because we arrived at the office about ten minutes ago and you've been sitting back there staring into space the whole time."

Shit. He grimaced inwardly. He'd zoned out so

completely that he hadn't noticed that the car was no longer in motion. "Kiss my ass," he snapped at his cousin before opening the door. He could say nothing in his defense, and Denny's laughter said that he knew it. Time to get it together and look like the ruthless businessman that he was. No need for the world to know that he'd been shaken to his foundation by a woman he called Angel. *Hashtag fucked,* he thought wryly. Thank God the other man couldn't read minds.

Chapter Twelve

Crystal arrived at her parents' house with just moments to spare. Apparently, Ella was running even later, because there was no sign of her car there. Grabbing her phone, she texted a quick *Where are you? You know how Mom gets when we're late.*

She was on the front walkway when Ella texted back. *What are you talking about?*

Crystal froze, quickly replying with *Mandatory family dinner at the parents. We're supposed to be here at seven. Did you forget?*

When she read her sister's next message, she wanted to drop, roll, and run. *She didn't contact me, Crys. Oh crap, ambush, run!*

She was backing away when the front door flung open and her mother stood on the threshold with her hands on her hips. "Honey, what are you doing out here?" Then, as if she couldn't resist, she sweetly added, "You're a little late. I was afraid you'd had an accident or something." Crystal could feel her phone chiming away with no-doubt-frantic messages from Ella, but it was too late now. She had officially entered the den of the spider, and escaping that particular web before she was released would be damn near impossible. And what was with the endearment? Why was her mother trying to be pleasant? That was even more frightening than the idea of a good verbal lashing.

"Er—where's Ella?" she asked, as if she didn't already know.

"Oh, you know how busy she is now, with the new baby." Her mother waved her hand as if to say, *What're you gonna do?* "Plus, Declan doesn't like to visit, so why force the issue?"

A sense of foreboding washed over her as she thought, *This is bad.* Her mother had taken only a small dig at Declan instead of her usual rant over her son-in-law. Either she was trying to turn over a new leaf or something was up in a big way. "We can do it another time," Crystal offered, hoping the desperate tone in her voice wasn't readily apparent.

Motioning to the still-open door, her mother said, "Oh, nonsense. Come on in."

Seeing no other choice, she edged around her mother and into the hallway of the house she'd grown up in. Not one for change, her mother was still clinging to the dark paneling on the walls that made the whole space seem small and dark.

Her father appeared just as her mother walked off to check on dinner. "Crystal—it's good to see you," he said before dropping a kiss on her forehead. Before he moved away, his voice dropped to a near whisper as he added, "Your mother invited Bill. I tried to talk her out of it, but you know how she is when she makes up her mind."

"Are you serious?" Crystal asked in a shrill voice

just as there was a knock on the door behind her. Her father gave her an apologetic half smile before opening the door to her ex-husband. She didn't even know why she was so surprised. Her mother did what she wanted, and in order to keep the peace, her father refrained from making waves. He'd managed to stand up to his wife a couple of times that Crystal could recall, the last being when Ella was in the hospital after being hit by a neglectful driver while she was crossing the street. Their father had kept her firmly in place then, refusing to let her continue to make snide comments to Ella's friends in the waiting room. That had been his last stand. He hadn't bothered to intervene as his wife continued to verbally bully his other daughter over her divorce and whatever else she could find fault with. Crystal loved him because, well, he was her father, but she'd lost her respect for the man years ago. He wasn't the head of the family—he'd abandoned that position without a fight.

"Bill, good to see you again." She heard him greet her ex-husband as warmly as if he were the long-lost son returning from war. In this household, it was obvious that Bill was the favorite and she was the disappointment. Oh, how she wished that she had the backbone to walk out and leave them all to gush over each other. But no, like the glutton for punishment that she was, she plastered on a smile and tried not to cringe when Bill stepped forward to kiss her cheek.

"How are you, Crystal?" he asked, sounding so formal she had a hard time remembering that she'd actually been married to the man for years. They'd had sex hundreds of times—maybe not good sex, but they'd joined together for brief encounters. How was it that they seemed so much like strangers now in such a short amount of time? It drove home to her the fact that she'd never really known him, and she certainly hadn't understood what love was when she'd said *I do*.

"I'm great," she finally replied to his question half-heartedly. Before she was forced to make further conversation, her mother rounded the corner and fussed over him as if he were some visiting dignitary.

"Bill, I'm so glad you could come tonight. It's been far too long since you two have been over for dinner." Crystal could only gape as her mother acted as if their divorce had never happened. She was almost afraid she would next be asking when they planned to have a baby.

Crystal stepped back from where her parents gathered around Bill and studied the man who'd once been her husband. She found it hard to believe that she'd ever thought him handsome, although many women would probably find him attractive. His brown hair was thick, and he kept it neatly styled. He pressed his dress pants perfectly, and his polo shirt had creases down the sleeves. She knew for a fact that he spent close to ten minutes picking any new lint off his black socks in the morning. He was so well put together that she'd always felt frumpy compared to him. Of course, the fact that he'd made subtle comments about her appearance hadn't helped.

Bill had needed a meek wife who wanted nothing more in life than to devote her attention to his happiness. One who wouldn't think twice about all of his OCD ways. What he'd gotten instead was her. And although she had spent years trying to please him, in the end, she'd discovered that to make him happy, she'd have to lose herself in the process. Sadly, without Ella having shown her what it was like to love and to be loved in return, she would more than likely still be attempting to be someone that she was not.

She found herself herded into the dining room and seated beside her ex-husband. Her mother generally served what she considered her prize-worthy meat loaf when she was entertaining, and tonight was no exception. She'd always found her mother's go-to dish dry and bland but had never had the nerve to admit that aloud.

Her mother dominated the conversation throughout the meal, with Bill and her father occasionally contributing. As was the norm, no one bothered to include her, and for once, she was grateful.

She'd been quietly planning her escape when she felt a hand on her arm. She looked up to see Bill studying her. He cleared his throat, swallowing audibly. "Could . . . um . . . I speak to you for a minute?" He seemed to notice at the same time as her that their exchange had her parents engrossed. "Alone," he added before getting to his feet. She considered his request for a moment before rising as well. She figured she'd have an easier time dealing with him than with her mother. And with any luck, she could make her getaway shortly afterward.

Feeling generous, since he was helping her escape, she smiled, saying, "Sure, how about we take a walk?"

It made her a little uneasy when he brightened as if she'd just handed him an early Christmas present. Maybe she wasn't the only one looking for an excuse to run tonight. Her mother had probably demanded that he show up for the mandatory dinner as well. Poor Bill—he wasn't about to say no to Dot Webber either. Apparently, Declan was the only one not intimidated by her. Well—him and Mark. He would be her mother's nightmare. Like Declan, he'd have no problem calling her on her behavior. She couldn't fathom how wonderful it would be to have that type of buffer. Ella had it now. Her sister still took a lot of crap from their mother, but Declan stepped in when he felt it was needed.

When they reached the back deck, Bill took her hand, helping her down the steps. They'd been walking through the wooded landscape for a few moments before she realized that he hadn't released her hand. He'd never been the hand-holding type, so this was foreign to her. She was relieved when he stopped next to a bench that her father liked to use for his bird-watching hobby. She thought it was possibly just an excuse to have some time alone when he was desperate to escape, which she certainly understood. She took a seat, freeing herself from his hold. "It's really nice out tonight," she said lamely. Shit, why could she no longer talk to someone with whom she'd once shared a home?

Without answering, he perched next to her, staring off into space. He looked every bit as uncomfortable as she felt. So she really wasn't surprised when he asked, "What happened to us, Crystal?"

Releasing her breath on a loud sigh, she said quietly, "I don't know, Bill. I guess it's inevitable after divorce that things would be awkward between us."

He raised a hand, pushing it through his hair in a gesture of agitation. She had to fight the urge to smooth down the strands that were now sticking up. It just seemed wrong to see Bill disheveled. She almost fell from her seat in shock when he said, "I know it's my fault that our marriage failed, and now we can't even say hello without it being strange."

"Bill . . . I'm sure they are things that we both could have done differently. But I've come to realize that we're just two people who are far too different to have a successful marriage. That doesn't mean that either of us was to blame. We just weren't compatible."

"But I loved you," he said without hesitation, "and I still do. I never wanted to let you go. I just didn't know how to keep you."

Feeling her throat go tight, she stared at the man she'd once thought she'd spend her life with. "I'm sorry I hurt you," she said sincerely. At the time, she wasn't even sure he really cared, but now she could see that she'd been very wrong.

He took her hand in his for the second time that night and absently rubbed her fingers. "You know the type of parents I come from. They're not very . . . demonstrative, and that's how I was raised. I knew—especially the last few years of our marriage—that you wanted more from me, but I couldn't give that to you. I just . . . didn't know how, Crystal. I felt like a total failure as a man because you were slipping away a little more each day and I was powerless to stop it. You'd look at me, and I could see the unhappiness there. I knew the day that Ella got married that I'd lost you. I watched you up there standing next to her as she took her vows, and I could see that it was over for you. I'm sure no one else noticed it because all eyes were on the bride and groom, but I saw the longing that you couldn't hide. You wanted what she had. Not Declan, but someone like him. I think, at that point, the part of me that had been holding out hope just gave up. I'm not that guy, and I never will be. After that, I was an ass to you—even more than usual, I know. But it was the only way I could face you leaving. I had to pretend that I didn't care anymore."

Letting her head rest against his arm, Crystal murmured, "Oh, Bill . . . why didn't you say all of this before? I was so lost myself that I would have been thrilled if you'd admitted you felt the same way."

With a laugh devoid of humor, he said, "Manly pride. I couldn't admit to you that I didn't know how to be the husband you needed. It's not a great feeling when you aren't giving the woman you love what she needs. Instead of trying, I kept ignoring the problem and just hoped it would go away." Shrugging his shoulders, he added, "If nothing else, months of therapy have made me accept that."

She had nodded before his words hit her. "Wait—what? You're going to a therapist?"

He looked embarrassed for a moment. "Yes, I am. I started a few months after we split up. I was so depressed I could barely function. I'd run into you at some gathering your mother insisted I attend, and you'd look so beautiful—and happy. You were flourishing without me, but I wasn't doing too well myself. Remember my cousin Calvin, who went through a divorce a few years back?" At her nod, he continued. "He recommended his marriage counselor, who also works with individuals."

"Wow." She blinked, hardly able to believe what she

was hearing. This was probably the sweetest and, strangely enough, the most intimate conversation that they'd ever had. "I don't really know what to say."

"What I'd like to hear," he began earnestly, "is that you'll go to counseling with me. I realize that it won't happen overnight, but I want a chance to show you that I can change. I hate to admit it, but it took you leaving for me to wake up. Would you consider giving me another chance?"

Oh, my God. This was the last thing she had expected from him. Sure, he'd tried to talk her out of the divorce, but in the end, he'd signed the papers and hadn't contested it. Her mother kept telling her that Bill wanted her back, and he'd admitted as much when he'd had the opportunity to talk to her. But it had been nothing like this. The man sitting beside her now was saying things that her husband would never have admitted to. He was shouldering the blame for their failed marriage and had sought help on his own. She was stunned and touched that he would let such vulnerability show. She wasn't sure if she wanted to run or give him the hug he looked as if he desperately needed. "This is—so unexpected," she stuttered out.

He laughed softly. "I can imagine that this is a lot to take in. I don't want you to give me your answer tonight. But if you'll at least say that you'll think about it, I would be extremely grateful."

She moved her hand to squeeze his leg, and then thought better of it. That might be misconstrued as an intimate gesture, especially with what he'd revealed. "Bill—so much has happened," she began speaking, only to halt when he got to his feet.

"Let's don't say anything else tonight until you've taken a few days to think it over. Please?"

He looked so hopeful as he stared down at her. There was no way she could say no, at least not right now. She really didn't have any desire to return to her previous life, but she felt as if she owed him this consideration after the years that they'd spent together. "Okay." She nodded.

"Thank you." He smiled and then turned to look toward her parents' house. "I'm, er—going to walk around front and leave, if you don't mind. I think I've had my fill of your mother for one evening."

She couldn't help it; she burst out laughing in delight. Dear Lord, maybe the man had changed. Even when she'd begged, he'd never skipped out on a long, extended farewell before. "Do you mind if I join you?" she asked before giving him a conspiratorial wink. "I'll text her before I pull out and let her know that we both had to leave."

"That works for me," he beamed as they walked quickly but quietly around the side of the house and to the driveway. "I'll call you soon, all right?"

She nodded her agreement and then sent off a text to her mother before following Bill down the road. He honked his horn once, when he took the turn that would lead to their old house, while she continued.

Her mother's emotional abuse tonight wasn't really a surprise. But Bill going to therapy and wanting to reconcile—there was the big shocker. She could tell that he hadn't been just telling her what he thought she wanted to hear either. He had been different. She would have never left the man who poured his heart out to her tonight. Though it was all too little, too late—wasn't it? She'd moved on with her life, and she liked the person she had become since her divorce. She loved her job and the friends that she had made. She'd barely existed outside of being Bill's wife when she was married.

Good grief, the man never even argued about visiting her parents—until tonight. Whenever she'd complained about her mother, he'd always seemed to take the other woman's side without even listening.

She was still playing their conversation over in her mind when she pulled into a parking spot at her apartment. Then it hit her—she was supposed to go to Mark's. She slumped back in her seat, feeling more tired that she had in a long time. She would love to curl into Mark's strong chest and sleep away the feelings of unease that were choking her. But they didn't know each other well enough for her to dump her problems at his door. She'd text him when she got inside and let him know she was too tired for a visit. She was beginning to see a pattern in texting to avoid confrontations— but wasn't that what everyone did now?

She pulled her phone from her purse when she walked in the door and ignored the string of responses from her mother. It was then that she realized that she didn't know Mark's number. Despite all of their recent interactions, apparently she'd never gotten that information. It took her another ten minutes and a rundown of the evening to Ella before she got Mark's number from Declan. Then she took an additional five minutes to compose her message. *Rough night. Tired so needed to come home. Talk soon.* She added a smiley face at the end, just to pretend that she was happy, before hitting SEND.

As she was putting her phone down, her mother sent another text, demanding an explanation for what happened with Bill. Crystal let out a snort of disgust, and then promptly turned the thing off. She then walked straight into her bedroom and face-planted onto her bed. As she started to drift off to sleep, she couldn't help but wish that Mark were beside her. She liked the woman that she had become with him—his Angel.

Mark looked at his watch and wondered what was keeping Crystal. He'd never admit the number of times that he'd looked out the window tonight thinking he heard her car—then swallowed a pang of disappointment when he was wrong. He got to his feet, intending to have a drink of something strong enough to take his mind off her when his phone chimed with a text. *Rough night. Tired so needed to come home. Talk soon.* What in the ever-loving fuck? She was standing him up? *So this is what the other side of things feels like.* He read her words again, looking for some hidden meaning. Was she blowing him off because she wasn't interested, or had her bitch of a mother upset her? Before he could talk himself out of it, he grabbed his keys off the kitchen counter and walked out to his Porsche. He wasn't some boy who was left hanging by a woman. He'd told her to come to him tonight, and he damn well planned to find out why she hadn't. If he found her lounging in front of the TV looking calm and relaxed, he wouldn't be responsible for his actions.

He was pissed when he pounded on her door. He had gone beyond that after a few minutes when there was no reply. He called her phone and it went immediately to voice mail. He was rapping on the door one last time, when he heard the security chain inside rattling. Then the door was flung open and a fully dressed—and quite angry—woman glared at him from inside the doorway. Crystal's clothing was wrinkled and her hair was sticking up in every direction—but, fuck, she looked beautiful. She opened her mouth, obviously intent on blasting him, but he stepped forward, pushing his way inside. Her shriek of outrage made his ears ring, but he ignored it. Instead of replying, he pushed her backward against the nearest wall and fastened his lips on hers. He ate at her mouth as if starving for her taste. She resisted for a moment before giving in with a groan of her own. "Angel," he breathed against her lips as he sucked her tongue into his mouth.

He had no idea how he managed it—possibly he was more talented than he knew, but almost before he could process it, they were both naked. Her legs wrapped around his waist, he was inches away from plunging into her when he remembered the condom. He cursed, extricating himself from their embrace and then feeling for his pants. As he pulled a condom from his wallet, he thanked whatever god was responsible for ensuring every guy over the age of fifteen had a rubber stored somewhere on him at all times. Her nails were raking his back in impatience as he deftly sheathed himself. His Angel was somewhat of an animal when she was turned on and he loved it. He'd proudly bear the marks of her eagerness tomorrow. "Now, please, Mark," she cried out, the impatience in her voice snapping his tenuous control. He hooked her leg around his hip and drove into her hard. "Yes!" she screamed as he pounded her greedy core. He was close, so he dropped his hand to rub her clit, but before he could make contact, she contracted around his cock as she came. Damn, this woman had no idea what a sexual creature she was. He'd yet to touch her when she wasn't eager, wet, and damn near halfway to orgasm before he penetrated her.

She was slumped against him once he found his release, and he used what little reserves he had left to follow her sleepy directions to the bedroom. He held her with one hand while stumbling along until he made contact with the lamp on her bedside table. He flipped it on, and then deposited her gently onto the bed. She immediately curled a hand under her cheek and shut her eyes. He located her bathroom and some washcloths. Returning, he cleaned between her legs and tossed the cloth toward the bathroom before flipping the light off. "Angel, baby, move over," he murmured against her cheek as he attempted to shift her lax body.

"I love it when you do that," she mumbled.

"What?" he asked as he finally managed to wedge in beside of her.

"Wash me. No one's ever taken care of me like that," she said softly before throwing a leg over his and collapsing on his chest.

He shifted until he had her cradled in his arms. He ran a hand idly through her dark tresses, rubbing her scalp soothingly. He didn't know if she was asleep yet, but he couldn't resist asking, "What happened at your parents' tonight, baby?"

There was nothing but silence for at least a full minute, and then she sighed. "It was a setup. I didn't find out until I was already there that Ella wasn't invited. Instead, my ex-husband showed up shortly after I arrived. My mother is still determined that I go back to him, and she never misses an opportunity to throw us together." When she hissed, "Ouch," he realized that his hand had tightened painfully in her hair.

"Sorry, Angel," he said as he forced himself to relax once again. He'd never even met the woman, but he wanted to strangle her meddling mother. Curious, he asked, "Why didn't you just leave?"

Her finger drew circles on his chest, making his cock twitch to life. It was getting to the point that if she even looked in his direction, he was hard. He'd jacked off more in the last few days while thinking of her than he had in years. He was so distracted when she finally answered him that he had to ask her to repeat herself. "It's always been easier to go with the flow and not rock the boat. Dad called it humoring her. Ella and I learned long ago that it was pointless to argue and that it just prolonged our misery if we did."

Blowing out an exasperated breath, he said, "Angel— that's not humoring her, that's being subservient. Plus, you're divorced now. Why in the world would she think it was okay for her to continue to invite your ex-husband over? If they have a close relationship, then she should see him when you aren't there. Unless you want him back." The words left a bitter taste in his mouth, and he fought the urge to get up and leave the room in a show of anger.

Her hand stilled, and he could feel her eyes on him in the dark. "What? No! Of course not. I was the one who left him. I mean, he said some things tonight that were surprising, and I'm flattered that he wants us to see a marriage counselor together—but it's too late."

Mark wondered if she was aware that the last part of her sentence sounded more like a question than a statement. So what did he do? Instead of being understanding and giving her the support that she no doubt needed after what she'd been through, he pushed her away and stood. Without saying a word, he made his way back through the dark apartment to the living room where their clothes were still lying in a pile. He dressed quickly and turned to find her standing just inches away. "I need to get home," he forced out. He was angry with her, and he had no right to be. He was being a complete and utter asshole, and he knew it.

He wanted her to say something snide to justify him stomping off, but she simply said, "All right." The part of him that wasn't a bastard had him walking to her and dropping a kiss on her mouth. And that was it. He'd made the trip across town, had amazing sex, and then turned his back when things got complicated. It was his MO and what he did best. He got what he wanted and didn't spare a thought for the woman afterward. Though as he got into his car and drove away, he knew that was no longer true. This time he'd taken off because he was shaken by the two things that were choking him—jealousy and fear.

For the first time in his life, he had something to lose. Why was he so scared to lose something that wasn't his to begin with?

Chapter Thirteen

"He treated you like a booty call," Mia snarled as soon as she had heard. "I don't care how hot he is, the man is a dickhead."

Gwen nodded solemnly, before taking a bite of her pizza. "I agree," she managed to say around the food in her mouth.

Crystal grimaced and chanced a look at her boss, Lydia, across the table. She hadn't intended to get into her night with Mark when she'd invited Lydia to lunch with them, but Mia as always had picked right up on her glum expression. "Maybe he's one of those guys who can only sleep in his own bed," Mia offered hopefully.

The truth was, she was beyond depressed over Mark's hasty exit from her bedroom and her apartment. He'd run out as if his ass were on fire. And, even more strange, he'd seemed pissed. She could understand if he was angry on her behalf at her mother's deception, but that wasn't what it was. She'd felt like his anger was directed at her, and she couldn't figure out why.

Lydia looked intrigued. Crystal had a feeling this was like a real-life soap opera playing out in front of her boss. "So who is this guy? You haven't mentioned that you were seeing anyone."

"It's Mark DeStudo—er . . . DeSanto," Mia blurted out before Crystal could stop her.

"Nooo!" Lydia gaped. "Not Mr. Big!"

"Mr. Big?" Gwen asked as she finished her pizza and laid a hand on her baby bump.

Lydia giggled, fanning herself. "That's what I call him. I swear, he reminds me of Mr. Big from *Sex and the City*. You know, in the first episodes when Chris Noth was younger. He's all tall, dark, brooding, and he flipping rocks those power suits." Then her eyes widened as she asked reverently, "Oh, my God, have you really slept with him?"

Crystal's mind was still stuck on how accurate the Mr. Big analogy was when Mia elbowed her. "The woman asked you a question, Crys, and since I've already let the cat out of the bag once, I'll let you take this one." She had managed to tell Mia, Gwen, and, of course, Ella, about her first sexual encounter with Mark, but that was the extent of it. Even though she was friends with Lydia, she'd been hesitant about sharing it with her. She hadn't wanted to upset the other woman since she was still mourning the loss of her fiancé. Now it looked like she didn't have a choice.

"Um—yeah, I have. I mean it's not serious between us or anything. Actually, I don't know what it is," she admitted.

Lydia propped her head in her hands and gave her a sappy smile. "Was it good?" Before Crystal could answer, Lydia slapped her forehead dramatically.

"What am I saying? Of course it was! That man is like a walking G-spot stimulator."

Mia started cackling so loud, Crystal was afraid she was going to pass out. Her face turned an alarming shade of red before she finally managed to take a breath. "You're my new best friend, Lydia," she managed to wheeze out. "That was brilliant!"

Lydia looked tickled with the compliment and did a fist bump with her new BFF. "Honey, I just call 'em like I see 'em. There's so much testosterone around Danvers that my hoo-ha is quivering some days." Pointing at Gwen, she shook her head before adding, "And your man and his band of G.I. Joes are prime panty-melting material. I don't know how you normally function because I'd be resorting to humping his leg or something during the workday."

Instead of looking offended, Gwen raised her glass of tea in a salute and chimed in with "Hear, hear. Don't I know it. You should try to live with a man who looks the way he does naked. I'm in perpetual heat."

Crystal could only gawk at her boss. Here she'd been avoiding talking about men in front of her out of respect for her feelings, and she was now finding out that the woman was something of a pervert. It was the best news she'd had all day! Deciding to test her theory, she asked, "So, Lydia . . . if you had to pick a favorite from the hot men of Danvers, who would it be? Don't be shy—Gwen won't beat you up if it's Dominic, and I'll certainly understand if it's Mr. Big."

Lydia pursed her lips, and then looked around the crowded restaurant as if to make sure that no one was listening to their conversation. Lowering her voice she said, "All right, please don't repeat this, but Jacob Hay makes me weak in the knees. I swear I'd agree to have the man's children, clean his house, and drive a freaking station wagon if he said the word."

"Who's that?" Crystal asked, racking her memory. "The name sounds familiar, but I can't place it."

"Oh, baby," Mia cooed, "you've got great taste there."

"I don't know him either," Gwen admitted. "Do you have any stalker pictures of him like Crystal has of Mark?"

Lydia looked at Crystal in surprise. "I can't believe you don't know him if you've been watching Mark. Jacob works for him. From what I've gathered through my . . . research, he's the number two man at DeSanto Group."

"So, Mr. Big, Junior," Gwen smirked. "I'm liking this a lot. How did you meet him?"

Laughing, Lydia admitted, "It was the whole damsel-in-distress thing. I worked late and then ended up in a deserted parking garage with a car that wouldn't start. I was on my way back in the building to call my auto club when I ran smack into someone." Looking slightly embarrassed, she added, "I kind of thought I was being mugged and started screaming for help."

"No way," Mia winced. "I bet he's not used to women yelling anything other than his name."

"I'm pretty sure he was afraid I was insane," Lydia agreed. "He held his hands out in front of him, and then actually showed me his company identification badge. When I finally calmed down, I was humiliated because this was the most gorgeous man I'd seen in ages and I'd made a total ass of myself."

Propping her elbows on the table, Gwen mused, "So I guess he didn't leave you stranded, right?"

Lydia fanned herself. "Nope, when I explained my car issue to him, he rolled up his sleeves and had me pop the hood latch. Then he proceeded to fix the thing right there. I still have no idea what was wrong with it, but can you believe the man was actually willing to work on my car? I know he was wearing expensive clothing. He ended up with an oil stain on his shirt-sleeve, but he refused to let me take care of the cleaning bill."

"Sweet mother," Mia moaned. "Now I want to have his babies too."

"I'm sorry"—Lydia shook her head—"but I'm Jacob's future baby mama. Plus, he's friends with your man, Seth, and his brother, Ash."

"I know." Mia snorted. "He's been to our place before. He does seem like a nice guy, and apparently, he's mechanical as well. You know what that means, right?" When everyone shook their heads, she added, "He's good with his hands."

"Ohhh!" Gwen wiggled her brows. "I like that in a man."

"Don't get any ideas about Lydia's man," Crystal teased. "You're Dominic's baby mama, and I have a feeling he doesn't share."

They joked around for a few more minutes before Mia asked, "So, what're you going to do about Mark?"

All humor left her as Crystal once again focused on her problem. "I don't know. I mean, it was kind of hot the way he showed up out of the blue and . . . took charge of things. We were lying in my bed afterward, and he asked how dinner went at my parents. I even told him about my ex-husband and how he wanted me to go to marriage counseling with him."

"Whoa," Gwen interrupted, holding her hand up. "I think I missed something here. What exactly happened with Bill?"

Crystal quickly filled them in on her latest unpleasant parental encounter. "So, as you can imagine, that was kind of unexpected. Bill had never admitted that he shared the blame in the breakup of our marriage. I was reeling when I left there, which is why I didn't go to Mark's as I'd planned to do. I just sent him a text and went home to bed. Then he showed up sometime later pounding on the door and acting all . . . sexy. Now you're up-to-date."

Lydia put her hand over Crystal's arm. "Honey, I know I've been out of the whole dating game for a while, but the problem here is obvious to me."

"Me too," Mia piped in, while Gwen nodded her agreement as well.

Confused, Crystal looked at her friends and said, "Well, then someone clue me in. Is this just how a booty call goes or something?"

"I don't think that's what his visit was about at all," Lydia began. "I believe he was upset because you broke your plans to go see him via a text message. You can rest assured that stuff like that doesn't happen to Mark DeStudo. Then after he rocked your world with his sexiness, you told him all about how your ex-husband wants you back."

"That's like two strikes against his manhood," Mia agreed.

"Well, what was the third strike that caused him to leave?" Crystal asked, beginning to understand that she might have been a tad too loose-lipped with him the previous night. Too much information—not good.

"I don't really know him," Gwen inserted, "but I'm guessing Mark is an alpha male, like Dominic. If so, then there are no three strikes. Two big hits like that would push him to leave and regroup."

"Bu-but," Crystal sputtered, before putting her hand over her face. "I'm so far out of my league. I've gone straight from a Toyota to some fancy sports car."

"Crys, if the hickey on the side of your neck is any indication, girl, then you're somewhere around a Ferrari level."

"What?" Crystal shrieked. She'd been so distracted when she was getting dressed this morning that she hadn't noticed anything. "Please tell me you're kidding."

Without looking, Lydia shook her head. "Afraid not, sweetie. I saw it myself but figured it was from a curling iron since neither you nor I have seen much action in a while."

"It's only noticeable when you turn your head a certain way," Gwen added helpfully. "Just stare straight ahead when you're talking to people."

"That's great," Crystal mumbled as she attempted to pull the collar of her blouse higher. "I have a hickey for the first time ever, and I ran Mark off last night by telling him the truth." Throwing her hands up in the air, she snapped, "There are just some weeks you're born to lose!"

"You haven't necessarily lost anything," Mia said

THE ONE FOR ME   159

thoughtfully. "Having an alpha man myself, I can tell you one thing. They're only pissed at a woman if she matters to him. The fact that Mark got his undies in a wad over you seeing Bill tells me that he was jealous, and it's probably not a feeling that he's well acquainted with."

"So true," Gwen agreed dryly. "In my long and disappointing love life before Dominic, I can tell you that men couldn't give a shit about stuff like that unless they are emotionally involved. I once dated a guy who brought up my ex-boyfriend constantly, even encouraging me to give the guy another chance. You're under Mark's skin, and he's out of his league with you as well."

"So what do I do now?" Crystal exhaled loudly. "I have one man wanting me back and another one running from me."

"It's quite simple." Lydia grinned. "Which one do you want to catch you?"

Gwen twisted her lips, looking the definition of devious as she said, "Actually, you don't need to do a thing, Crys. If Mark is who I think he is, then he'll come to you and your ex-husband will as well."

"But I don't need two men in my life," Crystal cried. "I just want one guy, the one who can give me what I need without me having to beg."

"Well, don't tell us." Mia chuckled evilly. "Tell it to Twitter."

Lydia left for a meeting after they returned from lunch. Crystal worked steadily for the next few hours before blowing out a long, frustrated breath and deciding that she needed a break. She got up and shut her office door before returning to her desk and Googling "booty call quotes." Even though Mia had encouraged her to tweet something at Mark, she'd been hesitant. That wasn't exactly the mature approach, was it? Scanning through the page, she read one that seemed to apply to how she was feeling about the previous night.

So, before she could talk herself out of it, she replied to Mark's last tweet with *"If you get a booty call at three a.m., you probably weren't first on the list."* Unknown. *#Angel.* Then she dusted her hands off in satisfaction. It took approximately sixty seconds for her to regret her impulsive social media slap down. She frantically pulled up the Twitter page and could hardly believe her eyes when she tried to log back in. *Sorry, we're overloaded. Please try again in a few moments.* "Shit!" she hissed as she desperately tried to enter the Twitter-sphere. Crystal had been pressing REFRESH for what seemed like hours with no luck, when she heard her office door open. Her head jerked up and the blood drained from her face. Mark stood there and if the way he was scowling was any indication, he'd already read her tweet. "Oh crap," she murmured.

He took what looked like carefully measured strides into her office before turning to close the door quietly behind him. "Good afternoon, Angel," he said in a neutral voice. "Having a good day?"

"Um, sure," she mumbled. His words were polite, but there was something about his eyes. They seemed to blaze down at her behind his careful veneer. "How about you?"

He strolled closer, stopping just inches from where she was sitting before propping a hip on her desk. "It was going well—until my assistant burst into my office to share something with me."

Should I beg for forgiveness or go the defiant route? Or maybe just act dumb for a bit longer and attempt to defuse the situation.

"Well, whatever it was, I'm sure the person meant no harm. Sometimes people say the first thing that pops into their head and then regret it. The person might even attempt to take it back, but is unable to."

Mark raised a brow as he studied her in silence for a time. Finally, he said, "Is that so? My question in that instance would be why say it to begin with? I've always found that unfiltered thoughts tend to contain the most truths."

Frustrated by his calm wordplay, Crystal snapped, "Oh, for heaven's sake, admit you're mad at me for dissing you on Twitter! I can't take much more of this civilized bullying."

She shut her eyes, waiting for him to blow. When nothing happened, she opened one eye, only to find him grinning at her with what almost looked like delight. "My Angel has claws. I've seen the evidence of that on my back—but I wasn't convinced until now. Even when you've been a bad girl, you still come out swinging. I like that—a lot."

Holy cow . . . I think I just had an orgasm—or wordgasm. Huffing, she could only manage an inelegant "Whatever" as he stepped close enough to trail a finger along the seam of her mouth. Without thinking, she parted her lips and touched her tongue to his digit, causing him to roughly inhale.

He leaned down, until his mouth was next to her

ear. "You've no idea how much I'd like to pull you to the end of your chair then part your legs, remove your panties, and lick you until you scream my name."

"Yes—please," she babbled in an aroused daze.

Mark gave a sexy chuckle that sent shivers down her spine. He sucked the sensitive skin of her neck, whispering, "Would that be considered a booty call, Angel? If I had you on my tongue, and then fucked you on your desk—is that what it would be to you?"

"Who cares?" she groaned, wanting to experience exactly what his velvety-smooth voice was describing.

His hand dropped to her thigh, stroking the smooth skin exposed by her dress. "I do, baby. When Denny tells me that you feel demeaned because of the way I handled last night, then I figure we need to clarify a few things before I have you again."

"O . . . kay," she managed to answer as he continued to drive her crazy with his maddening touch.

"Listen to me carefully, Angel," he instructed. When she nodded her agreement, he said, "You were my first choice. I waited for you to arrive as planned, and then when you blew me off, I came to you." When she opened her mouth to protest, wanting to point out that she'd had an upsetting evening, he tapped his finger against her lips. "No talking yet. Just give me a nod if you've heard and understood what I've said so far." She did as he asked and was rewarded with a "Good girl. Now, as I was saying, we agreed to spend the evening together, so I just made sure that happened when you didn't follow through. Although I'll admit that I didn't handle your revelation about your ex well."

Crystal gathered her wits enough to say sarcastically,

"Ya think? If you'll recall, you kept questioning me. I didn't just start unloading everything without encouragement."

Suddenly, he pulled from her the chair and into his arms. "I know, Angel," he admitted. "I'm sorry about that. I'm just—not used to something like that happening."

"Like what?" she asked absently as she snuggled closer, subtly inhaling his spicy, masculine scent. She wasn't sure if it was cologne or Mark's natural scent—but it was delicious.

He sighed. "I know this will sound bad, but I've never really cared what's going on in the life of the woman I'm having sex with." When she went stiff, he rubbed her back soothingly. "You know that I don't have relationships—at least I haven't until this point. What I'm trying to say—and I'm making a mess of it—is that everything about you and our time together is new to me. I've never had to deal with feelings such as jealousy. Apparently, it turns me into a bit of an asshole."

Her eyes widened as she stared up at Mark's rueful expression. "Really? You were jealous? I mean, the girls thought that you might be—but I didn't believe it. I mean you're—DeStudo." *Why, oh, why must I say one stupid thing after another?* Crystal thought to herself as Mark started laughing.

"We need to pause this conversation until later on this evening, Angel. I'm afraid it's very close to getting out of hand, and I don't know how Jason Danvers will feel about your vocal explosion during office hours."

Wrinkling her nose, she asked, "My what?"

He kissed her briefly, before setting her away from

him. "When you come, your voice hits levels that would put an opera star to shame, Angel."

Before she could reply, there was a knock on her door and Lydia stuck her head in before Crystal could call out to stop her. "Wanted to let you know I was back," the woman said before her voice trailed off as she noticed Mark. Crystal smothered a grin behind her hand as Lydia straightened, and then brushed a hand over her hair. "Hi, there," she said in a breathy voice. Apparently, even her boss wasn't immune to Mark's considerable charm.

He extended a hand to her. "I'm Mark, and you are?"

"Oh, I know," she whispered dreamily, before seeming to get a grip. "I—um, I'm Lydia. Nice to meet you."

"Lydia's my boss," Crystal said. "I believe she's met a colleague of yours, Jacob."

Mark looked at Lydia curiously. "Jacob's my right-hand man." Shooting Crystal a pointed look, he admitted, "He's doing a lot of my travel now as I've found—well, something that's keeping me home more."

"Tell him I said hello," Lydia said brightly before a mortified expression crossed her face.

"I'll do that." Mark smiled easily, then turned to Crystal. "I need to get back to my office. I'll see you at my house tonight around six?" It was phrased as a question for Lydia's benefit, but Crystal knew it was anything but. He didn't expect a repeat of last night—nor would he tolerate it.

"Okay," she accepted. "See you soon."

When he was gone, Lydia shut the door behind him and held her hand up. Crystal slapped it in a high five, and they both did some juvenile dance moves. "I swear, don't take this the wrong way, but sweet Jesus, that voice, those bedroom eyes—he's Mr. Big come to freaking life at Danvers."

"Calm down, girl," Crystal said soothingly before a giggle escaped. "I had no idea you were such a pervert. This is a whole other side of you, and I'm kind of digging it."

"Well, honey, you were a bit repressed when we started working together, and I was kind of screwed up over losing Brett, so I didn't bother to rock the boat. But now you've gone from sitting on the shore to swimming with the sharks, and I'm finding that I'm thrilled to live vicariously through you. Heck, I'm even acknowledging my lust for Jacob. Maybe this year we'll both shake off the past and do something that makes us happy. Or at the least, have a lot of meaningless sex along the way."

Impulsively, Crystal stepped forward and gave the other woman a quick hug. "I like your plan. And if Jacob has even a tiny bit of intelligence, he'll be knocking down your door to take a walk on the wild side with you."

Lydia looked thrilled by her comment. "I'm going to do my best to make that happen. And I don't think you have to worry about that with Mark. The man couldn't take his eyes off you, and he didn't give a damn if I noticed it or not."

"It's just sex, though." Crystal felt compelled to clarify things. "He's interested because I'm like the most inexperienced woman he's even known."

Lydia looked at her as if she was crazy before shaking her head. "I can't predict the future, but all I have to say is if I had the attention of a man like Mark, for whatever reason, I wouldn't squander it. Go forth my child, have sex—the dirty kind—and live in the moment. People come into our lives for a variety of reasons, and if we're smart, we take advantage of what they have to offer. Sometimes all we can do is grab on with both hands and enjoy the ride."

The words struck a chord inside Crystal as she acknowledged to herself that she was constantly trying to fit Mark into some neat category that she could label. Lydia was right; what she had with Mark might not last forever, but that didn't mean that they couldn't be good for each other. He'd said several times that she was different for him, and that was certainly true for her. What was wrong with just enjoying the company of a man she desired without expecting fancy words or heartfelt declarations? Happily ever after hadn't worked out so well before. She'd just do the very opposite of her marriage with Bill and base her nonrelationship with Mark on sex. If nothing else, it would drive her mother insane.

Chapter Fourteen

Crystal drove straight to Mark's house after work. Before she could knock on the door, it was flung open by a beaming Denny. "Hey—hey, Crystal. Come on in."

Unable to resist, she smiled back. Something about Denny's demeanor was infectious. He was a good-looking guy, but that wasn't his appeal to her. It was the fact that he always seemed so happy. Maybe if she spent more time with him, it would rub off on her. "Good to see you again," she replied as he shut the door behind her. Then she saw a sight that had her gawking in shock. Mark was standing at the kitchen island in well-worn jeans and a T-shirt, chopping vegetables as if it were the most natural thing in the world.

"Close your mouth, girl." Denny smirked as he walked to a barstool and plopped down.

Mark glanced up, giving her a sexy grin. His look went from relaxed to downright scalding as he took in her cut-off jean shorts and fitted tank top. She'd figured since they were staying in tonight that she'd dress for comfort. If the way the cousins were looking at her was any indication, they approved wholeheartedly of her casual attire—possibly a bit too much.

"Hungry, Angel?" Mark's searing gaze let her know he wasn't just talking about dinner.

She shifted her knees together before she could stop herself. "I—um, could eat." *Shit, they're still staring as if they've never seen a woman before.* "So . . . what are you making?" she asked brightly.

"Stir-fry," Mark said, before adding huskily, "Now come give me a kiss, Angel." She looked at him uncertainly, chancing a glance at Denny. Mark turned to the other man and snapped, "Go get something from the car."

"Like what?" Denny asked, clearly playing dumb to harass his cousin.

Mark put his hand on his hips, rolling his eyes. "I don't give a fuck—just walk out there and stand for a while." Denny grumbled under his breath, but Crystal could tell it was just for show. He looked vastly amused as he was essentially kicked out of the house. Mark turned back to her and crooked his finger. "Now come here so I can touch you. He'll be back soon just to be an asshole, so unless you want an audience, hustle, baby." That got her attention. She crossed the room, and before she could blink, he had her turned with her back pressed against the granite island. "You smell amazing," he murmured as his tongue licked up her neck. Mark, she'd discovered, loved tasting her.

"It's soap," she blurted out, unable to hold a coherent thought in her head. "Plus, I used the matching lotion as well, so that's probably what you smell. Although it could be my lip stuff. . . ." She trailed off, realizing she was rambling like a crazy woman.

Lifting his head, he said, "Angel—time's wasting."

She didn't need further encouragement. Going up on her toes, in a move that probably lacked grace, she locked her lips on his—and then he took over. His kiss consumed her, and even though she didn't realize it as he was repositioning her, she suddenly found her butt on the counter and him between her legs.

Crystal shamelessly pressed her aching core against his hardness as he gave her a deep kiss full of tongue and more than a little teeth nipping. "Oh, Mark," she moaned as she felt his hand pinching her nipple through her lacy bra. "God—yes!" she encouraged as his hand slipped into the back of her shorts before steadily moving toward the front. And for the second time that day, someone walked in while she and Mark were making out like teenagers.

A throat cleared nearby and a voice said, "Maybe you should have mentioned that you were planning to go all the way, instead of just kissing," Denny called out. "I could have walked around the block or something. Or picked up some takeout, since it doesn't look as if dinner is going to be ready anytime soon."

Mark broke the kiss, and Crystal let her legs slide down his body. She could only imagine how they must look to Denny. "I knew I'd regret letting you invite yourself to stay," Mark grumbled as he threw a carrot at Denny. They teased each other good-naturedly while she settled at the bar, listening to them bicker. They were very much how she imagined brothers would be like. Mark blustered and scowled, but there was no real heat behind his words. It was obvious that they loved each other and had an easiness between them that spoke of the years they'd spent together.

When Denny came over to throw an arm around her, she smiled over her shoulder at him. "Oh, Crystal, the stories I could tell you about the man you were slobbering all over," he teased.

"Denny," Mark snapped with a clear warning in his voice.

"Ah, come on. Sharing is caring. We've had some funny moments through the years. Crystal would really get a kick out of the chick who tattooed your name on her—"

"Denny! I swear—"

"Not her?" Denny continued as if he wasn't in the least concerned by Mark glowering at him from only inches away. "How about the one who sang that Britney song during the big event? What was it? '. . . Baby One More Time'? No, wait—'I'm A Slave 4 U'! Shit, that one was funny." By this point, both men, and she used that term loosely because they were behaving more like boys, were circling around the island. Mark was yelling threats and Denny was holding his sides while he continued with his trip down memory lane. "No—no, I've got it, the one you caught trying to make a mold of your—ouch! Dammit, I'm telling my mom that you hit me with a spatula. Your ass is in so much trouble!"

Crystal couldn't help it; she doubled over in her seat, laughing until tears rolled down her cheeks. "How in the world," she gasped out, "did that girl do that?" She wheezed.

Mark glared at Denny, who yelled, "Play-Doh," as he ran to the living room for cover.

Mark held his hands up as if trying to plead his innocence. "Don't listen to him. He's just messing with you."

Raising a brow, she teased, "So you're saying that none of that actually happened, right?"

"Whoops, looks like dinner's ready. Don't want to let it burn," he said hastily as he turned away and busied himself at the stove.

"Good save," she said lightly, letting the topic go. Oddly enough, hearing about his encounters with other women didn't really bother her that much. When Denny sidled back into the kitchen and gave her a wink, she felt like she'd passed some kind of initiation test by not overreacting to his stories. Even Mark gave her an easy grin when he set a steaming bowl of chicken stir-fry in front of her. If not for the way his gaze strayed to her breasts for a beat too long, she might have been afraid that she was officially one of the guys now, but it appeared there was no danger of that. As she sat joking and laughing with the two of them, she realized with a pang somewhere in the vicinity of her heart that it would be far too easy to become attached to these men—in fact, she was afraid that she already had grown rather attached.

Mark sat at the bar, sipping a glass of wine while Denny and Angel cleaned the kitchen and picked on each other like old friends. He wasn't jealous in the least that his cousin was getting along so well with the woman in his life. Strangely, he felt the most peaceful he had in years. It wasn't that he and Denny didn't have meals together often. In fact, it was normal for one of them to cook dinner when neither of them had plans that evening. What was unusual was how seamlessly she fit in with them, as if she'd always been a

part of their group. Denny liked Angel, he could tell—
and not in a sexual way. His connection from the first
had been more of that of a sibling.

After dinner, Crystal had dragged Denny up with
her and demanded he help her clean since Mark had
cooked for them. His cousin had put up a token argu-
ment, saying something about it being women's work,
which caused her to smack him lightly on the back of
the head. Mark had smiled, both amused and, fuck it
all, enchanted. That was what he was—charmed and
entranced by her. He kept waiting for the overwhelming urge to push her away and move on, but it never
came. Even when he'd freaked the previous night and
had taken off after their talk about her ex-husband, he
hadn't been able to stop thinking about her. He'd spent
the day wanting to go to her but trying to resist. Until
Denny told him to check his Twitter account. He'd
been pissed to see something like that from her—then,
strangely enough, he'd been upset that he'd hurt her.
Because clearly she'd misinterpreted the cause of his
abrupt departure.

He allowed himself to admit that he not only
wanted to be in a relationship—he was in one with
Crystal. Whether she knew it or not, all things Crystal
Webber captivated him, and he didn't see that changing anytime soon. When he thought of the future now,
she was always there. He didn't know what that meant,
but seeing as he was sitting there calmly watching her
flick water at his cousin and had no desire to run, he
figured it was a good sign. He knew most people
would consider this moving too fast. But to him, this
was reaching for something that he'd never dreamed

was possible. She was all goodness, light, and maybe even redemption, and he wanted it—needed it— because, after the first night with her had opened his eyes, he knew he couldn't go back to the meaningless life he'd been living all these years.

A thump on his shoulder suddenly pulled him from his thoughts. Angel stood in front of him with a mischievous grin, holding a towel. Obviously, she'd swatted him with it. He greedily took in the sight of her, looking so content. He wanted to take her to the bedroom and lose himself in her for hours. From the flush spreading across her cheeks, she knew exactly what he was thinking. Never taking his eyes from her, he said, "Good night, Denny." He heard his cousin laugh softly, but this time he held his playful comments and simply waved before leaving.

"I really like him," she said softly as the door closed behind his cousin. "He's a nice guy. I can tell that you two are close. Did you grow up together?"

He took her hand, pulling her closer until she was standing between his spread legs. "Do you really want to chat right now?"

She gave him what he figured was her best poker face, but he could see the corners of her mouth twitching. "What else are you offering?" And he told her in explicit detail with a few creative twists thrown in and watched her lips form a perfect O. "Talking's really overrated." She shrugged. And that right there was yet another reason she had succeeded where others had never tempted him into anything serious. He never knew what she would give him. Sometimes sweet and innocent, then there was sassy, and his personal favorite, purring kitten. She loved to be touched, stroked, and petted. The way her body arched when his hands were on her was one of the most beautiful sights he'd even seen. She responded to his touch as if she'd been made for him. He was becoming so accustomed to the unexpected from her that he barely blinked when she pulled back enough to shed her clothing. "Race you to the bedroom."

He attempted to sound stern when he said, "Angel," but he shot to his feet and ran after her. He grabbed her by the waist in the hallway, swinging her up into his arms as she shrieked. "Got you, baby. Looks like I'm the winner tonight." Looking down into her smiling eyes, he thought those words summed up perfectly how he was feeling about the whole evening.

Chapter Fifteen

Crystal sought Mia out during her break the next morning. She winced as she took a seat on the chair in front of her friend's desk. Mark had been insatiable the previous night, and her body felt battered in the most wonderful way. The man certainly had some stamina. They hadn't even made it to the bedroom the first time; instead he'd had her to lean on the arm of his sofa. He'd then spread her open wide and proceeded to lick her from end to end. She was certain she'd passed out a few times before he finished wringing a couple of orgasms out of her. He'd kept her in the same position and taken her hard from behind. She had been grateful that her feet weren't touching the floor because otherwise they would have buckled. Then they'd moved on to a bath, where she'd ended up riding him—while flooding the bathroom. And God, she couldn't forget the shower sex this morning. Wrapped around his waist and pushed against the wall. Sleepy, tousled Mark, all slippery and yummy.

Fingers snapped in front of her, and she flinched. "I don't know what you're thinking about over there,

Crys, but if the heavy breathing is any indication, it must be damn good." Mia winked. "Come on, tell me all about it. Seth's out of town, and I'm on a dry spell."

Rolling her eyes, Crystal asked, "How long have you been suffering this time? A whole day?"

"Hey, don't make light of my pain," Mia joked. "He's been gone eighteen hours, and he's not due back until later tonight."

"I don't know how you're going to make it," Crystal cried dramatically. "How are you able to work? To even function in society with that level of neglect? I'd just kick Seth to the curb and be done with it if he can't keep up with you properly."

Kicking her feet up on top of her desk, Mia nodded. "Yeah, I would—except he packs about five days' worth of loving into every session. So even though I don't like going without—I've got enough reserves to get by awhile longer." Giving her a questioning look, Mia said, "Now that we've got that out of the way, what brings you to my neck of the woods so early? I gathered from your text yesterday that you DeStudo have made up."

"Oh, yeah." Crystal grinned. "We sure did. And it was amazing as always. But that's not why I'm here." Mia flicked her hand, encouraging her to get on with it. Biting her lip, she admitted, "Well . . . I'm going to marriage counseling with Bill this evening."

"What?" Mia shrilled. Her friend looked like a guppy fish as her mouth flapped open and closed. "Bu-but I thought that was over. I mean, you're sleeping with Mark, right?"

"That's right," she agreed. "We're having a just sex nonrelationship."

Mia rubbed her temple as if in pain. "Er—honey, if you're sleeping with one man, should you really be trying to get back together with another one? I mean, no judgment here, but that sounds kind of . . . duplicitous."

"But I'm not going back to Bill," Crystal pointed out.

Enunciating each word carefully, Mia asked, "Then. Why. Are. You. Going. To. Counseling. With. Him?"

Crystal squirmed in her seat. "I can't help it. I feel sorry for him. He's called me for the past two days begging me to go. I caved under the pressure this morning when it sounded as if he was crying. It's not a big deal, though. We were married for a long time. What's a few more hours for old times' sake?"

Mia now looked as if she were close to beating her head against her desk. "Did you ever think that possibly he's just playing you? He, better than anyone, knows what a soft heart you have. You'd probably agree to go to marriage counseling with King Kong if he shed a tear or two. What does Mark have to say about this?"

"I can't tell him," Crystal whispered, after looking over her shoulder to make certain the door was still closed. "He doesn't like discussing Bill. Remember how he reacted a few nights ago when I told him about seeing him at my mother's?"

"Out of curiosity," Mia began, "how do you think you're going to hide this from him? What if he wants to see you tonight?"

"He left for Charleston this morning," she admitted.

"He said he won't be back until sometime tomorrow, so I'm good."

"You dumped all of this on me because you were afraid of putting Gwen in labor, weren't you?" Mia asked astutely. "Plus you knew that your sister would probably have a heart attack over it."

"Well . . ." Crystal hedged, "nothing really shakes you, and I had to tell someone in case Bill drags me off afterward."

"Well, hell," Mia huffed. "Now, I'm your enabler. I want to officially go on the record as being opposed to this crazy bleeding-heart sympathy counseling you're doing with Bill. I'll keep my mouth shut, but I want you to promise me that you'll talk to him after it's over tonight. Let him know where you stand and that this was a onetime thing for you."

Crystal crossed her heart. "I will. I'll invite him for coffee and tell him the truth."

"All right." Mia sighed, sounding resigned. "I just know this isn't gonna end well, but you're a grown woman. I hope you know what you're doing. Often it's better for someone to have no hope than the false kind."

Crystal was on her feet and almost to the door. Turning back, she asked, "Are you talking about me or Bill?"

"God knows at this point," Mia admitted.

What a mistake, Crystal thought dazedly as Bill used yet another tissue to wipe his eyes. She had to admit that the man who she'd always thought was oblivious to her feelings seemed to have a long and very detailed list of every time he'd hurt her in the past. As he listed each and every one of them, she nodded politely while he begged for forgiveness. As their hour drew to a close, she was physically and emotionally exhausted. She wasn't sure what she'd been expecting, but it wasn't to sit quietly the entire time while Bill talked nonstop and the counselor nodded approvingly before finally saying brightly, "This was a great session, you two. Bill, you communicated your feelings beautifully. And Crystal, next week we'll begin with you. After that, we can have joint discussions as we work to put your broken pieces back together again." Then she clapped—she honest-to-God clapped—her hands and said in a peppy shout, "Now stand up and take a bow—you both deserve it!" *Nightmare on my street.*

Bill jumped to his feet enthusiastically. When Crystal remained seated, mainly in shock, both the counselor and her ex-husband looked at her expectedly. So she had little choice but to stand and bow as if she'd just finished the starring role in a third-grade play. *Shoot me now.* After that, there was no way she could force herself to spend more time with Bill, even if they did need to talk. So she said the first thing that she could come up with, to get away quickly. "I've really got to go. It's that time of the month."

Thank the Lord that some things never changed. Bill looked like he was ready to bolt at her words, and he stammered out, "Oh, um, sure. You go do— whatever, um, you need to." She waved limply with one hand while holding her stomach for good measure with the other and shuffled quickly to her car.

And just to give her a swift kick, fate took that exact

moment to make her phone chime. She fumbled in her purse, pulling it out to see a message from her mother. *It's about time you got your head on right. Bill told me that you're getting back together. Don't mess it up this time!* Complete with an exclamation mark and a fucking emoticon with a frowny face.

The scales were officially out of balance in her life once again. The good side with her nonrelationship was rapidly being overwhelmed by the bad side with Bill and her ex-husband-loving mother. Joining the Peace Corps was sounding really good right about now.

Chapter Sixteen

It was almost two in the morning when Mark walked in the door of his Charleston home. He loosened his tie and tossed his suit jacket on the back of a chair. Evenings with his parents were freaking exhausting and he wanted nothing more than to leave the city and not come back. Every once in a great while, his father decided to make an ass of himself to get attention. And he'd done that yesterday afternoon. As usual, he'd been either drunk, high, or a combination of both.

He'd learned long ago that things would continue to escalate unless he gave his father the outlet he was seeking, which was usually an opportunity to flex his imaginary muscle. When his grandfather had turned the family company over to him, his father had nearly gone ballistic. Mark couldn't understand how his father was the only one who didn't see it coming. After all, Mark had taken a stagnant company and shot it straight to the top, ahead of all of their competition. His business instincts were spot-on almost without fail, and that was something that his shrewd grandfather had picked up on right away. Therefore, while his father lived the life of an overgrown playboy, Mark quietly took control and never looked back. And his parents cursed him for it even as they ran through the money he made for them like water.

His parents shared a bizarre relationship. He knew that they both had lovers and didn't bother to hide their affairs from each other. Yet they had each other's backs in a way that Mark would never comprehend, considering the state of their marriage. No doubt money played a part, as his mother was used to living the good life. When he was forced to spend time with them, he never ceased to be amazed by their actions, even though he should know what to expect from them by now. His mother would pretend for a few hours that she actually gave a damn about what was going on in Mark's life, and his father would go through a rehearsed list of all of the ways that Mark had embarrassed and failed them. It was almost like some childish bid for attention.

During the time that he was with them, his father would toss back one drink after another while his mother ate a couple of bites of salad. Then she would produce a compact from her purse and carefully reapply her lipstick and touch the skin under her eyes as if checking for any new wrinkles. If was as if she didn't hear a single word that her husband slurred out.

Looking at them tonight across the table, he'd felt something in addition to the usual anger and impatience. He'd had an epiphany of sorts. He'd avoided relationships all of his adult life because he'd been terrified of becoming what his parents were. Hell, it hadn't been long ago that his friend Brant had accused him of having mommy and daddy issues and he'd laughed in agreement and told him that he'd even throw in some grandparent issues as well. He'd been moody that day because he'd just finished dealing with his father's latest tantrum. He'd shown up drunk and disorderly at the DeSanto Group's Charleston headquarters, and Hank, one of the security guards there, had been forced to call Mark and ask what to do. That had been one of the worst instances since his father had swung at Hank before being subdued. Just another fucking moment of family embarrassment.

But tonight, when he'd been at his lowest point of the evening—ready to toss his napkin on the table, have the jet fueled, and leave the country—his phone had chimed. He'd pulled it from his pocket, welcoming any excuse to block out his father's grating voice. There had been a surprising text that instantly soothed his despair and brought a smile to his lips. *Hey, DeStudo . . . I'll never complain about being a booty call again. Could use one right about now. . . .* A smiley face followed the comment.

She would never know how much he had needed that text from her tonight. He'd quickly hit the REPLY button and typed, *Wish I could oblige, Angel. . . . You okay?* Regardless of her words, he didn't think she was necessarily trying to sext him. He had a feeling that like himself, she might have had a rough evening and just needed to reach out. It was already after ten, and he hoped like hell he could get out of here soon so he could call her before she went to bed. He longed to hear her sweet voice and her laughter tonight. Normally, after a hellish dinner like this, he'd be looking for someone to take the edge off for a few hours. Physical exertion followed by a release—or several of them. Right now, though, the idea of a one-night stand held no appeal for him.

He was still holding his phone when she responded, *I'm fine . . . but I miss you.* As he sat reading her words and wondering why the sentiment she'd expressed wasn't freaking him out, another one chimed right behind it. *Crap! I shouldn't have said that. I mean—we barely know each other and now you're going to think I'm some kind of clinger.* He'd no sooner finished reading that comment when another popped up. He couldn't help it; he started to laugh. She went on berating herself for at least two minutes before there was a lull in the action. God, he loved how adorably rattled she got when she was nervous. He could only imagine how flustered she was right about now.

Before she could continue on, he typed out, *It's fine, Angel.* Then, because it was very much true, he added something he'd never admitted to another woman. *Miss you too.*

Really?? Her reply was almost immediate.

Across the table, his mother had called his name and he'd known his reprieve was over. His fingers flew over his phone and he sent back, *Yeah, baby. Call you later,* before turning once again to his parents.

In the end, it was hours before he'd gotten away. He'd ended up taking them home since their driver was off for the rest of the night. His mother had insisted he come in and he figured that she needed his help with getting his father into bed after he passed out. He had no idea how she handled it on other nights, but some part of him couldn't leave her stranded. She'd never be mother of the year, but she was a damn sight better than her husband.

As he slumped back against the plush cushions of his sofa, he thought again of Angel. It was far too late to call her now—but he wanted to. He reached for his phone lying on the table beside him and waged an inner war. He could text her once and if she didn't reply, he'd know she was asleep. He chose to ignore his inner voice telling him that he'd wake her up either way. *Sorry was later than I expected. Bet you're already asleep.* He closed his eyes and tried to relax. He was dozing off when the sound of his phone ringing jolted him abruptly. He looked at the display and chuckled. "What're you doing awake, Angel?"

"Waiting for you to call," she responded softly and without hesitation.

His gut clenched, and his heart did a funny flip. So fucking sweet and innocent. He should walk away and leave her alone. If only he didn't want her so damned much. She was changing him—changing everything. "Baby . . . ," he said, unable to get anything else out.

"You sound tired," she added. "Is your trip going okay?"

"Yeah, Angel," he said huskily. "Just dealing with some family shit."

She sounded curious now. "Problem?"

"The usual." He had no idea why he was compelled to add, "My father makes your mother seem like June Cleaver, if that gives you any idea."

All was quiet before she let out an "Ohhh. Wow, I had no idea. I'm sorry."

He was moved by the sincerity in her voice, but he didn't want to think about his parents anymore for a while. "It is what it is, Angel. So, tell me about your evening. What had you stressed enough earlier to request a DeStudo drive-by?"

She giggled at his attempt to lighten the mood. "It was . . . nothing specific really. The usual long day."

Even though she tried to sound light and airy, Mark could tell there was more to it than that. She seemed happy to talk to him, but he could detect a note of strain beneath the surface. "Did you speak to your mother today?" he asked casually, figuring that was the source of her unhappiness.

In a rapid-fire change of subject, she asked playfully, "So . . . what're you wearing, DeStudo?"

If her evening had been anything like his, then he figured she needed an escape, because he certainly did. So, he went along with her diversion and replied, "Still dressed in everything except my jacket. How about you, Angel? What's touching that beautiful body of yours?"

She hesitated for a moment. "A T-shirt and panties. I wanted to say something more exciting, but I'm going with the truth."

"I can't imagine anything better than what you've just described. I bet that shirt is riding up and the curve of your sweet ass is peeking out. If I were there, I'd have my hand right on that spot where it connects with your thigh. You're so sensitive that you'd shudder as I stroked you."

"Oh, wow." He heard her breath hitch, and he knew without seeing her that she was biting her plump lip. That mouth drove him crazy. He spent far too much time thinking of it wrapped around his cock. Then she surprised him by asking—or more like mumbling shyly—"Do you . . . I mean, have you ever tried . . . phone sex?"

He couldn't help it; her question had him bursting into laughter. He heard her huffing in irritation before he finally got himself back under control enough to say, "Yeah, but it's been a long time."

"Oh," she murmured, "I guess it was never something that the great DeStudo had to resort to very often."

"That's true," he agreed truthfully. "I think we both know I haven't lacked for female company, Angel, but I will say this. Right now, other than being with you in person, there is nothing else I'd rather be doing. In the past I would have gone out tonight and found someone. Fuck knows I needed the release, but it just didn't interest me."

"Really?" she asked, sounding almost giddy at his words. He'd never been one for flowery speeches, and to him, what he'd just said didn't even come close to romantic. But it seemed to make her happy, and it was certainly the truth. All he wanted right now was her, and phone sex sounded pretty damn appealing.

"Baby, I could drag this out for a while, tease you with taking off one article of clothing at a time, but I think we need to cut to the chase. So how about you be a good girl for me and remove that shirt and your panties. While you're doing that, I'm going to take my clothes off and then I'm going to stroke my cock while you touch yourself. Does that work for you?"

"Um—yes!" she squeaked. "I'm er . . . going to do that—what you said—right now. Hang on, okay?"

Chuckling under his breath, he said, "All right, baby." Then he laid the phone down before tossing off his clothing. Instead of returning to the sofa, he went to the bed. The sheets felt smooth and cool against his overheated skin. "You back, Angel?" he asked as his hand encircled his hard length. He clicked the SPEAKER button on his phone and dropped it on the bed beside him.

"I'm here," she answered right away. "I'm naked. Should I be on top of the covers or under them? Is there like a certain position that you're supposed to assume for this?"

He smiled, wanting to laugh at her question but managing to bite it back. "Put your phone on speaker and lie on top of your comforter, Angel—then spread your legs for me. Now touch yourself and tell me if you're wet." He heard a rustling sound and knew that she was doing as he instructed.

He pinched the tip of his cock, attempting to relieve a little pressure, as she suddenly moaned low in her throat, admitting, "I'm really wet. And my hand feels good—but not as good as yours."

"Ah, baby," he groaned, while pumping his dick. "Slip a finger inside you." He knew by the sounds she was making that she'd done exactly as he asked. "Rub your clit with your other hand."

"That feels so good," she whimpered. "Are you . . . doing it too?"

As his balls tightened painfully, he said, "Yeah,

Angel. I'm imagining plunging deep inside of your wet heat while I bury my tongue in your mouth. I'm so hard right now that I can hardly stand it. And it's all for you, baby. Now add another finger and stretch yourself."

"I'm close," she wailed, and he could hear her how close she was to her orgasm through the phone line. "Oh, Mark—I wish you were here."

"Me too, baby," he gasped out as his hips surged forward. With the sounds of her cries in his ears, he shot streams of cum onto his belly. He knew he called her name as she continued to call his. "Are you okay, Angel?" he managed to ask when he finally recovered. She'd been quiet for the last minute or so, not saying anything.

"Mmm-hmm," she sighed, sounding both tired and satisfied. "That was awesome. I mean, it's not the same as—you know, but it was still one of the best ever."

"For me as well," he admitted, and he meant it. He'd come harder from phone sex with her than he had being intimate with most of the other women who'd passed briefly through his life. "It's late, baby," he said gruffly, unused to dealing with these types of tender feelings. "You should go to sleep now. You're working tomorrow, right?"

"Yes," she answered quietly, and he knew that she was already practically dozing. "When are you coming home?"

He yawned, relaxing further into his pillow before remembering he had some cleanup to take care of. "I'll be back sometime tomorrow evening. We'll have dinner if it's not too late."

"Mmmm K," she agreed. "Night, Mark."

He said his good nights and waited until she ended the call before tossing his phone aside. He left the bed and took a quick shower before collapsing back onto the soft surface. As his mind relaxed and his body drifted, he couldn't help but find it strange that after a shitty evening, he was going to sleep happier than he had been in a while. And somehow he didn't think it had anything at all to do with phone sex.

Chapter Seventeen

"Please tell me you aren't still going to marriage counseling with Bill," Ella pleaded.

"I've only been one time," Crystal said defensively. "But he's pressuring me to go again."

Ella ran a hand through her hair in frustration before looking at the baby monitor on the table beside her. Sofia had gone down for a nap right after Crystal arrived, and she was still moving restlessly in her crib. When the baby quieted again, Ella said, "Tell me the absolute truth. Are you thinking of taking Bill back?"

"What?" Crystal gasped. "No! Of course not. I'm happy as I am."

"Okayyy." Ella drew the word out as if her patience were being tested. "Then why are you going to marriage counseling with him? For God's sake, Crys, that's whacked. Do you realize what kind of message you're sending the man? He no doubt thinks you're going to end up remarrying sometime in the not so distant future. That's certainly what most would believe. And what about Mark?"

"Things are good with him," she said happily.

Actually, things *were* great there. They'd been going out for over a month, and the only times they weren't together in the evening were the few times he'd been out of town on business.

"That's good." Ella smiled before lowering the boom. "And what does he think about you attending a therapy session with your ex-husband? I can tell you what Declan's opinion would be on the matter, and it's hard to believe that Mark is that understanding."

Crystal shifted in her seat before dropping her head back on the sofa and staring up at the ceiling. "I—er, I haven't really told him," she mumbled, hoping that her sister couldn't understand what she was saying. She should have known better.

"That's pretty much what I thought." Ella snorted unhappily. "Crys, are you trying to ruin your life? I'll admit, when you and Mark first started spending time together, I was a tad concerned that you would get hurt, and Declan was frantic. But you two have been so good for each other. Everyone says that Mark is a changed man, and you're just . . . glowing. I've never seen you this happy before, even when you were a newlywed. But you're playing with fire here, and I don't understand why."

Crystal pinched the bridge of her nose before looking at her sister and admitting softly, "He keeps crying."

"Mark?" Ella shrilled, looking amazed.

"What? No! Of course not. Bill. It's as if he's broken out of the cold shell he's always lived in and now he's this whole new emotional person that I don't recognize. Each time I try to tell him that I've moved on and there is no hope of us getting back together, he breaks down. He said that he just needed me to be his friend and support him while he's getting help. I mean, he doesn't have anyone else, and he wants to change."

Ella blinked rapidly before pursing her lips. "Honey, I think it's great that Bill is attempting to better himself. And, of course, knowing how softhearted you are and the history between you both, I would expect nothing less than for you to be a friend to him. But, that being said, you're going to marriage counseling at his request. Which indicates that you're working on issues as a couple—to have a future together again. I'm very much afraid that Bill is manipulating you and taking advantage of your good nature."

Crystal chewed her bottom lip as she pondered her sister's words. In truth, she'd wondered the same thing more than once. But he seemed so sincere. And he hadn't made a move on her romantically—well, other than holding her hand during the session. "I don't know what to do," she finally admitted. "I know I shouldn't care whether he suffers or not because he never cared or noticed when I was. But he just seems so lonely and lost, and I feel kind guilty that I've caused it."

Ella reached over and put a hand on top of hers. "That's why you're the woman you are, sis. You have a huge heart, and you don't want the person who made you miserable to be sad. But regardless of whether it's genuine or if he's messing with your head, it has to end. It's not fair to you, to Bill, or most of all, to Mark to keep this going. Tomorrow, you need to call him and tell him that you can't do it anymore. Don't meet him in person, because you won't be able to handle it if he gets emotional."

"All right." Crystal sighed. "I know you're right. I guess I'd just been hoping that Bill would lose interest in me again—you know, kind of like when we were married." Smiling, she added, "I certainly don't want to lose Mark."

"How are things with DeStudo?" Ella asked with a mischievous grin. "You know everyone's talking about the whole romance of the year, right?"

Baffled, Crystal asked, "Romance of the year? Us?"

"Well, heck yeah," Ella enthused. "No one has ever seen Mark walk around at Danvers holding a woman's hand. You two are joined at the hip almost every day when you come through the door, and trust me, it's been a hot topic. Did you know that your boss calls him . . ."

"Mr. Big," Crystal filled in with a laugh. "Yep, she's convinced that we're the Danvers/DeSanto version of Carrie and Mr. Big from *Sex and the City*. Of course, I think she's concentrating on Mark's right-hand man, Jacob, more than anything."

"She mentioned that too," Ella agreed with a grin. "It's nice to see her smiling again every day, though, isn't it? I mean, I knew Lydia a little before you went to work as her assistant, and she always seemed so sad. I'm not saying that anything will ever come of her crush on Jacob, but it's great to see her living life again."

"I've been trying to get Mark to set them up," Crystal confessed sheepishly. "He says he's not getting involved, though, and that Jacob doesn't really do long-term commitments."

"Well, neither did Mark," Ella argued.

"We aren't exactly engaged; it's been like a month," Crystal pointed out.

"For a man like Mark, that's major," Ella added. "I'm just saying that sometimes people do things a certain way because they haven't found someone who makes them want more. Look at Declan—he wasn't looking for love, marriage, or a family, but that changed."

"That's true," Crystal said thoughtfully. "Whatever it is, I'm enjoying what we have. I never knew that a man could make me feel so much." Dropping a hand over her eyes, she whispered, "I flat out lust after him as much as I did back when I used to stalk him around the office. And it's not just that. He's funny, thoughtful, and one of the most interesting people I've ever met."

Moving in for the kill, Ella asked bluntly, "And are you willing to lose that to keep from hurting Bill's feelings?"

"No"—Crystal cringed—"not at all. Of course, you're right. I'll do something about it."

"Thank God," Ella deadpanned. "Now, are you two coming to Suzy's party this weekend? I have no idea what's going on because she's been really secretive about it."

"I think Gwen knows something." Crystal nodded. "When we were having lunch the other day, she acted really funny when Mia brought up the party."

"Same thing here from Beth. She's a horrible liar, and I can normally get her to break, but this time she's keeping her mouth shut, which is highly unusual."

"Mark doesn't know anything," Crystal said thoughtfully. "He asked Gray if there was some special occasion, but instead of answering, he said Gray just smiled and walked off. I tried to get him to ask Nick or Jason, but he told me that men don't harass other men for information like that."

"Oh bullshit." Ella snorted. "They try to pretend that women are so much worse about gossip, but I've heard Declan in action, and they're every bit as nosy. He probably already tried it but didn't want to admit to failing."

Before Crystal could reply, her phone chimed and she fished it from her purse. Her insides went all gooey as soon as she saw the text from Mark. *When're you going to be home, Angel?*

"Dear Lord, let me see that." Ella chuckled as he grabbed the phone from Crystal's fingers. When she read the message, she said, "Awww, that's so sweet. Is he waiting at your place or something?"

Crystal knew she was blushing as she admitted, "No . . . he's talking about his house. He calls it 'home' because—it is, right?"

Wiggling her brows, Ella said, "Mmm-hmm, it's his place all right. But he's referring to it as *your* home. That's a big difference." When her sister started humming the bridal march, Crystal got up from the sofa and threw a pillow at her.

"Keep it together, crazy. If Mark hears you doing that, then no doubt he'll run for the hills." Picking up her purse and snatching her phone away from Ella, she walked backward to the door. "I'm leaving now before you start ordering wedding invitations and creating a song list."

Ella laid back full-length against the couch cushions, putting her hands behind her head. "Come on over to the dark side, Crys—it's pretty sweet here."

Crystal shook her head and gave a wave before leaving. She quickly typed out a response to Mark's text letting him know she was on her way as she settled in her car. She didn't want to admit it to her sister or anyone else, but she'd started to let herself think of Mark's place as home. She only hoped for the sake of her heart that it was a permanent residence and not temporary housing.

She and Mark had just finished a dinner of Chinese takeout and were curled up on the sofa watching television. It seemed so domestic and normal that Crystal had pinched herself once just to prove that she was awake. Somehow, she'd always imagined being with a man like Mark would mean lots of socializing, but they'd actually developed a fairly low-key routine. Most evenings they cooked, ordered in, or went out to eat, and then went back to either her apartment or Mark's place—mostly his. They had gone to the movies a few times and spent lazy days on the beach in front of his house. She loved it since she'd never been one who liked to be constantly on the go.

His arm was around her shoulders, and he was absently twirling a piece of her hair when his phone rang. She saw Denny's name on the display before Mark answered the call with a simple "Yeah?" Then there was nothing but silence, followed by an explosion of profanity. She jumped in her seat, looking at him in alarm. "You've got to be fucking kidding me!" He removed his arm and hunched forward. "I swear to Christ, I'm about sick of dealing with this." He said a few more sentences before ending the call and dropping his head in his hands.

She tentatively touched his back, rubbing at the tense muscles there. "Is everything okay, babe?" Quite obviously, it wasn't, and she felt kind of stupid for asking, but she had to start somewhere.

"Not really, Angel," he snapped, before softening his voice. "Sorry, baby." He rubbed at his neck before straightening to look at her. "You need to go home. My parents are coming into town unexpectedly, and it won't be good if you're here."

Wow, she hadn't been expecting that. She knew from the few things that both he and Denny had shared with her that his parents were about as bad as hers. From his reaction, she had to think they could even be worse. "I don't mind," she protested, not wanting to leave him in his hour of need.

Pulling her back into his arms, he dropped a kiss on her neck before saying, "Remember when I said that my parents made yours look tame?" When she nodded, he added, "Well, that was somewhat of an understatement. Your mother may be a bitch and your father may let her get away with it, but that's where the similarities end. In my family dynamic, my father is the asshole and my mother is the enabler. And to make matters worse, he's also a drunk who abuses alcohol and God knows what else. He's weak, selfish, and spineless. My mother tries to smooth his rough edges by pretending to care about us, and possibly a part of her does, but I'll always be a distant second to her. They both sleep with whomever they want, but at the end of the day, they're a team and anyone else is just on the outside looking in."

Unable to process his words, she stared at him for a moment before saying, "Wow, I thought I had the parents from hell."

That appeared to have surprised him enough to get a laugh out of him, which he'd looked sorely in need of. "I believe we both do," he agreed, "just in different ways. They're toxic, Angel, and I don't want you to have to deal with it. You have enough to handle with your mother. Chances are that my father will be wasted, and when that happens, he can be nastier than usual. So it would make me very happy to know that you're home enjoying your evening and away from their toxic behavior."

"Are they staying with you?" she asked, still feeling as if she was abandoning him to the wolves.

"Hell no," he responded immediately. "I'll be their first stop, but luckily they prefer an expensive hotel. They generally stay at the Oceanix, so I figure I only have to survive a few hours—at least tonight."

"All right," she agreed. "I don't want you to be stressed over them and have to worry about me, so I'll go." She was pulling away to stand, when he managed to halt her progress and lift her neatly into his lap.

"Thanks, baby," he growled, "but I'm going to need a little something to get me by before you leave."

"And what would that be?" she purred as his lips locked on hers. Dear God, the man could kiss. She might not have much to compare him to, but somehow she knew he'd be at the top of most women's lists. He didn't just kiss, he owned. He was in control, unless he was feeling playful and allowed her to take charge for a brief time. He believed in lots of tongue. When Mark took your mouth, you damn well knew it. Her clit throbbed and her nipples hardened, even though she tried to silently warn her body that there would be no satisfaction tonight—unless it was self-induced.

"Fuck," he grated out against her lips. "I can't believe I'm sending you away after that." She felt the hard length of him pressing into her bottom. They were both worked up and in no way ready to see it end.

She curved her palm along his jaw, rubbing the stubble already showing there. "If you get rid of them quickly tonight, then come to me. You still have my key, right?"

He nodded, looking almost hopeful at her suggestion. She'd given him a key to her place the last time he'd left to go out of town. He hadn't wanted to scare her by knocking on her door if he was late getting back, and she'd hadn't wanted to wait until the next day to see him. "We'll see, Angel. Leave the security chain off."

"I will," she promised, before getting to her feet. He walked her through the house and into the kitchen where she picked up her purse. She gave his arm a squeeze of reassurance. "It'll be okay. Maybe they just want to see their son tonight." Even as she said the words, she didn't really believe them. If his father was anything like her mother, then there was no such thing as a simple social call. There was always some agenda, and it was never good.

"Could be," he replied with a forced smile. He kissed her lightly, and then held the door open for her to get in the car. "If I don't see you later, then I'll come by your office in the morning."

"Good luck." She smiled brightly. As she was driving away, she took one last look, and her heart broke for him. He looked so alone and solemn standing there with his hands in his pockets. Crystal wanted to go back and demand that he allow her be there for him, but she knew well from her own experience that the last thing you wanted was to have an audience while you were verbally attacked.

She'd carefully tried to keep her parents away from Mark for the same reason. Deep down inside, she thought that was why she'd continued to attend the marriage counseling sessions. It satisfied her mother to some degree, and while she was happy, she left Crystal alone for the most part. And regardless of what Bill said about wanting to avoid her mother, she knew the moment she stopped going, he would go straight to her parents to enlist their support. Then, once again, Crystal would be the difficult daughter who never did as she was told. Unfortunately, she could no longer hide from the fact that going on as she had been made her nothing but a liar and a coward. If she went to these kinds of lengths to avoid conflict, then where did it end? How could she ever truly be the strong person that she wanted to be, while still letting others run her life? Even though she'd finally divorced Bill, she still wasn't free of him, and she wouldn't be until she learned to stand up for herself in all areas of her life. Maybe that was something that she and Mark could work on together, because it appeared that they were both suffering at the hands of the very people supposed to love them the most.

Chapter Eighteen

His mother had the grace to at least look apologetic when he opened the door an hour later. "Sorry, dear," she murmured as she preceded her husband in the door.

"To what do I owe the unexpected pleasure?" Mark asked dryly. His father, he noted, actually looked marginally sober, which was a rare occurrence. Apparently, that wasn't going to last long, though, because he ignored Mark's question and started opening cabinets in the kitchen until he found the one with liquor in it. He rummaged around next for a glass and poured it nearly full of bourbon. *Great.* It looked as if tonight Mark would get to deal with both his father's drinking and the aftereffects.

"Why don't we all go have a seat in the living room," his mother suggested. "I'm sure we'd be far more comfortable there." He wanted to point out that the last thing he wanted was for them to make themselves at home, but he held his tongue. At least his mother was trying to be civil. He turned and led the way, hoping to God he could get rid of them soon so he could go to Angel and forget all about his messed-up family.

Mark took one of the armchairs, while his mother reclined back on the sofa where he'd so recently been seated with Angel. Something about that seemed wrong, and he wanted to ask her to move. Dammit, must they taint anything good in his life? His father chose to remain standing, which would probably turn to swaying soon after the large glass of liquor. "So, son," he said, making Mark's back go ramrod straight. They were playing the parental card tonight—how fucking spectacular. "We're here to meet your girl-friend. According to Oliver, you've been seeing some-one for quite a while now."

Freaking Oliver. How did he even know what was going on in Mark's life? Oliver was his father's brother and lived in Santa Barbara, California. Mark spoke to him about as often as he did his parents, which wasn't much. But the bastard was nosy and about as bitter as his brother that he hadn't been left controlling interest in the DeSanto Group. He was also more than happy to cash his dividend checks and enjoy the life that Mark provided them all. "My personal affairs aren't open for discussion." Lifting a brow, he asked, "Now, was there anything else?"

His mother moved from her perch and put a mani-cured hand on his shoulder. "Mark, we'd just like to meet her. Surely, you can understand why we'd be curious. You've never been in a relationship before."

"Plus, there's more to consider here than picking out goddamned china, boy," his father interjected. "You come from a very wealthy family and this woman doesn't. We have to make sure that she under-stands her place."

"Her place?" Mark parroted, unable to comprehend what he was hearing. His mother's hand tightened, and he thought that her husband's crazy ramblings might have surprised even her. "What exactly are you talking about?" he asked, trying to rein in a temper that was threatening to blow out of control.

"Honey, I believe what your father is trying to say— and maybe not well—is that we'd love to meet Crystal. I'm sure she's a lovely young woman, but we're a little concerned about the difference in your backgrounds."

Mark could only gape at her. "You grew up sharing a bedroom with three sisters and your mother made your clothes. Tell me how you're suddenly better than the woman I'm seeing or how you could possibly stand here and have the audacity to participate in this absurd conversation? Unless I'm mistaken, you weren't raised rich—actually, Crystal probably had it much better than you did."

"Now listen here, son," his father blustered. "Don't talk to your mother in that tone. We're tired of being treated like lepers every time we visit our son. After all we've done for you, is it too much to ask for some respect?"

"Respect?" he spat out. "Is that what you're showing me when you barge into my home and immediately begin hurling insults at the woman I'm dating? By the way, I'd like to know how you know so much about her. Because I swear to God, if someone on my payroll had her investigated, then their ass will be out the door before they know what hit them."

He could tell by the momentary shift on his father's face that it had indeed been someone at DeSanto.

Great, he was officially picking up the tab for invading Crystal's privacy. A few of the older employees who were loyal to first his grandfather, and then his father, were still employed, and he could easily see his father finagling some favors with the assistance of Oliver. No one in his father's family was capable of arranging anything complicated on their own. They were too used to making one simple call and getting what they needed. "This girl is divorced; were you even aware of that?"

"Of course," Mark huffed. "We're not living in the Stone Age. People get married and sometimes it doesn't work out. Should they stay together when that's the case?" He didn't bother adding that he'd pegged his parents for a future divorced couple from a young age and was constantly amazed that it hadn't happened yet.

"We understand that, Mark," his mother again injected. "We have friends who are no longer together. We're not saying that it doesn't happen." *Great, another organized tag team session,* he thought as she paused for a moment before continuing. "What we're distressed about is the fact that while she's seeing you, she's also attempting to reconcile with her ex-husband. I assume that you know that, so could you explain that behavior to your father and me as well?"

Mark froze, staring up at his mother. She looked genuinely perplexed, which made two of them. Surely, they'd gotten something wrong somewhere. He knew that Crystal's mother had ambushed her into dinner with her ex-husband several weeks back, but she hadn't made mention of him once since then. That was probably what this whole thing was about. The investigator had found out about it. His chest lightened as he looked over at his now-pacing father. "Her ex is close with her parents, so naturally she's run into him there. That's all it is, though. She spends most of her free time here."

Mark felt a sick feeling in the pit of his stomach as his father gave him a look that was a cross between pity and compassion. That unsettled him more than any words that he could have said. He knew something— goddammit, what was going on? Instead of his usual booming voice, this one was quiet as he said, "Son, she's been going to marriage counseling while you've been involved. The counselor's name is Celia Mulkey, and she has an office downtown." Then the evening took an even stranger turn when without saying anything other than good-bye, his parents left as quickly as they'd arrived. Either they felt that their work at dismantling his life was complete or they felt sorry for him and decided not to kick him again while he was down. To Mark, it just drove home the fact that he'd been caught completely unawares and hadn't been able to hide it.

What was Crystal doing going to marriage counseling? There was no way that information was a mistake. Owing to the nature of the business, his employees went through a rigorous background screening as part of the hiring process. He had an entire department dedicated to designing and maintaining an advanced encryption system for the routers they manufactured, and security breaches were always a threat. He hired only the best to ensure that didn't happen. So he knew that they wouldn't pull something like that out of the blue. So why wasn't he picking up his phone and calling her to demand an explanation? Perhaps he didn't want to hear her explanation. This was the first real relationship he'd ever been in, and he liked how his life was with her in it.

Laying his head back wearily, he admitted the truth—he was afraid of what she'd say. He knew they couldn't go on as they had been without him knowing what in the hell was going on. He'd never had anyone that he was scared to lose, and he didn't like how it felt at all. She'd gotten closer to him in the short time they'd known each other than any woman ever had—including his own mother. And he had no idea how to deal with it.

Mark stayed in the same position for another hour before getting to his feet and going to pack a bag. A quick call to his pilot ensured the plane would be ready in an hour. Jacob was still in Boston dealing with problems there, and he was going to join him. Right now, he needed distance from Angel until he could come to terms with what she'd done.

Crystal checked her phone yet again, hoping to see a message from Mark. She'd been worried about him since last night, and he hadn't attempted to contact her. She'd called him as soon as she woke that morning, but his phone had gone straight to voice mail. She'd left a message and then texted him a few hours later when she reached the office. Since they'd been together, he was seldom out of contact. If he didn't take her call, then he returned it, usually within the hour. So this silence from him was unusual and worrisome. Now it was time for her break, and she was going to drop by his office and see if he was in.

When she reached the door with DESANTO GROUP on it, she gently pushed it open and was met by a smiling, middle-aged receptionist. Crystal had met her several times before when she'd waited for Mark after work. "Hi, Ginny, is Mark in yet?"

The other woman looked momentarily confused as she said, "No, honey, he's in Boston. He left last night, I believe. Jacob is already there, so obviously there was some issue to make Mark leave so suddenly."

Crystal was stunned and from the look of sympathy on Ginny's face, it showed. "I . . . um . . . oh, that's right," she stuttered, "I'd forgotten about that."

As she turned to leave, Ginny called out, "Did you want to leave a message for him?"

"Oh no, that's okay. I'll talk to him later," she managed to choke out before hurrying out the door. *What is going on?* she wondered frantically as she walked back to her own office. It wasn't like him not to let her know he was leaving town. Had the visit with his parents been upsetting to the point that he'd fled without a word? Well, that wasn't quite true. Ginny knew he was gone.

She was distracted for the rest of the day. Lydia asked her a few times if everything was all right, and she'd attempted to smile and assure her that she was just tired. Not technically a lie since she'd tossed and turned most of the night, worried about Mark.

When five o'clock finally came, she gathered her things and was grateful that Lydia was on the phone. She gave her a wave as she walked by and went straight to her car without stopping on the way to speak to Gwen or Mia. Normally, she'd pop in and chat for a few minutes, but today she wanted only to get home and make sense of what had happened.

"Care to tell me again why we packed up in the middle of the night like a bunch of outlaws running for our lives? Don't get me wrong, I can see you trying to avoid your parents again, but I've heard through the family grapevine that they're out of Myrtle Beach today," Denny said between mouthfuls of his breakfast. He might be complaining about their last-minute trip, but he was certainly enjoying the food at their hotel.

Mark had opted for just coffee, not feeling up to a large meal this morning. He took his time taking a sip before answering his nosy cousin. "Jacob's been tied up here for too long. If Williams can't run this fucking location without having his hand held, then I need to make some changes. We shouldn't have to constantly bail him out." Williams was the new general manager and was having issues with those loyal to the one who had been recently terminated. The other manager hadn't been doing his job, and the company had suffered as a direct result. Mark had given him ample opportunity time and again to get his act together. Yet nothing had ever changed. He'd continued to come in late or not at all, while contracts went unfulfilled. The man was single-handedly ruining the reputation of the DeSanto Group and he had to go. Unfortunately, thanks to his lax work ethic, he was popular with the employees, and they were making it hard for their new boss.

None of it was Cal Williams's fault, and he was doing a fantastic job while dealing with a lot of hostility. Mark was just frustrated with the world right now and using him as an outlet to deal with it. The look on Denny's face said that he knew exactly that. "O-*kay*," Denny replied, before wiping his mouth and tossing his napkin on the table. "Now that you have that little tirade out of the way, could we possibly get to the real problem? I mean, don't get me wrong, I like Boston and all. There are some fine-looking women here. But I know you didn't come to micromanage Jacob or Cal. And since you've been ignoring a lot of calls and texts—which you never do—I have to assume that they're from Crystal. So . . . is there trouble in paradise?"

Sounding completely childish, Mark snapped, "If you weren't my cousin, I'd fire you so that you could torture someone else for a while."

"You say that at least once a week." Denny waved it off. "It's still hurtful, but the threat doesn't hold much water," he added with a smirk. "Now, what's the problem with your girlfriend? God, I can't believe I'm using the *G* word in relation to a woman in your life."

Mark listened to him rattle on about the shock of him actually seeing someone for more than a few hours. He had to give the man credit, though: even as shitty as his current mood was, he was fighting a smile by the time Denny ran out of steam. Then he found himself opening his mouth and saying more than he'd planned. "I found out that Crystal's been going to marriage counseling with her ex-husband while we've been together. And I had to learn this from my mother, while my dad looked at me in pity when it became obvious I didn't have a clue."

"Pardon?" Denny choked out. "Holy crap, that's creative even for them. You're not seriously buying into that, are you? They're probably just worried that you'll get married, pop out some kids, and not have enough money to support them."

"Oh, it's true enough." Mark grimaced. "They had Oliver use Craig at DeSanto to run a background check on Crystal." Her name felt strange on his tongue, and the lift of Denny's brow told him that he'd caught the fact that he hadn't called her "Angel" as he normally did.

"I'm guessing Craig is looking for another job this morning?" Denny asked, knowing how Mark would feel about an employee invading his privacy.

"Within an hour of their departure last night, Craig was fired," Mark confirmed. "I spoke to him, and he didn't bother to deny it. He admitted that he knew it was wrong, and he should have gone to his supervisor when the request was made. If I wanted to dig into the private life of the woman I'm seeing, I damn sure wouldn't have someone who worked for me do it. No doubt, that shit has probably already made the rounds by now."

Looking confused, Denny said, "Let's get back to Crystal. Have you asked her what's going on? Because I find it really hard to believe that she's trying to reconcile with her ex. That woman is crazy about you."

"You think so?" Mark asked before he could stop himself. Shit, he sounded like some lovesick teenager. Maybe he could send her a note asking if she liked him and ask her to check the box for yes or no.

"Hell yes, I do," Denny stated firmly. "What did she say when you asked her about it?"

Mark shifted uncomfortably in his seat before admitting, "I haven't talked to her about it yet."

Denny looked at him incredulously before putting both of his hands on the table as if to brace himself. "So let me get this straight. You found out about this last night. Freaked the fuck out. Packed your shit and left the state. Is that an accurate assessment?"

Suddenly becoming fascinated with his coffee cup, Mark stared into it while muttering, "Pretty close."

Denny gave a long, drawn-out sigh of disgust. "You're not too good at this whole relationship thing, are you?" When Mark started to protest, Denny held up a hand, stopping him. "I'll grant you, it does sound a touch . . . bad. But come on, this is Crystal—your Angel. You have sleepovers with her. You flitter with Mae West quotes. You took care of her for two days while she was barfing all over your house. For the love of God, man, you even cook for her. And after all that, you're sitting there with your tail tucked between your legs after fleeing town? Shit, come on! What happened to confrontation and fit throwing? You should have gone straight to her place last night and had a minirant before demanding some answers. Instead, you've done everything short of burying your phone in the sand to avoid speaking to her."

"I don't know how to do this," Mark murmured glumly. "I don't get involved with women beyond fucking. I've never had to deal with something like this. I need space to figure everything out, and that's what we're doing here now."

"All right." Denny surprised him by agreeing. "I can see how this would be difficult with you being a dating newborn. Possibly, it's even better that you decided on distance rather than saying something you might regret later. But you do need to let her know where you are. Taking off like that without any explanation, regardless of the circumstances, was kind of an asshole move."

Staring at Denny in bewilderment, Mark asked, "It's okay for her to be pursuing happily ever after with her ex and I'm supposed to keep her updated as to my whereabouts during the meantime? If that's the case, how does anyone ever get married and stay that way?"

Denny rubbed his temples before adopting a soothing tone. "That's not what I'm saying, cousin. Let her know that you're alive and out of town. Then, when you're ready, go home and talk to her." Snapping his fingers, he added, "Gray and Suzy's party is this weekend. Were you two planning to go together?"

"Yeah, of course." Mark shrugged, not understanding where this was going. Denny had picked up his phone and was typing out a text as if their conversation was over. "Were you making some kind of point that I missed?"

Denny looked up after a few more taps on his screen. "What? Oh, right. I was just letting the pilot know we're flying out Friday night. You'll go home and take Crystal to the party. You'll be polite and cordial to everyone— and not drain the positive energy from the event. Then afterward, you'll take her back to your place and have a rational conversation about what you've learned. She'll probably be pissed that you were checking up on her, and you'll have to deal with that."

By this point, his head was spinning. Rubbing the bridge of his nose, he snapped, "Don't you think maybe you should have consulted me before filing a flight plan? Plus, I'm not in the mood for a freaking party right now. And last, Angel's going to be the one pissed and not me?" The twitch of Denny's lips let him know that he'd slipped and gone back to Crystal's nickname.

Denny got to his feet and clapped Mark on the back. "Welcome to the wonderful world of dating—where no matter what they do, it's always your fault."

"Fuck me," Mark hissed as his assistant walked away.

Is eight in the morning too early for alcohol? Because I damn sure need it right about now.

Chapter Nineteen

Mark was due home today after his unexpected business trip, and she was beyond anxious to see him. He'd finally returned her call the afternoon following his departure, telling her briefly that Jacob needed his help in Boston and it had been a last-minute thing, which was why he hadn't called. When she'd tried questioning him about his parents' visit, he'd simply said that it was fine.

The whole call had sounded stiff and formal. She had been certain that he was trying to blow her off, so she'd been surprised when he'd confirmed their date for Suzy's gathering on Saturday night, saying he would meet her there.

Since then, he'd given brief responses when she texted, but she had been too uncertain about what was going on between them to call him again. She spent the rest of the week in a depressed funk, avoiding her friends and her meddling mother. Bill had made the mistake of calling an hour earlier to badger her about another counseling session and she'd let him have it. She'd told him in no uncertain terms that it was over, and that although she wished him well, she had moved on and he needed to do the same.

Of course, less than half an hour after that, her mother had started calling. There was no way that was a coincidence. Bill, the bastard, must have ratted her out. Before turning her phone off, she'd texted Mark just to make sure he knew that Suzy's party had been moved to Ella's house. There had been some severe storms in the area the last few nights and both Suzy and Claire had been dealing with some coastal flooding on their properties. Rather than trying to get everything cleaned up in time, Ella had volunteered her house since she and Declan had escaped the worst part of it.

She took one last look in the mirror and decided that she needed another coat of concealer. The dark circles under her eyes gave testament to the fact that she hadn't slept well while Mark had been away. Funny how she would often sneak away to the sofa or spare bedroom because she needed some personal space during her marriage to Bill, but with Mark, she'd slept practically wrapped around his hard body and had loved it. She'd done nothing but toss and turn without him.

After touching up her makeup, she made the drive to Ella's far too quickly. Traffic had been unusually light for a Saturday evening. She saw Mark's car almost immediately and gave a small prayer of thanks that he'd actually shown up. Taking a deep breath to calm her jittery nerves, she left the safety of her car and made her way to the door of her sister's home. *Everything's fine. He's a busy man, and this is probably normal behavior for him. Be cool and don't wrap yourself around his leg.* She repeated the same thought a few more times before opening the door and walking in.

Ella spotted her immediately and walked forward, looking strained. "I know I told you to ditch Bill, but did you have to do it today? Mother is driving me freaking crazy!" she whisper-hissed, before plastering a fake smile on for anyone looking at them.

"I know," Crystal murmured back. "She's probably bothering you because I turned my phone off. I couldn't deal with it today. I figure I'll give her some time to get past the initial shock before calling her back."

"It's probably going to take a while." Ella cringed before throwing an arm around her waist. "I'm proud of you for talking to Bill, though. It had to be done, and let's face it, there was never going to be a good time for it."

Changing the subject, Crystal asked, "So, if you're hosting this party now, then surely you've been let in what's going on?"

"Oh, come on." Ella rolled her eyes. "Do you think I could make Suzy do anything that she didn't want to?" Rubbing her hands together like a child, she rocked on her feet. "Plus, I love surprises! It wouldn't be very exciting if I found out ahead of time."

Ella's mouth continued to move, but Crystal had completely lost track of the conversation as she spotted Mark and Denny across the room chatting with Jason Danvers. "Oh God," she squeaked.

"What?" Ella asked, looking at her in confusion. When she didn't answer, her sister turned to see what she was looking at and said, "Oh, yeah, he got here a few minutes ago. Is he still acting weird?" She had confided in Ella on the second day that Mark was in Boston. It was not that she wanted to, but more that Ella was too good at sensing when something was bothering her. Apparently, she hadn't been able to hide her anxiety over Mark's behavior very well.

"Kind of." She nodded. "I don't know . . . maybe it's because of the visit from his parents. He's said that they're pretty bad, and I can certainly understand the need to pack your bags after an unpleasant encounter."

Still studying Mark, Ella asked, "So tell me, if this were a week ago, what would you do now?" At her baffled look, Ella added, "Would you be standing over here or would you be over there with him?" At her wistful look, she sighed. "That's what I thought. So go see your man. He's been out of town, and you don't even know that anything is wrong. Stop slumping and hiding in the doorway. Channel your inner Suzy and sashay right up to him."

"Did you just say . . . ?" Crystal smirked.

"Get your ass moving!" Ella huffed, putting a hand on her shoulders and giving a shove that was surprisingly strong. Crystal bobbled around like a drunken chicken for a minute, before catching herself and giving her sister an evil look.

"Oops, sorry." Ella winced before making a shooing motion.

By this point, almost everyone was looking at her. Mia was waving from within the circle of Seth Jackson's arms, while a hugely pregnant Gwen was looking back and forth between her and Mark as if watching a reality television show. Even Lydia was there and mouthing the name *Mr. Big*. Something about that cracked her up and made her move across the floor to Mark's side more easily. She was still smiling when she reached him. And then she saw it—he went noticeably stiff when she touched his arm, a split second before he relaxed. Dammit, what was going on? What had happened since the last time they'd been together? "Hey," she said brightly. Jason gave her a warm smile, while Denny seemed to be trying to communicate something with his eyes.

"It's good to see you again, Crystal," Jason said. He opened his mouth to say something else when Claire motioned to him from across the room. "Excuse me, the wife calls." He smiled ruefully as he walked away.

Right on his heels, Denny said, "I'm just going to go do—that thing." Once again, Denny shot her the same strange look before leaving.

"Geez, was it something I said?" she joked as she looked up into Mark's closed expression.

"Possibly it was more of what you left out," he added cryptically.

"What?" She stared at him in puzzlement.

"Crystal . . ." he began, before she cut him off.

"You're angry with me about something. Either that or you're breaking up with me. Because I don't remember a time when you've called me by my given name." Feeling herself on the verge of tears, she asked quietly, "Please tell me what's going on. I've been worried all week, and I don't want to continue being in the dark."

He had taken her hand and was leading her toward the double doors to the deck when a dinging sound had everyone looking toward the other side of the room. Mark bit off a curse and pulled them both to a halt.

"Thanks for coming this evening," Gray Merimon began with Suzy tucked into his side. "We do have some good news, but we also realize that there are those who aren't aware of the struggles that we've

THE ONE FOR ME   221

faced that have brought us to this point." He looked down briefly, giving his wife a tender look before clearing his throat and continuing. "Suzy and I have been trying to have a child for quite a while now."

Crystal could tell by the bright smiles in the crowd that most thought a pregnancy announcement was forthcoming. She wasn't so sure, though. There was something about the way they looked at each other that spoke of pain—and a lot of it. Gray's arm tightened around Suzy before adding, "But it's been a difficult road for us. We've tried medical intervention, only to suffer numerous miscarriages. After our last loss, we decided that we couldn't continue to put ourselves through that anymore." The women in the room were all teary-eyed as he dropped a kiss on Suzy's forehead before speaking again. "Then my amazing wife told me that she felt we were meant to go down a different road. I've long been in awe of the woman that I love, but her strength and conviction that day showed me that if I lived to be a thousand years old, I'd only have just enough time to scratch the surface of all that she is."

Crystal jerked as Mark pressed a napkin in her hand. She hadn't been aware that she was crying until that moment. She wiped her eyes and gave him a grateful smile when he put his arm around her for support. Regardless of what was going on between them, she snuggled into the strength he offered as Gray continued. "Sorry. I didn't mean to move the ladies to tears," he joked. "Declan, make sure you have the alcohol flowing as soon as I'm finished." Crystal's brother-in-law held his beer up in acknowledgment, causing Gray to chuckle. "Anyway, that's the history part. Now on to what we wanted to tell you all tonight. Suzy and I decided to build our family through adoption. We both felt that we had so much love to offer a child and at every point of the process, it felt right. As if we were finally doing what we were meant to all along."

Suzy suddenly stepped forward, wiping her eyes before throwing her hands in the air. "What Gray is trying to say is that it has happened for us! We're meeting our son soon!"

The room exploded into pandemonium. Crystal found herself jumping up and down as if she'd just won the lottery. "Oh, my God, did you hear that?" she beamed at Mark. "I'm so happy for them."

"It's wonderful," Mark agreed, looking just as thrilled as she felt. "I don't know Suzy that well, but Gray is a good guy. I had no idea that they'd been going through so much, though." Mark propelled them forward until they reached the other couple to offer their congratulations. He kept his hand on Crystal the entire time and she was beginning to think that whatever was wrong, it was going to be okay. Until she heard her sister's voice above the noise in the living room and looked over to see their mother standing in the foyer with her hands on her hips.

"Oh no," she breathed, hoping she was seeing things. But after blinking a few times to clear away the disastrous scene before her eyes, it didn't change.

"What's wrong?" Mark asked as she stopped abruptly as he was attempting to lead her away from the crowd.

"I—um, need to go help Ella for a moment," she stuttered as she tried to pull her hand away.

Mark looked around, before zeroing in on her sister. "Who's Ella arguing with?"

"It's our mother," she said with forced cheerfulness. "I just need a second to see . . ."

Crystal got no further. Mark was now in the lead and pulling her toward her now-gawking mother. "Mrs. Webber, I've heard a lot about you," he said in a voice that was pure ice. The fact that he didn't offer his hand also indicated his lack of friendliness toward the woman staring back.

"Who, pray tell, are you?" Dot Webber sniffed. "And why are you holding my daughter's hand? That's not appropriate at all, young man."

"Mother," Crystal said warningly.

Without missing a beat, Mark piped in, "My name is Mark DeSanto, and I'm involved with Crystal— which would be why I'm touching her."

Her mother's face bloomed red so suddenly that it was fascinating to watch—until she opened her mouth. "Well, doesn't this just explain so much!" Turning to Crystal she said, "I swear, girl, you've been difficult since the day you were born. There's a troublemaker in every family, and Lord knows you're ours."

"Mother," Ella gasped, looking horrified. Crystal had heard some version of that same theme so many times; it had almost lost its power to hurt her anymore—but not quite.

"Ella, you always were a bleeding heart. Your sister's a bad seed. I mean, just look at how she's been leading poor Bill on by going to marriage counseling with him one day," then, pointing at Mark, she added, "and fornicating with this guy the next. It's not the behavior of a lady and certainly not a Webber."

Crystal could feel the blood drain from her face as her eyes flew to Mark's. Oh no . . . he looked beyond furious, but strangely enough, not surprised. How could that be? Maybe all of her mother's malicious statement hadn't registered with him yet. "That's enough!" His hiss came out like a clap of thunder, causing the three of them to jerk. A vein throbbed visibly on his forehead as he asked, "What's wrong with you? You come to your daughter's house, uninvited I'm guessing, and then proceed to tear your other daughter to shreds in front of guests? And you've appointed yourself judge and jury of moral conduct. Clue the fuck in, lady. Before you pass judgment on someone, take a long look in the mirror."

"What's going on here?" Declan asked as he walked up.

"Mrs. Webber was just leaving," Mark answered, giving Declan a hard look. It seemed that volumes were spoken between the two men as Declan's lips thinned.

He turned to his wife, asking, "Are you okay, Ellie?"

Ella gave him a slight shake of her head before surprising them all by saying, "Yes, Mother is leaving. Could you walk her out, honey?"

Crystal stood frozen to her spot as a sputtering Dot Webber was escorted gently but firmly from the foyer and out the door. She looked over her shoulder to see everyone attempting to look like they weren't riveted by what had just taken place. "I'm so sorry, Crys," Ella whispered as she wiped a tear from her cheek. "I can't even make excuses for her anymore because there are none."

Declan walked back in, looking irritated. "I swear to God, that woman is fucking insane. What did she do this time?"

Crystal sent Ella a pleading look, not wanting to get into it again. The damage had already been done tonight, and she just wanted to go home and enjoy one hell of a pity party. Her sister turned to her husband and lightly patted his arm. "We'll talk about it later, babe. Let's go make sure everyone has enough to eat and drink."

Declan gave Crystal a concerned look as if noticing her pallor. "You all right, sweetheart?" he asked before dropping a kiss on her cheek.

"Sure," Crystal managed to get out past the lump in her throat. "It's been a long day, though, so I'm going to head home now. Please give my congratulations to Suzy and Gray again."

"Let me get my keys and I'll take you," Declan offered, already walking away to collect what he needed. Her brother-in-law was such an amazing man.

"I've got her, Dec," Mark spoke up, still sounding tense from the earlier scene. *This is probably the last thing he needed tonight,* Crystal thought, after having to deal with his own parents just days earlier. "We'll take her car. If you'll just tell Denny to go on home when he's ready . . ."

"Sure thing, man," Declan agreed easily.

Ella gave her a hug, whispering in her ear, "Call me later. I love you."

In another few moments, they were out the door and Mark was helping her into the passenger seat of her Volkswagen Beetle. Then he gave her what she was in desperate need of—laughter. Just watching him trying to fold his tall frame into her tiny car was hilarious. And when he finally managed to get in and close the door, his eyes fell on the built-in vase with the bright flowers inside of it and the look of astonishment he gave her was comical. When he reached out to touch it, she started giggling so hard she could barely remain upright. "Did you put that there?" he asked, studying the floral arrangement as if it were a science experiment.

"It came with the car," she managed to wheeze.

He looked around him for another moment before putting the key in the ignition. "I can't see a man ever buying one of these. I'm going to have to turn in my man card after driving the damn thing home."

"Ah, come on," she teased. "Aren't you secure enough in your masculinity to handle a small vehicle? Your Porsche is about the same size."

"Angel, a Porsche is all testosterone. This—whatever it is—is strictly for those with a vagina."

He teased her about her beloved Beetle for the five minutes it took to get to his house. Despite the ugly scene with her mother, she found herself able to relax for the first time in days. He'd brought her here instead of taking her home. Obviously, he hadn't caught the part in her mother's rant about Bill. She had to tell him, though, before something that was essentially inno-cent was blown out of proportion.

Mark parked the car and then took one last look at the flower vase before shaking his head and getting out. He walked to her side, opening her door and holding out a hand to her. He didn't release his hold on her as he punched in some numbers on the garage keypad, raising the door so that they could walk through and access the kitchen entrance. He led her to a barstool, then took a bottle of amber-colored liquor from the cabinet and poured generous measures into two glasses. He pushed one of them in front of her, saying, "I believe this evening calls for something more than wine."

She took a tentative sip and felt like her throat was flaming. She gasped as she tried to breathe. Mark chuckled while tapping her on the back. "Holy crap," she croaked. "What is this stuff? Gasoline?"

"That's scotch, Angel—the good stuff. Now be a good girl and drink up." She had just taken another sip when he added, "Because when you're finished, we're going to discuss the fact that you've been seeing a marriage counselor with your ex-husband one day and riding my cock the next."

That was all it took; she spit the fiery liquid across the granite countertop, with some of it splattering the front of Mark's suit. "I—you . . . heard," she blurted out before stopping abruptly. God, that didn't sound good at all. Instead of her knee-jerk reaction, it might have been a better idea to play dumb, at least until she'd collected her wits enough to have a rational discussion.

"I already knew, Angel," he said flatly.

"You did?" She gaped up at him. Shit, she just kept making this worse on herself.

He removed his now-damp suit jacket and tie, draping them over one of the spare stools. Then he settled across from her. When she remained quiet, he rubbed the bridge of his nose. "My parents told me about it on their surprise visit this week."

She couldn't have heard him correctly. How could

his parents possibly know what she did in her private life? "Could you repeat that?" she asked, unable to make sense of anything at this point.

He sighed. "When my parents showed up, it was to nose into my personal life. Apparently, it had trickled down the family grapevine that I was seeing a woman. Since it's . . . unusual, they felt the need to invade not only my privacy, but yours as well. During the course of that, they ran across the fact that you were divorced but appeared to be on the verge of reconciling with your husband. Or at least your recent trip to a marriage counselor seemed to suggest that."

"Oh, my God," Crystal gasped, before jumping to her feet. "They told you that?" When he nodded, she put her hands in her hair, more embarrassed than she'd probably ever been in her life—and that was saying something. What kind of person must they think she was to be dating their son while trying to get back together with her husband? *A harlot, that's what they think. Probably the gold-digging variety, no less.* As she paced the kitchen, she muttered to herself, "Their son finally has a girlfriend, and she's a bona fide tramp. Boy, that's just something you want to put on your family newsletter and holiday cards. Oh look, here's Mark and his slut of a lady friend. They're very happy together—when she's not dating her ex-husband." Crystal paused in her rant when it registered that Mark was laughing so hard he was shaking. "What in the world do you find so funny?" she yelled. "This is a disaster of epic proportions, and you're amused?"

He held up a finger as if asking for one second while he fought to control his mirth. "Sorry, Angel," he managed to get out. She stood with her hands on her hips, glaring, which didn't seem to faze him at all. He got up and walked to where she was standing and slid an arm around her waist, pulling her into his arms. She stood stiffly before letting out a huff and melting into his embrace. "I'm sorry they did that to you, Angel, and I promise that it's been dealt with. But you do owe me an explanation, don't you think?"

"You're right. I do," she answered quietly. "Can we go in the living room and sit down?" Instead of answering, he tucked her under his shoulder and they walked down the hallway together before he dropped down to the sofa and pulled her into a similar position.

"Now, what's going on?" he asked, not sounding angry, but rather determined.

"This is why you took off without telling me, isn't it?" she asked, already knowing the answer.

"That's correct," he replied, without hesitation. "I was pissed and uncertain as to how to handle it. It seemed better that I take the adult version of a time-out, so to speak, than stay here and say something stupid."

"We'll get back to that in a moment," she said before telling him exactly why she had agreed to attend the first counseling session with Bill. He remained quiet, letting her talk until she reached the part of her telling her ex-husband that she wouldn't be accompanying him again and that she wished him well.

"So that's what brought on the visit from your mother this evening?" he guessed correctly.

"Yep. I wasn't taking her calls, so she must have decided to corner her other daughter, probably in hopes that I was there hiding from her. Most people might have left it for another day when they saw a driveway full of strange cars, but not my mother. She's not shy at all about causing a scene, as you witnessed firsthand."

Mark dropped his head back, looking up at the ceiling. "Even after everything you told me about her, I still never expected her to be as bad as she was. I may have joked about it before, but she truly is the female version of my father, and you have no idea how much I hate that for you, Angel."

Crystal stroked a hand up and down his chest, enjoying being close to him once again. "It's not a good feeling to know that I'll probably never have many peaceful moments in my life because of her. Sometimes I wonder if I'll eventually just crack under the pressure of it all."

His arm around her had tensed before relaxing once again. "You're stronger than that, baby. Your mother is a bully and needs to be put in her place."

Looking up at his handsome face, she quirked a brow in wry amusement. "And how's that working out for you with your father?"

"Touché." He winced. "Possibly, this is one of those instances when you need to do as I say and not as I do. Believe me, I know how hard it is, Angel. I've lived it for most of my life. And I don't want that for you."

Allowing her hand to slide downward until it reached the bulge behind his zipper, she lowered her voice and told him, "What I want is to not think of parents at all for the rest of the night. I've missed you so much."

"Fuck, I've missed you too," he hissed when she

unbuckled his belt, before dealing with the fastening and zipper on his pants. He was already semihard when she lowered the material of his boxer briefs, releasing his heavy weight. "Angel," Mark shuddered, thrusting his hips upward to meet her stroking touch.

His mind was still on everything that had happened earlier at Ella's, but his body was firmly aligned with Angel. When she wrapped her plump lips around his cock, a groan escaped his throat. He threaded a hand through her hair, guiding her wet mouth up and down his length. "Fuck yeah, baby," he moaned. "Relax your throat and take it all." She gagged as she attempted to go too far. The vibrations were enough to nearly make him lose his load far too soon. It took her a few more attempts, but then she was working him exactly the way he needed. "That's right, Angel," he praised. "You feel so goddamn good."

His balls tightened and his spine tingled, proof that he was close. He tried to pull back, not wanting to catch her by surprise. "No," she mumbled around his cock and took him in farther. That was it for him. He was coming and powerless to stop. He only hoped she would push him away before she suffocated on his cum.

Instead, she took everything that he gave her and sucked him dry. "Angel." He found himself begging for mercy. "Baby, stop before I pass out."

As spent as he was, when she sat back on her knees and licked her lips, he felt his dick twitch. Then he lost his heart to her when she gave him a saucy smile and asked, "Good, right?" At this defining moment, he knew he was in love for the first time in his life. Most men were probably prone to some fuzzy thoughts after a blow job, but an outstanding one was enough to make the biggest of bastards sentimental. Since none of those had ever applied to him, he knew this was different. He could easily picture himself having moments such as this with her for the rest of his life, which was the real confirmation that she was different. "It was amazing," he agreed as he stroked her cheek. He stood, pulling his pants up so that he wouldn't trip over them, before extending a hand to her. "Come on, baby; let's go to bed." She allowed him to lead her down the hallway and into his darkened bedroom. He left her at the doorway while he walked across the room and turned on a bedside lamp. Then he quickly stripped and took a seat at the foot of the bed. She looked at him uncertainly as if awaiting his instructions. *Good girl.* "Do you need my help taking your dress off?"

She shook her head, saying quietly, "No."

He palmed his rapidly hardening cock, stroking it from tip to root lightly as he said, "Remove it—now." She only hesitated briefly before bending to grip the hem of her dress and pulling it slowly over her head. Before she could release the material from her hands, he said, "Now place it on the chair close to you."

"Yes . . . ," she replied.

Mark had a feeling that it was on the tip of her tongue to add "sir," but she didn't. Thank Christ, because he wasn't sure how he would have handled it. The urge to dominate her was already overwhelming, and she wasn't ready for that. Something about her demeanor told him that she wouldn't be averse to it, but to him, she wasn't like the others. He'd never been a tender lover, but with her, that was his first inclination. He could far too easily imagine a life where they could both express themselves sexually, secure in the unconditional acceptance that their love for each other would bring.

"Take your bra off for me." Again, without question, she flicked the clasp between her breasts and released it before putting it on top of her dress. He continued to pull on his cock, content to watch as she bared herself to him. "Now the panties, beautiful girl," he directed. She was absolutely gorgeous as she shimmied out of a scrap of lace and added it to the pile. A look of surprise flashed across her face when he pointed to the other chair and said, "Now have a seat. Spread your legs and put them over each armrest." Again, she barely faltered before doing as he instructed.

When she parted her thighs, revealing her neatly trimmed sex, Mark felt his renowned control beginning to slip. While he was attempting to regroup, she asked shyly, "Now what?"

Now I come in my hand like an inexperienced teenager, he thought dryly. Clearing his throat, he said huskily, "Touch yourself, baby. Show me what you do when you're alone."

He almost choked on his tongue when she looked around and asked, "Do you—um, have a vibrator?"

Sweet heaven. Count to ten . . . do anything but focus on the visual of what she's implying. "I—not at the present, Angel," he wheezed. "Make do without it."

She shrugged her shoulders and then dropped a hand between her legs. She began circling her clit as if she had all the time in the world. His cock was so hard by this point, it could be used as a fucking battering ram. He squeezed the tip and attempted to blank his mind. Not easily done when Angel was sitting just feet away with a finger now buried in her wet heat. "Mark," she moaned as her motions went from languid to feverish.

She was close—almost at the edge. "Keep your eyes open and on me, Angel," he called out, bringing her head up immediately. She was magnificent. She embraced her sexuality in a way that made him weak with desire. She was his perfect match. She made him a better version of himself, and he gave her the freedom to shine in a way that she had always been denied.

Never looking away from him, she thrust two fingers deep into her channel and her body clenched. He could smell her arousal as she came by her own hand while chanting, "Mark . . . Oh God, Mark . . ."

Her words were his undoing. Taking her slowly at first never seemed to be an option. The edge had to be taken off before he could take his time and make love to her. He didn't even bother to tell himself tonight that it was anything other than that. If it were, she would have been long gone like the women he had known before her. "Come to me, Angel," he demanded softly. He watched as she rose to her feet before moving gracefully across the dimly lit room, stopping just inches from him. He reached for the hand that she had so recently pleasured herself with and sucked the two fingers he knew she had used into his mouth. He couldn't get enough of her sweet, musky flavor. He licked until nothing remained before releasing her digits. He raised his arms to encircle her waist, and then surprised them both by laying his head on her stomach.

After a moment, he felt her fingers run through his hair, stroking him gently.

"I love pleasing you," she murmured as she continued to touch him. He kept his face averted for a bit longer, not wanting her to see how deeply her words affected him. He had employees all over the world that he paid to do his bidding. But, other than maybe Denny, when had anyone ever wanted to do something for him out of the goodness of their heart? Sure, he knew she was talking about something sexual at this moment, but in the short time that they had been together, she was constantly doing thoughtful things. When she found out in an earlier conversation that he loved Mallo Cups, from that point forward, she always stopped on her way to his house and bought him a pack. And even though he had a housekeeper and used a dry cleaner for his suits, she still insisted on washing his other clothing and putting it away when she stayed over. Angel, he'd learned, was the nurturing type, and he'd been surprised to find that he liked it.

She gripped his head, tugging back until she was looking at him in question. "Yeah, baby," he agreed. "I'm all yours." She gave him a grin before motioning him backward against the headboard. When he settled there, she climbed on the bed and encircled his cock with one hand. She positioned him at her entrance and lowered herself onto him inch by inch. "Fuck," he hissed, feeling his eyes roll back in his head. He fought the urge to thrust upward, not wanting to give her too much, too soon. Instead, he let her set the pace, gritting his teeth until she was finally snug against his root.

"I need you to move, Angel," he grunted, digging his fingers into her hips to help her upward movement.

She let him guide her hips, while she gripped the headboard to propel herself up and down. "So good . . ." she cried out as he bumped against her cervix on each thrust.

"Not gonna last for long, baby," he warned as he tried to hold off long enough for her to come first. He moved one hand from her hip and circled his thumb around her clit. That was all it took. Within seconds, spasms shook her body as she came. He was unable to stop himself from following closely behind as she milked his cock of everything he had. Then it hit him like a bolt of lightning. He stiffened as she slumped against him. "Angel," he said urgently. "Shit, baby, I didn't wear a condom." He couldn't believe it. He'd never had intercourse in his life without protection. He'd never been in a committed relationship, so the issue hadn't come up. A few women had assured him that they were clean and on the pill, but he wasn't ever tempted to risk it.

"I'm on the pill," she mumbled from her position on his shoulder. Then, with him still inside her, she curled even closer, and he could have sworn he heard a light snore beside him.

Shaking her slumbering body lightly, he asked, "Since when?" He knew when they first started dating that she wasn't on anything, or at least that was what she'd said.

"A couple of weeks ago. I was going to surprise you," she whispered before adding, "Oh—surprise."

He relaxed, breathing a sigh of relief. It rattled him

that he'd forgotten something that he'd always considered so vitally important. But luckily, Angel at least had been thinking ahead. And God had it felt amazing being inside of her bare. He'd known while he was sliding in and out of her that it was somehow impossibly better than ever, and now he knew why. Skin on skin. Unbelievable.

Mark enjoyed their closeness for another few moments before he lifted her from his body so that he could go to the bathroom. He washed up and then brought a cloth to take care of her. She didn't even stir while he cleaned between her legs. When he got back in the bed and wrapped his arms around her, she snuggled into his hold with a murmur of approval before going still once again.

He wanted to go over what had happened tonight in his mind but found that he didn't have the energy. Tomorrow would be soon enough to figure out the next step. Tonight he just wanted to hold his Angel and believe that he was the type of man who ended up with a woman like her.

Chapter Twenty

As Crystal flitted around his kitchen making pancakes, Mark relaxed at the bar reading the paper and sipping his coffee. Finally, he gave up on trying to focus on the news and simply watched her. She was wearing one of his T-shirts and had her hair up in a ponytail. Her face was freshly scrubbed, and she could have passed for years younger. When she flipped a pancake in the air and managed to catch it neatly in the pan, she turned to him with glee as if wanting to share her accomplishment with him. "Good job, Angel," he praised, bringing a soft flush to her cheeks.

After another ten minutes, she was finished and settling in beside him on a barstool. He put his arm around her shoulders and they ate their breakfast nestled against each other. Again, he had the feeling that he would be content to do this for the rest of his life. He was firmly in that fantasyland when his doorbell rang. The garage door was already open since he'd walked down the driveway to retrieve the paper earlier, and the knock that followed the bell came from that direction. "Are you expecting anyone?" Crystal asked, still looking relaxed. "I'll just go to the bedroom and change before you open the door."

"Baby, you're fine," Mark assured her. His shirt practically reached her knees, which was about the length of the dresses that she normally wore. "It's probably either Denny or, God forbid, someone selling something. Although that doesn't usually happen on Sundays."

"Maybe you're being recruited for the church." She giggled.

Mark gave her a mock scowl as he walked toward the door. "We're going to talk later about why you think that idea is so funny, Angel," he warned as he slung open the door without bothering to check the peephole first.

Crystal was still laughing over his threat when he felt his first jolt of alarm. For the second time in mere days, his parents stood facing him. Visiting him at home was so unlike them that he could only blink for a few moments as he attempted to regain his composure. "Good morning, son," his mother said brightly, but again there was a hint of apology in her expression before she motioned for him to invite her inside.

He stayed where he was, blocking their entry into his home. "This isn't a good time," he stated firmly. "I had no idea you were back in town, so I'll have to call you later and arrange another time."

"We never left," his father spoke up, already sounding well on his way to being intoxicated at ten in the morning. "I'm sure you can spare us a few moments. We wanted to follow up on what we were discussing on our last visit."

His mother turned to his father and put a hand on his chest. "Honey, let's go have breakfast and let Mark finish with whatever he's in the middle of. It was rude of us to barge in on him. We should have called first."

His father snorted his disdain. "He's not some business associate, Celine. He's our son. I don't think we need to make an appointment to talk to him."

Then at the worst possible moment, Mark felt a hand on his back as Crystal asked in a voice filled with concern, "Is everything okay?" He shut his eyes briefly, hoping his parents hadn't heard her, but luck wasn't on his side at all.

"Who do we have here?" his father asked as he pushed his way closer.

"Um—hi, I'm Crystal," she stammered, looking taken aback by his father's loud demeanor.

Instead of taking the hand that Crystal had hesitantly extended, his father let out a startled oath before bellowing, "Are you kidding me?" His eyes were drilling Crystal to her spot, but his words were directed at Mark when he snapped, "After all that we told you about her, she's still around? And from the looks of things, she's damn comfortable in your home. What're you planning to do, let both her and her husband live with you after they reconcile?"

His mother and Crystal both gasped simultaneously. "Marcus, that's enough," his mother hissed, looking appalled. "This isn't what we came here for."

"It's exactly why we're here," his father insisted. "Do you want to see some moneygrubbing tramp take *your* son to the cleaners, Celine? Because that's what going to happen unless we intervene. He plainly can't see the forest for the trees."

"Get out *now*," Mark boomed. He knew by the way that her hand shook against his back that he had startled Crystal with his forceful tone. His parents also appeared to be shocked by his command. Good, maybe he finally had their attention. "You have no right to come to my home and speak to or about Crystal in that manner. Besides the fact that you don't know what in the hell you're talking about, it's just downright rude. I don't think I've ever been more embarrassed to say you're my parents than right now—and believe me, that's saying something."

His father's chest puffed out as he snapped, "Well, I don't have to stand here and take this from you."

Throwing his hands in the air, Mark said, "No, and please don't. Leave now before this gets even more out of hand." His father was sputtering insults and in general blustering about everything he could toss out. His mother, for probably the first time in his life, looked disgusted at her husband's behavior and maybe just a little fed up. Was it possible that the rose-colored glasses were finally off and Celine DeSanto didn't like what she was seeing?

"I'm leaving now, Marcus, and so are you," she stated firmly. Turning back to Mark, she added softly, "I'm sorry, son. We shouldn't have come." Then her gaze moved beyond him to Crystal. "It was nice to have met you, dear, and I apologize for both my husband and myself." Crystal murmured something in reply that he couldn't make out, but it brought a brief smile to his mother's face before she grabbed her husband's arm firmly and all but dragged him away from the door and down the driveway.

Mark shut and locked the door behind them, then turned to check on Angel. What he saw there made his gut clench in despair. Her violet eyes looked impossibly large in her pale face. Her body still trembled in reaction to the verbal assault from his asshole of a father. Mark wanted to go after the man who had sired him and kick his ass for upsetting her in this way. He'd gotten far too used to dealing with the drunken tantrums, but obviously, even with her shrewish mother, Angel still wasn't accustomed to such ugliness from strangers. Fuck, he was angry and embarrassed. "I'm sorry, baby," he said against the top of her head as he pulled her into his arms. "I had no idea they were still in town."

"Aren't I just the popular one this week," she joked weakly against his chest. "First my mother and now your parents. Maybe we should introduce them; I think they'd have a lot in common."

He chuckled lightly at her attempt at humor, but his heart wasn't in it and from the sound of her voice, neither was hers. She'd been the victim of far too many angry words in the last twenty-four hours. None of which she'd deserved. She'd attended marriage counseling with her ex-husband because she was a nice person and he was hurting. Not the best idea, but that was the type of caring person she was. And for that, her mother had ripped into her in public for not being the malleable puppet that she wanted her to be. Now his own parents had joined the fray on the premise that he needed to be protected from a money-grubber.

What a joke. The only thing his father was afraid of was that there would be another person with a claim to the DeSanto money or, hell, even more if he had children. "Ah, Angel, I'm sorry that I don't bring anything better to the table than what you've already got. I've never given much thought to it beyond the usual misery, but right now I really wish I had better to offer you in that area."

She hugged him to her tightly. "It's not your fault." She still looked ashen when she pulled back. "Do you mind if I go lie down for a while? I woke up with a bit of a headache, and it's still bothering me." He knew she was lying by the way her eyes shifted to the side. She needed space and some time to regroup. She'd probably actually like to go home but didn't want him to feel worse than he already did.

"Sure, baby," he agreed. "Go on in and I'll bring you some Tylenol and water in a few moments, okay?" He had dropped a kiss on her upturned mouth before she walked down the hallway and out of sight.

When she was gone, he sank down onto a barstool and ran a hand over the stiff muscles in his neck. He was feeling pissed off and helpless. Why couldn't anything ever be simple? The usual meet-a-girl-and-fall-in-love scenario didn't seem to matter here. Instead, the woman whom he adored had a bitch of a mother intent on tearing her down at every opportunity. Mark was a big boy and figured he could handle that. But then toss his own parents into the mix, also intent on making his woman miserable, and you had a lynch mob of sorts. He'd gotten pretty good at blocking them out or pretending they didn't exist, but now it wasn't just him. Sure, he could go on the attack. They might even back off for a while afterward, but there was one thing he'd learned through the years—that didn't last for long. It was amazing how resilient the mean bullies of the world were. He wished that everyone could bounce back from discord that quickly and easily.

His Angel was a sweet, kind, and loving woman who'd already had to deal with a hostile mother and possibly a manipulative ex-husband for years. Was it fair to ask her to continue that trend with him? If there was one thing he knew about his father, it was the fact that he was like a bloodhound when he was obsessed with something. And right now, he feared that Angel was the object of that fixation. Mark couldn't be sure that he would always be there to put a buffer between them, and he didn't want to think of her as she was right now: wounded over thoughtless words from a man who drank too much and cared too little. How much peace would she ever have if they remained together? As much as it tore him apart inside to admit, he was very much afraid that he loved her enough to let her go. He had nothing more to offer her than himself and how much would that mean after a few more run-ins with his father? Where would she escape to for sanctuary after a nasty encounter with her mother? To his house, where she would be nervous every time the doorbell rang? Goddammit to hell.

It looked as if this would be the one time that he walked away and left his heart behind, along with any future happiness that he had dared to envision. If love was the subject of so many fairy tales, then why did it fucking hurt so much?

*   *   *

Crystal curled up in the soft sheets of Mark's bed. She'd chosen his side so she could smell his scent on the pillow she'd pulled in close to her. He'd been in just a few moments earlier to bring her the promised pain relievers. Not that she actually needed them. She'd made up the headache excuse to get a few moments to feel sorry for herself. The horror she'd felt over having the parents of the man that she loved thinking she was trash was devastating.

Even with her mother constantly putting her down, she'd never actually thought of herself as not good enough for someone she cared about. Possibly not the best daughter or even wife, but never inferior to others. She considered herself an average woman who dressed nicely enough and worked hard to support herself. It was quite obvious that those were not qualities admired by the DeSantos. Instead, she'd been labeled as a tramp who was out to deceive Mark into allowing her access to his money and his bed. She'd read stuff like that in novels but never thought she'd encounter it in real life. It hadn't been an issue with Bill because they were both of similar upbringings.

Mark came from money and a different set of circumstances from anything she'd ever known. Of course, he had an amazing house and cars that she was certain cost a lot of money. But he'd never made her feel as if he was better than her because of it. She had found him to be very levelheaded and . . . normal. He cooked when the situation called for it, he cleaned up after himself, and yes, he had a driver, but in his defense, he spent a lot of his travel time working. She'd

also heard Denny mention the company plane, but
again, that was to be expected of a man in his position.
He owned a company and had to travel sometimes at
the last minute. He didn't lord it over her and brag
about the riches that were available to him. He was
just Mark, the man who made her feel better than she
ever had about herself. The man who called her "Angel"
and treated her like one.

His parents, though—that was a different story.
He'd told her that his father would make her mother
look nice, but she hadn't actually believed it until
today. Marcus DeSanto was a nasty piece of business.
She wasn't as certain about his wife. Celine DeSanto
had tried to defuse the situation and had apologized
for her husband. Then she'd literally hauled him away.
From the conversations Crystal had had with Mark,
she didn't think that was a usual occurrence. Maybe
Marcus had even gone so far this time as to have
embarrassed his wife.

She'd always thought that the disdain her mother
showed her was an isolated incident. Bill's parents,
while being aloof and rather cold, had never been ugly.
She didn't get the sense from them that they were disappointed that he'd married her. She didn't think it
really mattered much to them either way. And they'd
never been insulting over anything—even the divorce.

Looking back, Crystal realized now that she had
loved the idea of escaping her mother more than she'd
actually loved Bill when she got married. For years,
that had been enough for her. She'd been content to
take the scraps of affection he'd tossed her way because
it was preferable to being at home and constantly

criticized by her mother. It had also been one of the first times in her life that her mother had seemed almost proud of her. Or at the very least, she hadn't been as disappointed. But when Ella and Declan had shown her what true love actually looked like, that had been the end of that happy bubble. She'd wanted Bill to be more like Declan—which hadn't worked at all. And in truth, it wasn't really his place to change. He had stayed exactly the man she'd married. If anything, he had more right to argue that she wasn't the woman he'd married.

Poor Bill. Even though she was a bit pissed that he'd run straight to her mother over her quitting the counseling sessions, she couldn't really hate him for it. He'd been reeling since she'd asked for a divorce, and he had yet to recover. She didn't think it was because he was heartbroken as much as he was struggling to adjust to the change in his life. He couldn't fathom why she was suddenly not content to be his wife. She'd been truthful when she'd told him the day she left him that they both needed to be free to find what they were looking for. When he did finally move on, she sincerely hoped he would meet the one for him—because it wasn't her. That had never been clearer to her than it was now. After being with Mark, she couldn't go back to settling again for less than what she needed. She knew what true passion, desire, and—God help her—love felt like. It was a fire that consumed you. It took your very worst parts and made them into something new—better than you had ever been before. The fire burned so brightly, you wondered if you'd survive the flames. And rolled up within all of those exhilarating feelings was the counterbalance of peace. Just a feeling of knowing that you'd found the ultimate connection. The one that would spin you higher than you'd ever been before and then be waiting to catch you as you came down.

With these thoughts racing through her head, Crystal pushed the cover back and slid from Mark's bed. Even at her worst moments, she'd never been the type to hide away from the world, and this wasn't the time to start. She quickly splashed some water on her face in the bathroom before running a brush through her hair. Then she went in search of Mark.

She had almost given up and was going to get her phone to call him when she noticed someone sitting on the back deck facing the beach. She halted and turned that way, silently opening the door and walking barefoot across the warm wood to where he was seated. She ran a hand over his shoulder, letting him know she was there, before saying softly, "I was wondering where you were. I couldn't find you."

He reached back, capturing her fingers in his and pulling her around to sit on his lap. She cuddled closer to him, and for a while, they were content to watch the waves crash against the shore. In the distance, she could see people on the sand enjoying the warm day, but strangely enough, it still seemed as if they were in their own private world. "Feeling better, Angel?" he finally asked against her ear, causing her to shiver.

"Yeah, I'm good." She smiled. "Nothing an hour in the DeStudo bed couldn't take care of."

He snorted, squeezing her lightly before relaxing his grip. Then he began speaking and by the end of what he had to say, she realized that she'd never really known what true fear was until that moment. "My parents weren't that different from the ones that my friends had growing up. They weren't like the ones on television shows, but they were all I knew, so I adjusted to their quirks pretty early on in life. Then I started spending a lot of time with Denny, and things were different at his house. He had a mother who did all of her own cooking and cleaning. Plus, she actually enjoyed having us around. His father was quiet and worked long hours at the auto shop he owned, but he was never too tired to toss around a baseball or spend time teasing us about some girl we liked. The funny thing, as we got older, I liked staying at Denny's because his parents cared, even though it came with rules, and he liked staying at my house because mine didn't give a damn where we went or how late we stayed out. I could have a party most anytime I wanted to because they either weren't around or didn't care if we used the pool house."

"So each of you wanted what the other had?" Crystal asked when Mark paused to gather his thoughts.

"Yes, for a while, that was exactly it. Then, as my father started to drink more and more and the arguments between him and I ramped up, Denny gained a new appreciation for what he had at home. By the time we were eighteen, he avoided my house about as much as I did. That saying that you need to be a drunk to live with one is very true. Other than my mother, no one wanted to be around my dad when he was intoxicated. I've even blamed her through the years, thinking if she'd just get fed up enough to force him to get help, maybe he would change—or at least want to. But she's always been right there, his enabler. I guess I should admire her unconditional love, but who is that helping? It's certainly not good for him, and I can't see how it can be for her either."

"She seemed as if she wasn't happy about it earlier," Crystal pointed out. "She forced him to leave when he clearly wasn't ready to."

Mark nodded. "That was unusual. It did prove what I've long believed. She could so easily bend him to her will if only she would try. But I dare not hope that today was anything more than a momentary lapse in patience on her part. Celine has always been a permanent fixture in Team Marcus's camp, and I don't see that changing."

"I'm sorry, honey," Crystal stated honestly. Her heart broke for him. She, better than anyone, understood the kind of pain dealing with a foul parent could bring, and the fact that his father was also an alcoholic brought a whole different element to the equation for him. It made her shudder to think of how bad her own mother might be if she were drinking as well. The term *hell on wheels* would certainly apply.

He fitted his hand to hers before weaving their fingers together. He watched the act as if fascinated by it. "My father has been angry with me for years because my grandfather left his company in my hands. It wasn't because he loved me more, it was simply because he didn't want to see the family fortune or reputation go down the toilet because my father couldn't stay away from booze. Since then, my father goes to the main headquarters every so often and makes an ass out of himself until he has my attention.

It makes him feel powerful to jerk my chain because he knows I'll come to save my employees from dealing with him. It's been the same for so long that it's almost part of my regular routine now. I'll go to Charleston, pretend we're one big happy family, and then I'll have a short reprieve before we do it all over again. It's my life, Angel, just as your mother's behavior is in yours."

"I know," she agreed. "And you're right; it does become somewhat routine after a while. It doesn't mean that it's any easier to deal with, though, does it?"

"No, baby, it doesn't," he sighed. "Which is why I can't do this to you anymore. I saw what it did to you last night to have your mother say those things to you. Then you had but a few hours to recover before my parents were in your face saying even worse. I would have had to be blind this morning not to have noticed how much that hurt you. I may be able to shrug off the ugliness and go on, but I can't ask or expect you to do the same."

In a voice thick with panic, she croaked, "Mark, what are you saying?"

Instead of shying away, he faced her fully. His eyes were sad, but there was also a determination there that scared her to death. "You're such a beautiful person, Angel—both inside and out. And I feel more for you than I could have ever imagined. If I didn't, we wouldn't be having this conversation. But I do, and I can't let someone who I care so much for suffer because of me. And that's what it would be. I can threaten and lay down the law at every turn with my parents, but eventually they'll manage to get you alone and unload some more vile accusations on you. With me, you'll never get away from that. You'll bounce back and forth from one bad situation to another. Eventually, you'll grow to hate me for doing that to you, and that would kill me, baby."

With tears rolling down her cheeks, she cupped his face as she shook her head. "No—baby, no. I could never hate you. God, I—I love you. I would deal with anything as long as we're together. Please . . ."

He put his hands up, rubbing the tears from her face with his thumbs, only to repeat it again as they continued to fall. "Shhh, Angel, don't you see it's because I love you that I'm doing this? Baby, parts of my life are ugly, and they're not going anywhere. One of the things that I love so much about you is that you've always seemed so bright I could have sworn you were lit from within. But after my parents left this morning, that light was so dim that it was almost nonexistent. And I won't be the one to extinguish it forever."

"Mark," she cried, "you don't have to do this. I can be stronger. They just surprised me today. I promise you, I'll be okay. Just—"

"But you shouldn't have to be," he interrupted. "That's the point here, baby. They'll always catch you by surprise because you can't and shouldn't have to plan to be attacked." Before she could argue, he lowered his head and locked his lips on her. Even as she responded to the frantic touch of his mouth, she knew it for what it was— good-bye. He was sitting here with her after professing his love, but he was already gone. Men like Mark didn't make decisions lightly, and he'd decided to sacrifice his happiness, thinking he was saving her own.

He got to his feet and lowered her back into the

chair. "Denny's here to take you home. He'll have your car delivered later. He'll give you his card so that you can call him if you need anything at all." Then he drove the final arrow into her heart. "Take care of yourself, Crystal."

I'm no longer "Angel" to him. He's letting me go.

She reached out and grabbed his hand before he could walk away. "Don't do this to me—to us," she begged, as she tossed her pride aside.

For a brief moment, she saw past his blank expression to the pain that blazed from his eyes. He cupped the side of her face, stroking her cheek. "Can't you see, baby? I have no choice. This is hurting me too, but it's better this way. I'm giving you a future of happiness and laughter instead of a life spent looking over your shoulder." When she opened her mouth to protest, he put a finger to her lips, silencing her. "Don't, Angel—this is hard enough already. Please just go with Denny."

"I love you," she whispered as he pulled his hand away. He closed his eyes and looked unsteady on his feet as he walked away.

Crystal was dimly aware of Denny showing up at some point and helping her into the car. He cursed under his breath, and she had no idea if it was directed at her or Mark, but she couldn't find it in herself to care either way.

As she walked numbly down the hallway toward her apartment with Denny keeping a firm hand on her back, she was surprised to see her sister standing in front of her door, looking at her in concern. "Mark called me," Ella answered her unspoken question as she got closer.

Crystal winced before focusing on finding her key

in her purse. Ella took it from her hand and opened the door. Denny followed them inside and insisted on doing a walk-through of the apartment before coming back to her with a card in his hand. The look of sympathy on his face was almost her undoing. "I don't need that, Denny. I'll be fine," she insisted as he tried to give her his contact information.

He put his hands on her arms, pulling her gently against his chest. "I know you will," he murmured, "but humor me anyway. One night you might need someone to buy you a beer while you talk about what a dumbass my cousin is."

Crystal laughed weakly despite herself. "What are you doing right now?"

He chuckled along with her, not appearing in any hurry to leave. When she finally pulled away, she was mortified to realize that she'd been crying hard enough to soak the front of his shirt. "Crap," she hissed, wiping her cheeks. "Don't you dare tell him about this," she threatened. "If he asks, say that I was fine when you left."

"You got it." He nodded. "I'll be the person that you both lie to about how not miserable you are without each other."

Her sorrow turned to anger as she put her hands on her hips and glared. "This wasn't what I wanted, Denny. I pretty much begged him not to walk away from me."

"I know, Crystal," he agreed solemnly. "It was a rather unexpected time for Mark to be so damn noble. But, in his defense, he's doing what he feels is best for you. And I've been around the DeSantos long enough to know how ugly things can get. For the record, though, I don't agree with him, and he knows that. He's been happier since meeting you than I've ever seen him, and I think that scares him."

"Why would he possibly be afraid of me?" Crystal asked in frustration.

Denny looked conflicted for a moment as if afraid of betraying Mark by talking to her. Finally, he shrugged his shoulders and said, "You got past the public Mark to the private one, and he doesn't let that happen. He has many acquaintances, but no one close. He let you in, though, and discovered how good love could be with someone more than a one-night stand. Then the whole scene happened with his parents this morning, and it hit him hard how it would feel to get even more attached and then lose you. Which he feels like is inevitable due to the fact that they'll always be crazy and ride his ass at every opportunity."

"I swear. What is it with you men and this honorable, do-the-right-thing crap?" Ella shouted, shocking them both. "Declan was the same way, and it took me getting hit by a car to bring him to his senses. For God's sake, if not for being scraped off a bumper, I might still be single!"

"Um—Ells . . . are you okay over there?" Crystal asked tentatively. A glance at Denny showed him opening and closing his mouth as if unsure whether to speak or not.

"Of course," Ella sniffed. "I'm just tired of the Webber sisters having to deal with this bullshit. I'm telling you, though, if I didn't like Declan's guy part so much,

I'd go home and cut the sucker off just for putting me through this."

"Is this some kind of weird flashback?" Denny whispered.

"It may not be safe for you to be here, since you have a penis," she whispered back. "You'd better leave while you can."

She saw his hand drop down for a moment and wondered if he'd cupped the family jewels out of fear. "So, I should run along now," he began as he edged toward the door. "I'm going to leave my card right here, Crystal," he added as he laid a white rectangle on the coffee table. "Call me if you need anything at all."

"Thanks, Denny," Crystal called out as he opened the door to leave.

Looking from Ella to her, he cringed, saying, "Um, good luck with all of this," before closing the door behind him.

"Damn, I thought I'd have to go after him with a pair of scissors next," Ella huffed. "Talk about not getting the message."

Crystal stared at her sister incredulously. "Are you saying that whole thing was an act to get rid of Denny?"

"Well, duh," Ella snorted. "Although I was serious about men being stupid. Don't think I haven't pointed that out to my hubby a few times either. He agrees that he was out of his ever-loving mind back then to consider walking away from me."

Looking at her normally sweet sister in amazement, Crystal said, "You're just a little scary sometimes, Ells. And possibly a bit nuts. But I like it, and I sure needed it today."

Ella closed the distance between them, pulling her into a hug. "I'm so sorry, Crys. If it makes you feel any better, Mark sounded miserable when I talked to him."

"I'm glad you're here, but I have no idea why he called you," Crystal admitted.

Ella kept an arm around her as they walked to the sofa and then collapsed onto it. "He told me briefly that you two had broken up and that he was worried about you. He asked if I could come here and stay with you. So of course, I told Declan to watch Sofia and came right over." Pushing a piece of hair from Crystal's face in a motherly gesture, Ella asked, "What happened, Crys?"

Crystal repeated everything that had occurred that morning before, during, and after Mark's parents' visit. She was proud that she managed to get through it without choking on another wave of tears. "So, I guess, points to our mother for starting the downward spiral of my weekend and also planting the seeds in Mark's head that I couldn't handle any more drama in my life."

"Crap." Ella dropped her head back onto the sofa. They both had stared at the ceiling for a few moments before Ella said, "I don't think he's right in his decision, but I can understand him trying to protect you. I mean, what you described about the way his parents treated you sounds even worse than Mom. I can't imagine how it would feel to have three people in my life who were always gunning for me. Look at how you and I text and call each other when Mom is on one of her rolls. Sometimes we spend hours a week trying to coordinate our efforts to avoid her until she calms down. How draining would it be to add two more people to that kind of toxic mix?"

"Trust me, Ells, I get that part," she sighed. "Is it wrong that I wished he'd loved me enough to at least attempt to look for another answer other than walking away? I mean, we didn't even try. He just made the decision and sent me on my way."

"I wasn't kidding when I said that Mark sounded bad when I talked to him. He might have thought he didn't have any other choice, but he's suffering as well."

"Good." Crystal smiled weakly before closing her eyes and resting against her sister's shoulder. She was no happier about Mark's misery than she was her own. She wasn't sure what the answer was or even if there was one. The only thing she did know was that she was going to have to be stronger than she ever had before; otherwise, losing him would destroy her.

Chapter Twenty-one

"So, we're back to running away again, huh?" Denny asked as he settled next to Mark on the company plane. "Plus, I know you've been dodging me for the last week."

"How would that even be possible?" Mark asked out of curiosity, even though it was true. He had been avoiding being alone with the other man since his breakup with Crystal on Sunday.

Denny held up his hand and started ticking off his supporting evidence. "First, you've been driving yourself to the office every day. You never do that, so that's a bit suspect. Second, you haven't been answering your phone when I call—only replying to texts. Third, I've never known you to have so many meetings at other locations. People generally come to you, not the other way around. Fourth . . ."

"I get the picture," Mark acknowledged dryly. "It's nothing personal; I just haven't been very good company this week. I did bring you on this trip, though, so it's not a case of complete avoidance."

Denny smirked. "I figure that's mainly because you don't want to make your own arrangements everywhere you go, but I'll let it slide."

Mark looked out the window of the plane as they taxied down the runway and started climbing. When they'd finally reached the correct altitude, he asked softly, "How is she?"

Denny didn't bother to pretend he didn't know to whom the question pertained. "She hasn't called me for anything, but I've managed to catch sight of her a few times at the office. She's been there every day, according to Lydia, but she looks about like you do."

"Who's Lydia?" Mark asked, thinking the name sounded familiar, but unable to place it.

Lifting a brow, Denny said, "Crystal's boss—who, incidentally, I promised you'd put in a good word for her with Jacob in exchange for a little information."

"Okay," Mark said automatically, before frowning. "Why would I do that? Oh, never mind, I remember Angel mentioning that Jacob had helped a coworker out with a car problem, and she had been rather taken with him. I'm assuming that was Lydia."

"I've already mentioned it to Jacob and asked that he take one for the team, so he'll handle that when he's back in town," Denny said as if he played matchmaker every day of the week.

"Can we get back to Angel?" Mark said impatiently.

"There isn't much more to tell." Denny shrugged. "Lydia said that she hadn't missed any work but was quiet. She told her that you two were no longer seeing each other, but she didn't want to talk any further about it. I saw her from a distance in the cafeteria yesterday, and she looked kind of washed-out—like you, actually." Mark knew that he had dark circles under his eyes from lack of sleep. Not holding Angel each night had been a difficult adjustment. Add in the fact that he worried about her almost every hour of the day, and it wasn't conducive to any type of relaxation.

Mark pinched the bridge of his nose before opening his briefcase and attempting to distract himself with work. "Let's go through some of these messages that you e-mailed over this morning."

"It doesn't have to be this way. Both of you are miserable without each other. Turn the plane around and go to her," Denny advised earnestly.

Mark stared at his cousin, torn between the urge to hug him for caring and to choke him for meddling. Instead, he went the direct route that Denny couldn't argue with. "Has my situation changed at all in the last week?"

Denny knew what—or whom—he was talking about immediately. "No," he answered quietly, "not that I'm aware of."

"And is that likely to happen?" Mark continued to drive his point home.

"Probably not," Denny acknowledged.

"Then why are we still talking about it? You, better than anyone, know how bad it can get when my father goes on a real bender. He was fairly mild on Sunday, all things considered. Would you want to inflict that on your girlfriend or wife on a regular basis?"

Instead of answering the question, Denny growled, "I fucking hate this!"

"As do I," Mark agreed. And truer words were never spoken. Instead of it getting easier without Angel, each day was worse to endure than the previous. He walked around feeling as if his shoes were made of lead and bullet holes riddled his heart. Work was his only escape, and he'd been at it like a maniac. When he was so tired, though, that he couldn't go a moment longer, he'd remember how she looked that morning when she begged him not to walk away. She was the first woman in his life to say *I love you* to him, and he'd left her behind as if she didn't matter. He was raw and gutted. In order to keep the light burning within her, he'd completely extinguished his own, and he had no idea if it would ever burn for anyone other than her again.

Crystal looked up as her office door opened. She plastered on a smile, but inwardly groaned as both Mia and Gwen walked in. God, she couldn't handle another relationship postmortem right now. She was barely hanging on as it was. At least after the first day, Lydia had done her a favor and had not mentioned Mark again, even though she could see the concern in the woman's eyes. "Hey, you two," she said brightly. *If you can't dazzle them with brilliance, then baffle them with bullshit,* she thought to herself. That was a saying she'd relied on a lot in the last week. Smiling and pretending everything was perfectly fine—when it was anything but.

"Oh God, she's doing it again," Mia groaned to Gwen. "It's starting to kind of freak me out."

"Me too," Gwen whispered back loud enough for Crystal to hear, before turning to stare at her. "Honey, we don't want to rain on your happy train, but we're a bit worried about you."

Crystal thought that statement was a bit comical, since Gwen looked as if she'd swallowed a beach ball and was presently rubbing her back while looking at

THE ONE FOR ME   263

Crystal in concern. "Shouldn't I be saying that to you?"
she asked, with real amusement this time.

"She's deflecting." Mia sighed. "It's worse than I
thought."

Crystal bit her lip, trying to stay in her carefree zone
while faced with her friend's attempts to push her into
reality. "I really should get back to work," she said,
pointing to the stack of papers on the corner of her
desk. "Lydia needs this done by the afternoon."

"We talked to her on the way in," Gwen inserted.
"She said to take all the time you needed." To punctuate
the fact that they weren't leaving, each of the women
took a seat in front of her desk and settled in. *Shit.*

Desperately grasping at straws, Crystal pointed out,
"I don't think we should be having a long personal conversation at work. We could meet up later and talk."

Mia nodded. "Ordinarily, I'd agree, but since you've
been blowing us off for days, obviously that isn't going
to happen. You run out of here like your ass is on fire
in the afternoon and somehow manage to get by us in
the lobby each morning. Then you hardly answer your
phone in the evenings, or your door for that matter. So
this is our last resort."

"Honey, we're worried about you," Gwen added
softly. "You told us about Mark on Monday, but after
that, you've buried yourself in here. The few times one
of us has managed to see you, you've been effusively
happy, which we know is bullshit."

Crystal had the words of denial on the tip of her
tongue. She was all ready for a glib reply with a big
smile for reassurance. Which was why she was so
baffled when she opened her mouth and blurted out,

"I'm dying inside without him. When my friends said stuff like that in high school, I thought they were pathetic. Now I understand the meaning of those words all too well. I'm working, eating some, and sleeping for the most part. I'm alive and doing most everything that I normally would, but a part of me isn't there anymore. Which seems absurd, even to my ears, considering Mark and I were barely together a month. It wasn't long enough to fall in love . . . was it?" she asked, needing someone to be the voice of reason, because it apparently wasn't her right now.

Mia leaned forward to grip Crystal's hand, stopping her from nervously shredding papers on the desk. "I knew Seth was different from anyone else I'd ever dated almost from the start. It took me a while longer to admit it, but it was what I consider love at first sight." Smacking her lips, she grinned. "Well, maybe lust, followed quickly by the other L word."

"Yep, me too," Gwen agreed. "I was drawn to Dominic even while I was dating Mac. If I'm honest, I may not have wanted to admit it at the time, but it was always him. When we were finally together as a couple, I knew in my heart that I was in love with him. I was scared because my romantic life had always been something of a disaster. But I know exactly what you're saying about missing a part of yourself. "

"I think the next question here is what do you intend to do about it?" Mia demanded. "Mark may have some full-blown crazy in his family, but so do you, Crys."

"No offense," Gwen added sheepishly. "I'm sure your mother has her good days. . . ."

Shaking her head with a smile, despite herself Crystal said, "Um—no, she really doesn't."

"All righty, then." Mia stood and began pacing the small office. "So you'll talk to her and then move on to Mark's parents. If you can show them all that you won't be cowering in the corner like some wallflower, then Mark's concerns won't matter. He'll know you're capable of kicking ass and taking names whenever you want. Maybe we could even get you some of those platform boots—kind of like a uniform, or . . ."

Slashing her hands in a cutting motion, Gwen looked at Mia and said, "Rein it in, Rambo. I think Crystal gets the point. There's no need for us to dress her like Xena the Warrior Princess."

Crystal waited until their bickering had subsided before saying, "I can deal with my mother, but Mark's parents? I have no clue where to even find them if I wanted to. Plus, his father would probably squash me like a bug."

"Oh, screw that old goat," Mia snapped. "Why don't you talk to his cousin—what's his name? Kenny?"

"Denny," Crystal answered absently. Pushing a hand through her hair, she stared at her friends before finally blowing out a breath. "Let me think about it, okay? I don't want to take a bad situation and make it worse."

"Absolutely," Gwen encouraged softly. "Give it some thought and let us know how we can help you. Just don't give up, Crys. I've seen you and Mark together, and you're perfect for each other. You click."

After the other women had left with promises to check on her later, Crystal relaxed back in her chair and thought of their suggestion to confront the three people responsible for taking Mark away from her. She'd never been a person who dealt well with conflict. As much as it pained her to admit it, Mark was correct in the respect that it would be hard on her if his parents continued to attack her. But she had learned that she wanted to be with someone who could meet her needs, both physically and emotionally. What it all boiled down to was she would either have to be stronger than she'd ever imagined possible or leave him without a fight so that he could someday find another woman who was willing to fight for him. And, oh, how the last thought stung.

Chapter Twenty-two

A charity fund-raiser was the last place that Mark wanted to be. He stood off to the side of the banquet room, brooding as he drank ridiculously expensive scotch from fine crystal. It had always seemed ironic to him that fund-raisers served only the best to help the less fortunate. Hell, why didn't they just have a simple gathering and donate the event money? It would probably be enough to feed the homeless of Charleston for months.

He had already dropped off a check from the DeSanto Group and was preparing to make his exit when a hand wrapped around his arm. "Mark, I thought that was you," said a vaguely familiar female voice. Turning, he gave his first genuine smile of the evening as Margot Rush beamed up at him. They'd grown up together and had connected from time to time when he was in town. She was a gorgeous woman, but he'd never had the desire to sleep with her, and luckily, she'd always felt the same. Much like his relationship with Ava Stone, Margot was a friend who he enjoyed spending time with when their paths crossed.

"It's good to see to see you again, beautiful." He

grinned as he pulled her into an embrace before dropping a brief kiss on her upturned lips. That affectionate gesture was as far as it ever went with them. It felt comforting and familiar, which he very much appreciated tonight. As they stood catching up on each other's lives, he could almost pretend for a moment that he wasn't a truly miserable fuck. Seeing her tonight could well save him from another evening of staring at the walls at home and missing Angel. Maybe the tide was beginning to turn for him.

Crystal stood before the double doors of the Oceanix penthouse suite. Her stomach roiled, and she fought the urge to throw up in the opulent hallway. Ever since Denny had called to let her know that, strangely enough, the DeSantos were still in Myrtle Beach, she'd wanted to call a halt to this crazy plan to get Mark back. Really, how much of her would possibly be left after Marcus DeSanto chewed her up and spit her out? Denny had offered to accompany her, but that wouldn't be the same. She would still be depending on someone else to fight her battles. Even if things went south— which they were likely to—at least she'd have the comfort of knowing that she'd tried.

So, taking a deep breath, she stood ramrod straight and knocked on the door. When it opened, she felt her shoulders slump slightly at the sight of Celine DeSanto staring at her in shock. Finally, her good manners appeared to kick in and she said smoothly, "This is surprising. Crystal, isn't it?" Then looking around, she asked in confusion, "Is Mark with you?"

"No, he isn't," Crystal replied. "I wondered if I could speak to you for a few moments."

Celine looked uncertain before glancing behind her and lowering her voice. "Give me five minutes and I'll meet you in the coffee shop in the lobby."

Please tell me she won't be bringing her husband, Crystal prayed inwardly as she took the elevator back down to the bottom floor. She walked past some of the swank boutiques before finding the place that Celine had indicated. She ordered a vanilla latte and found a quiet table in the corner.

Surprisingly, Celine was on time, and after giving her a nod of acknowledgment, she bought a drink for herself, and then slowly approached, pulling out a chair. Crystal had to give the other woman credit. Even on short notice, she looked cool, elegant, and polished. Plus, she could have easily passed for Mark's sister rather than his mother. Her hair didn't appear to have any gray and her figure was one that most women would envy. Aside from her coloring, though, it was her eyes that resembled her son the most. Striving to keep the quaver from her voice, Crystal said, "Thank for you agreeing to see me. I know I should have called first, but . . ."

"You wanted to have the upper hand?" Celine inserted, looking faintly amused and maybe a tad impressed. Although possibly that was wishful thinking on Crystal's part.

"I had hoped it would make it more difficult to turn me away," Crystal corrected before adding, "But a phone call would have certainly been easier, I think."

Celine picked up her coffee and took a sip before

leveling another direct look at her. "You're here about what happened at Mark's, aren't you?"

"Yes, I am," she agreed without hesitation. "You see, I love your son and he loves me. But that scene with your husband was the catalyst that split us apart."

The other woman swallowed audibly before picking up her cup once again with an unsteady hand. "I didn't want to come that day. I tried my best to talk Marcus out of it, but as usual, he acted without thinking it through." Looking at Crystal with eyes that seemed to plead for understanding, she continued. "I've loved Marcus for most of my life. We were best friends before he finally saw me as more. And since that moment, we've rarely been apart for more than a day. Loving him doesn't mean that I'm blind to his demons. It's because of them that I never planned to have children." When Crystal gasped, Celine smiled sadly. "I love my son, but I realized early on that Marcus and I didn't lead a life that would make us good parents. Unfortunately, though, sometimes things don't turn out as you plan. One oversight on our part led to a surprise pregnancy, and nine months later, Mark was born."

"What happened afterward?" Crystal prodded when the other woman paused as if lost in time.

"For a while, things were good," Celine said. "Marcus wasn't drinking as much and seemed to dote on Mark. Then as our son got older and turned into some kind of child prodigy, things went downhill. Marcus's father picked up on Mark's intelligence, and that turn of events signaled the end of the peace in our household. From then on, Marcus mostly ignored his son, but as he got older, they began butting heads. As that became a regular occurrence, Marcus's drinking picked up as well. Then, when the DeSanto Group was left to Mark, that was it. Since then, I've watched the husband I love play a cat-and-mouse game with the son I've never known how to save."

Crystal's head was spinning as Celine finished the summary of Mark's life. From the boy who was never wanted to the man who no one had ever stood up for. It broke her heart. He'd been defending himself since he was a child, and now he was trying to protect her in the only way he knew how. *Oh, my love.* Crystal didn't think she had anything to lose by being completely honest with Celine, so she admitted, "Mark left me because he doesn't want his father to inflict the same pain on me that he has on him. He's afraid that I'll grow to hate him after a while and can't bear the thought."

Celine gave up all pretense of drinking her coffee. For the first time, Crystal thought the woman probably looked close to her real age. There was a fatigue about her now that had little to do with sleep. She was a woman who had buried her head in the sand for years and was now having to face the consequences of her actions. "I don't know what to do," she murmured. "I'm tired of living this way, but Marcus would implode fully without me. We both have our own . . . lives at times, but we always come back to each other."

"How about your son?" Crystal snapped, tired of hearing excuses made for the older man. Had anyone even considered some tough love where he was concerned? God knows giving her mother some of that was next up on her agenda.

"I can only help Mark by getting control of his

father," Celine hissed back. "I know you don't want to
hear this, but I need some time to make decisions.
After what happened at Mark's, I've already been
attempting to put a plan in place." Crystal wanted to
argue when the woman got to her feet, but she could
tell by the closed-off expression on her face that she'd
said as much as she was going to for now. "I'll get your
number from Denny and call you when I'm ready."

Crystal nodded. "I'd appreciate anything you can do."

As they went to part ways in the lobby, Celine
turned back to her and said earnestly, "I am sorry. You
seem as if you really care about my son, and I promise
you that I'm going to do everything in my power to
help him."

Crystal made it a few more feet to the plush sofa in
the lobby before collapsing down on weak legs. She'd
done it. She'd faced one of the obstacles in her path to
Mark. She dearly hoped that in doing it, she wasn't
making things worse for the man she loved.

Chapter Twenty-three

Mark looked at his Twitter account for the first time in a few days as he sat in his office. Yeah, he had more important things to do than check his social media accounts, but as usual, lately his focus was shit just knowing Angel was somewhere in the building. They'd been apart for almost three weeks now, and he was still a mess. He was pretty sure he hadn't gone this long without sex since his first time, and the sad thing was that he had no desire at all to do anything to remedy that dry spell.

He was scrolling through his Twitter stream, pathetically hoping for something from Angel when he saw a picture that had him yelling, "Denny!"

As usual, the other man took his time strolling into Mark's office with a resigned "Yes?"

Mark flipped his iPad around, showing his cousin the picture of him kissing Margot at the charity event in Charleston a few weeks back. "Who in the hell posted this?" he asked, now in a panic. "What if Angel saw that? Oh God, do you think she has?" He frantically scrolled through the remaining posts to see if she had left him a message, but there was nothing.

"You need to calm down." Denny rolled his eyes in exasperation. "You broke up with her, so it's not like this is an admission of cheating. What's the big deal? I mean, I'm sure that she assumes you've returned to your loose ways by now."

Mark felt like his head was going to explode. He got to his feet and rounded his desk, intent on wringing the other man's neck. "This would upset her!" he shouted, waving his hands in agitation. "And you know that's Margot. We've never even kissed, much less slept together."

"Um—looks kind of like you're kissing in that picture," Denny pointed out helpfully.

"I swear—" Mark began, only to be cut off when Denny suddenly snapped.

"I really don't want to hear any more of this whining! I liked you when you were with Crystal. Hell, I even liked you okay when you were banging everything on the East Coast. Now you mope from one city to another because you're miserable without her. But you're too much of a pussy to do anything about it! So your dad's a big asshole. Do you think you've got the market cornered on that or something? Big—fucking—deal. Crystal's mom is a rabid bitch from what I've heard too, but at least she has some balls. How about you grow a pair and take charge of your life again. Or, at the very least, borrow Crystal's for a while. *Now*, I'm taking the afternoon off because I'm at my limit with you for today. And you can call a cab when you're ready to leave." With those final parting words, Denny slammed the outer door impressively and left Mark in oppressive silence.

Without giving himself time to think about his actions, he called Declan and, after a fair amount of ass chewing, got the information that he needed. Then he looked up the number for a cab company and ordered one to arrive in fifteen minutes. If Denny's fit had done nothing else, it had given Mark an idea—or really a plan. And fuck it all. When you had nothing, what was left to lose? It was time to find the balls that he'd obviously lost, and he knew where he wanted to look first.

"What are you doing here?" an angry voice demanded. Mark almost smiled. He was pissing off people everywhere he went today, it seemed.

"I'd like to speak with you for a moment, Mrs. Webber."

Angel's mother stood before him looking like an angry pit bull. He had a hard time figuring out where Angel and Ella got their looks, because there didn't seem to be anything attractive about the bitter woman snarling at him. "First you put my daughter up to cutting me out of her life, and now you're here to what? Give me one final kick?"

Mark couldn't control his surprise. "Crystal's been here?"

Giving him a hateful glare, she said, "Oh, like you didn't know? She was a good girl before she met you. But ever since then, she's been nothing but disrespectful to me. I've given those girls my whole life, and they don't appreciate it. Instead, they both come here and tell me that unless I can turn over a new leaf, I'm not their mother anymore."

As belligerent as she was trying to appear, Mark could see the cracks in her tough armor. Whatever had happened, the Webber sisters had struck a chord deep within their mother, and she was still reeling from it. He'd come here today to tell her to leave Angel alone, but it appeared to be rather anticlimactic now. She'd done it. She'd stood up to her mother and obviously not backed down. Shit, he was so proud of her. It looked like she possessed the balls, as Denny had suggested earlier, and this was one time that he was okay with letting her borrow them.

"Mrs. Webber, I can see that you're upset, and I don't want make it worse. But I want you to know that I love your daughter. I may not be the man that you envisioned her being with, but as of now, I'm going to dedicate myself to pulling my head out of my ass and being the only one she'll ever want or need."

He expected to catch some hell for his less than delicate terminology, but then something amazing happened. He blinked several times, thinking he must be hallucinating. But no, Dot Webber, the female equivalent of his father, was smiling. Okay, so maybe it was more like the grin of someone with really bad gas pains, but it was there. It fucking counted. When she opened her mouth, he braced for another smackdown, but instead he got, "Well, what are you doing standing here in your fancy suit wasting my time, then?" She looked past him to the cab idling at the curb and added, "After you've groveled to my daughter, maybe you should go buy yourself a car. I'm assuming you've got enough credit to pull it, because I'm not cosigning for a loan."

He grinned broadly before walking backward. "I think I've got it covered, but thanks for the tip. Be seeing you." She raised a brow before shaking her head and walking away. Amazing. The woman might never be more than passingly pleasant, but it appeared Angel had reenacted *The Taming of the Shrew*. God, he'd been such a fool. But he didn't intend to let another day pass him by before he begged for her forgiveness.

Chapter Twenty-four

Across town at almost the same time, Crystal opened the door to find Celine DeSanto standing there. She made a mental note to kick Denny's butt later for not giving her any warning. "I'm sorry to show up unannounced, but that seems to work best for us, doesn't it?" Celine smiled briefly before asking, "Can I come in?"

Crystal waved her inside, and then led the way to her small living room. The other woman looked far different from her normal polished appearance in her jeans and a pair of running shoes. A black turtleneck rounded out the casual look. "How have you been?" She felt compelled to ask because she was genuinely curious.

"Marcus is in rehab," Celine admitted. "He checked in a week ago after I threatened to leave if he didn't get help. Nothing else worked. I begged, pleaded, and tried a healthy dose of guilt, but it took me packing a bag and opening the door before he caved."

Without thinking, Crystal leaned forward and placed a hand on Celine's. "I'm so sorry; I can't imagine how difficult that must have been."

"It was horrible," she shuddered. "He started crying when he knew I was serious. I told him that he either got the help he needed and learned to be a father to his son or we were over. As hard as it was, I meant it and he knew that. He checked himself into rehab the next morning in Charleston. I just drove up today to tell you in person and also to talk to Mark."

Before she could say anything, there was a knock at the door. It seemed as if this was the day for unexpected visitors. She knew Ella was planning to come by later that evening, but figured she might have gotten away earlier than she thought. The last thing she expected when she opened the door was to see Mark standing there looking like some kind of Armani dream in his dark suit. She knew she was gaping at him, but she couldn't seem to find her voice.

"Angel," he said in that soft, sexy voice that enchanted her. "Oh, baby, I've . . ."

"Mark?" She heard from somewhere behind her. He gave her a questioning look before gently tugging her aside.

"Mother?" he muttered in shock. "What're you doing here?" Crystal took the hand that was still holding on to her arm and pulled him gently forward so that she could shut the door behind him.

"Come in and sit down with us," she invited. In a testament to how stunned he was, he did as he was told, settling beside her on the sofa while Celine took a nearby chair. Unable to stand the silence that had fallen over the room, Crystal turned to Mark and made a full confession. "I went to see your parents a few weeks ago while they were still in town. Your mother and I ended up talking alone, and I told her how much I loved you and that I was miserable without you."

The day just kept getting stranger, because instead of anger, a smile played around his full lips. He reached out to run a hand over her leg, before giving it a squeeze. "You've been a busy girl, haven't you, Angel? I should have expected something like this, since I just left your mother's house with similar intentions in mind."

"Wait—what?" Crystal gaped at him. "You went to see my mother? Are you nuts?" Dear Lord, was the man suicidal? Of course, he had no way of knowing that she had already poked the dragon with a stick before he'd walked into her lair. The poor guy.

"I don't know," he replied, while darting a look toward his own mother, "are *you*?" *So possibly, we have both lost our minds a bit,* Crystal wryly acknowledged to herself.

Probably feeling a little lost over their conversation, Celine sat forward in her chair and blurted out, "Mark, I came by to tell Crystal that your father has entered a rehabilitation facility."

This time it was Mark stammering out, "What are you talking about?"

At that point, Crystal decided that mother and son could use some alone time together. Mark was so riveted by his mother's explanation that he didn't appear to notice when she slipped away to her bedroom, closing the door behind her. She kicked off her shoes and relaxed back on her bed, content to wait for him to find her.

She had no idea much time had passed when something jolted her awake. She jerked as a shape beside her took focus. "How long have you been there?" she asked dreamily as Mark smiled gently down at her.

"A little while," he admitted. "I was happy just

being in the same room with you after not seeing you for so long."

"Is your mom gone?" she asked, looking beyond him to the open bedroom door.

"Yeah, Angel, she's gone back to Charleston to see my dad."

"I hope you're not mad at me for going to see her," Crystal began hesitantly. "I thought if you could see that I'm strong enough to handle anything our parents could dish out, then you'd reconsider your decision. I never expected your father to actually seek help, so that was an added bonus."

He turned for a moment to push his shoes off then climbed into bed, taking her into his arms. He kissed her for long, drugging moments before pulling back slightly. "I was wrong, baby. I was so blinded by my need to save you from the world that I damn near took away both of our reasons for living. I've only been existing without you, Angel—nothing has meant anything to me. I can't tell you how much I regret shutting down on you like that. I thought I was doing what was best, but I should have talked to you instead of pushing you away. I'm not proud of it, but it took Denny throwing some kind of girl tantrum and threatening to kick my ass before I figured out what a fool I've been."

Crystal squeezed a hand up in the air and smirked. "Mia and Gwen pointed something similar out to me. Which pretty much lit a fire under me to stop feeling sorry for myself and take action."

Mark laughed softly. "So how long do you think we would have gone on if not for our friends stepping in to save the day?"

Shuddering, Crystal said, "I don't even want to know. I couldn't care less how much hell we catch from our parental units in the future. I love you, Mark DeSanto, and you're not getting rid of me again."

Giving her a tender look full of promise for the future, Mark kissed the tip of her nose before saying, "I love you too, Crystal Webber, and thank you for being strong enough to slay both of our dragons."

"Whatever," she huffed playfully. "Now would you please shut up and make love to me already? You know how cranky I get when I haven't had sex for a while."

Mark burst out in relieved laughter, jumping to his feet and pulling at his clothes. "I'll take care of that right now, Angel. Does 'hashtag multiple orgasms' work for you?"

"Hashtag hell yeah!" She giggled as he moved to join her. Within moments, only the sighs of pleasure and words of love filled the room.

Epilogue

"Are you sure this is a good idea?" Ella asked yet again as she looked nervously around the crowded restaurant. The DeSantos were meeting the Webbers for the first time, and it was anyone's guess as to how it would go.

The day had started out with the news that Gwen was in labor. So Crystal had rushed to the hospital—actually, Denny had taken her at Mark's insistence, and she had arrived just an hour before Gwen had given birth. Since Dominic and Gwen had elected not to find out the sex beforehand, it was truly a surprise when baby boy Brady made his way into the world. His parents had decided on a name for both a boy and a girl ahead of time. Mac and Gage were not only Dominic's best friends but also business partners. And they had served two tours in the military together prior to opening East Coast Security. Gage's middle name was Cameron, and Mac's first name was McKinley, so those were combined to Cameron McKinley Brady. Gage was thrilled to get first billing in little Cameron's name, and Dominic was afraid that they'd never be able to live with his ego now. Gwen had told them after Gage was gone that they just liked the way it sounded and it was in no way because Gage was more important, as he had been insinuating. Whatever the reason, Crystal thought it was a wonderful name for the most beautiful baby boy ever.

"Here comes your crazy . . ." Declan began, only to stop abruptly as Ella shot him a reproachful look. Crystal tried to hide her smirk as their mother walked into the restaurant trailed by their father.

"Well, at least she showed," Ella pointed out. Bless her; she was always looking for the bright side. Crystal had to admit that even though things were far from perfect with her mother, they were better than they had been in some time. She even thought that Mark was winning over the tough-as-nails woman. She wasn't sure if it was because her mother actually liked him or if it was just because she knew that Mark wouldn't put up with any of her negative behavior.

When their parents stopped before them, her father gave them both a brief hug before shaking Declan's hand. Then their mother gave them each a peck on the cheek. "Hello, girls. Where is Sofia?" she directed to Ella.

"Oh, we got a sitter for her tonight. Declan and I thought we could use a date night since it's been a while." Their mother couldn't resist a small eye roll, but didn't comment. "Oh look," Ella pointed across the room. "There's Denny, Mark, and his parents, I presume."

Crystal grinned before excusing herself and going to her boyfriend's side. "Angel." He smiled in return as she slid into the circle of his arms. "I missed you, baby," he murmured for her ears alone as he brushed his lips against her temple.

Denny wrestled her from Mark and dropped a loud, smacking kiss on her cheek before going to greet Declan and Ella. She returned to Mark and mentally braced herself to face the man she hadn't seen since that day in Mark's house almost two months earlier. "Mr. and Mrs. DeSanto, it's so good to see you again," she said politely as she extended a hand.

Mark's mother took her hand and pulled her forward, hugging her. "It's Celine, and it's wonderful to see you again, Crystal." Then, in a surprise move, still holding on to Crystal, she moved her husband closer. "This is my husband, Marcus. I don't believe you've been formally introduced before."

And then in what would be the biggest shock of the night, an obviously sober Marcus DeSanto took her face in his hands and kissed both of her cheeks. "It's a real pleasure, Crystal. I'm looking forward to getting to know you, and I hope you're open to meeting the real me."

"That sounds amazing," she replied honestly. *Wow.* It was not what she had been expecting at all—it was so much better. She'd expected hostility at the very least, but the couple she saw before her now only resembled their former selves in looks. Their demeanor was completely different and, dare she say, friendly. She glanced quickly at Mark to gauge his reaction, and he looked so happy and not a little relieved. Mark had admitted earlier that he hoped somewhere down the road when his father was further along in his recovery, he might be able to take a position with the DeSanto Group. But for now, they were all taking things one day at a time, while attempting to establish a relationship with each other.

And then the moment was upon them. Her mother,

pulling her husband along behind her, marched over to the DeSantos looking like a drill sergeant. As Ella crept up beside Crystal, she whispered, "Oh shit, I tried to distract her, but she's relentless."

But the DeSantos, proving they were more astute than anyone could have guessed, performed a small miracle. Marcus went directly to Crystal's mother and Celine went to her father. When her mother extended a hand stiffly to Marcus, he took it in his own and brought it to his lips. "Mrs. Webber, I would know you anywhere. You look so much like your beautiful daughter that it's uncanny." Out of the corner of her eye, she saw Declan smirking, while Ella jammed an elbow into his side. Celine seemed to be trying a similar approach with her father, and from the look of bliss on his face, he was eating the attention up.

"Well." Her mother snorted, but there was no heat behind it. Instead, she gazed at Marcus helplessly as if she didn't know how to handle his charm. "Please call me Dot. Nice to meet you." She pointed at Mark, and then shocked them all by saying, "I'm real fond of your son. He's a hard worker, and he takes care of my daughter. He gets a bit cheeky sometimes, but boys will be boys, won't they, Marcus?"

Marcus threw back his head and laughed before extending an elbow to her mother. "Shall we find our table?" he asked, and she blushed like a schoolgirl and hastily accepted.

As both sets of parents walked away, Crystal turned to gape at Mark. "I can't believe it. The DeStudo magic has worked again. How in the world did you and your father manage to do the impossible?"

Giving her a devilish grin, Mark said, "Just call me big . . . Mr. Big."

"Oh brother." She giggled, loving this silly side of him. Going up on her tiptoes, she murmured for him alone, "How about later, you show me if you can live up to that name?"

Pinching her on the butt, he looked around to make sure no one was near before saying, "There's a broom closet somewhere around here with our names on it. Let's go find it now. I've got something to prove to the woman I love, and it can't wait."

"By all means, lead the way, Mr. DeStudo," she teased. "In case you didn't already know it, I've always got your back—but I'm more than happy to handle your front as well." Within moments, they found their own little corner of the world and they were happily lost in each other, just as they would be for the rest of their lives. If anyone in the other room missed them, Crystal was certain that Declan would stop them from looking in any closets.

Don't miss the next book
in the bestselling Danvers series,

WISHING FOR US

Coming in November 2016!

———

Continue reading for a glimpse
at Emma and Brant's story in

NO DENYING YOU

Available now.

"Honey, have you given any more thought to getting some bigger tits?"

Emma rolled her eyes and dropped her head onto her desk. Why couldn't her mother bake cookies, knit sweaters or do any of that other Betty Crocker shit? No-o-o, she couldn't be that lucky. Katrina Davis—or Kat, as she liked to be called—had always wanted to be the cool mom on the block. Heck, most of Emma's childhood friends still called her mother for advice. The woman didn't pull any punches. "God, Mom, can we please not talk about my tits today? Or lack of them?"

"Em, it's for your own good. You're too attractive to sit at home all the time. Men are visual creatures, so maybe a new rack is exactly what you need. Your father can't keep his hands off mine. And you're not getting any younger. You don't want to wake up one day and have them fall out of bed before you do."

"Gross, Mom. This whole conversation is really gross. I don't want to hear anything about your sex life with Daddy. Ever. I'd like to be able to look him in the eyes just once without the constant stream of images in my head of the things you feel the need to confide to me.

Maybe you should just go Catholic—then you could confess to someone with a more professional opinion."

"Oh, Em, get over it. I'm just trying to help. You know what? I'll even pay if I can pick them out. I'll e-mail you some information and you can let me know what you think."

"Mom, for the last time, I like my tits just fine!" As soon as she shouted that last bit, Emma froze at the sound of a throat clearing behind her. *Please tell me that the asswipe isn't behind me, ple-e-ease.* As she swiveled slowly in her chair, she groaned. Fate definitely wasn't on her side. Her boss, Brant Stone, stood behind her with his usual condescending smirk. She quickly said her good-byes to her mother although she could hear her still speaking as she gingerly placed the receiver back in the cradle. Determined not to give him the satisfaction of seeing her rattled, she raised a brow, asking as politely as she could manage, "Did you need something?"

"Apparently not as badly as you do, Emma."

Oh great, here it comes, another jab at my work performance. I wonder how much jail time I would get if I choked him with the paisley tie he's wearing. Turning her back to nonchalantly pick up her coffee cup, she said, "Pardon?"

"I am positively riveted by your plight," he replied.

More obscure code to unravel. She spent half of her time trying to figure out what in the hell he was talking about. She knew he did it on purpose, the sneaky bastard. "I bet you are, considering you cause most of my misery." She knew it was unprofessional as well as career suicide to talk to her boss this way, but she kept hoping he would have her transferred to another department so that he could find someone more suitable for his assistant. So far, that hadn't happened. She had even started dropping hints, but, like every suggestion she made, he seemed to completely ignore it.

"That's flattering, Emma, but I don't think I can accept responsibility for your . . . shortcomings."

Her coffee cup fell from her suddenly limp fingers and crashed to the floor. Then she plowed into him as she jumped back to avoid the hot liquid. "Shit!" The carnage continued as they both fell backward like dominoes. When she managed to get her bearings, she was horrified to realize that Brant was laid out on the floor underneath her, and her butt was nestled firmly near his crotch. Coffee stains were splattered all over his perfectly creased slacks, and it took her a moment to realize why her legs seemed so bare as they lay tangled with his. Her short skirt had blown up during their fall and was now resting well above the level considered legal in most states. Was that . . . ? No, it couldn't be. . . .

Without thinking, she wiggled around experimentally. *No way!* Her boss, the spawn from hell, was not growing hard against her bottom. *Oh my God, he was!*

"I didn't realize that ruining my clothing also came with a lap dance." When she froze, he chuckled. "Oh, by all means, don't stop now. Even someone with small tits is a turn-on when she's grinding against your lap."

Emma jumped up as if she were on fire. "You are such an asshole. I should file sexual harassment charges against you. I'm pretty sure there are rules in the *Danvers Handbook* against discussing my tits."

Brant snorted as he rose to his feet. "I'm pretty sure there are also rules in there about talking about said tits on a company telephone on company time, and I'm even more sure there is a section about job performance."

If she didn't hate the man so much, she would be impressed by the way he excelled at sarcasm. She had worked for Brant Stone for about six months at the communications company Danvers International. Jason Danvers, owner of the company, had bought out the family company that was previously run by Brant and his sister, Ava. They had both come to work at Danvers in vice presidential roles after the merger.

Brant's younger brother, Declan, also worked for Danvers, although he hadn't been involved in the Stone family business. He had recently married Ella Webber, a receptionist on the fourth floor who had become a good friend of Emma's. It was the most recent wedding in a string of couplings at the company. Jason had married his secretary, Claire, and the Merimon brothers, Grayson and Nick, had also settled down. Gray was married to Suzy, who handled the special events for Danvers; Nick was married to Beth, Suzy's sister and assistant. They had recently had a new baby.

As far as romance was concerned, Danvers seemed to be the place to work if you were looking to find a significant other. So far it hadn't helped her, though. Instead, she was stuck with a shit head for a boss and a vibrator for date night. Life sucked in that area.

When Brant snapped his fingers in front of her face to get her attention, she stuck her tongue out at him. She simply couldn't resist, although she did refrain from giving him the verbal slapdown he so richly deserved. She settled for muttering, "Yeah, yeah, whatever." He actually looked disappointed before he turned and stalked off to his office.

When her phone rang yet again, she groaned, praying it wasn't her mother. "Brant Stone's office."

"You sound like someone pissed in your corn flakes."

Emma released a sigh of relief as she heard her friend Suzy's voice on the line. They may not have known each other for very long, but recognizing fellow smart-asses in each other, they had bonded pretty quickly. "Ugh . . . just the usual kind of morning nonsense with Mr. Sunshine. Maybe a little worse than usual."

"You'll have to tell me more; I could use a laugh. How about lunch today? Claire, Beth and Ella are going to the mall for some baby stuff and I'd really like to pass on that."

"I hear you, girl," Emma agreed. "I'll meet you downstairs around noon if that works for you?"

"Sounds good; stay out of trouble."

Emma did manage to work with Brant the rest of the morning without incident until he came out of his office as she was preparing to go to lunch. "Where are you eating? You don't mind if I go, do you?"

For a minute Emma stood there gaping at him. "Are you kidding?"

"Actually, yes. Going to Taco Bell and watching you drip your taco fixings all over the table isn't my idea of a relaxing lunch. I would like you to pick me up something at the deli around the corner, though, on your way back in."

Emma huffed in dramatic fashion. She didn't bother telling him that she was having lunch with Suzy there. "I guess it's asking too much that you get your own lunch.

Who runs all of your errands in the evening? Do you have a maid that you keep chained up in your kitchen?"

Brant perched on the corner of her desk, grinning. "What a great idea; are you looking for a second job? If you were on the clock for twenty-four hours, I might be able to get eight hours of actual work out of you."

She gave him a sympathetic look before saying, "You've really got it bad. You deserve so much better than me."

Brant gave her a wary look before saying, "True."

"How about I bring you back a nice lunch and then we fill out the paperwork to have me transferred to another department? Somewhere in this building is the uptight assistant of your dreams. Just think, by Monday you could both be boring each other to death. Just say the word."

He was already shaking his head before she finished speaking. "I don't think so, Miss Davis. If you would like to quit, that is your choice, but I won't be transferring you. If you're going to work at Danvers, then you are going to be working here."

Emma looked at him, truly puzzled. "I really don't get it, you know. You hate everything about me. Our personalities don't mesh at all and you'd be much happier with someone else in this position, but you won't sign the transfer request. Why? Are you like one of those guys who enjoy being tortured? Do you have mommy issues? What gives?"

He gave her that superior look that he did so well and said, "I have no idea what you're talking about." Walking straight back into his office, he tossed out, "Don't forget my lunch," before he shut the door behind him.

She knew it was childish, but she flipped the bird toward his door before going to meet Suzy for lunch.

About the Author

Sydney Landon is the *New York Times* and *USA Today* bestselling author of the Danvers novels, including *Watch over Me*, *Always Loving You*, and *No Denying You*. She lives in South Carolina with her husband and two children, who keep life interesting and borderline insane but never boring. When she isn't writing, Sydney enjoys reading, swimming, and being a minivan-driving soccer mom.

CONNECT ONLINE

sydneylandon.com
facebook.com/sydney.landonauthor
twitter.com/sydneylandon1

Also available from
New York Times bestselling author
Sydney Landon

THE DANVERS NOVELS

Weekends Required
Claire Walters has worked for Jason Danvers as his assistant for three years, but he never appreciated her as a woman—until the day she jumps out of a cake at his friend's bachelor party...

Not Planning on You
Suzy Denton thought she had it all: a great job as an event planner and a committed relationship with her high school sweetheart. But life is never quite so simple...

Fall for Me
All her life, Beth Denton battled both her weight and her controlling parents. And now that she's declared victory, she's looking for one good man to share the spoils of war...

Fighting for You
Ella Webber has spent years uncomfortable around the opposite sex, but as soon as she meets the handsome Declan Stone, she's smitten. But can she persuade Declan that they're a perfect match?

No Denying You
Working for uptight workaholic Brant Stone is more than Emma Davis can bear. But when the tension between them explodes, hate will turn into lust, and then to something much more...

Always Loving You
Ava Stone has spent her entire life looking over her shoulder. But when she's forced to rely on the one man who has never let her down, can he break through the protective walls she's needed for so long?

Watch Over Me
Gwen Day has never been lucky in love, but now she's betting on one man ready to care for her like no one ever has...

Available wherever books are sold or at
penguin.com

sydneylandon.com

s0436